Cavender pretended sleep as he listened to them . . .

Rose lay in McLaughlin's arms, talking earnestly of Cavender.

"Listen to me, Brendan, darling," the woman was saying. "I'm really afraid of Cavender. Of his greed. A man who works only for money—he's dangerous."

"Get rid of him? Is that what you're saying?" asked McLaughlin.

"Exactly."

McLaughlin did not reply.

"But you'll do it then?" she asked anxiously.

"I'll think about it in the morning," he said.

Cavender turned onto his side and went to sleep. He needed the rest.

APPOINTMENT IN CALCUTTA

by

Elliot Tokson

FAWCETT GOLD MEDAL • NEW YORK

For Deanna

APPOINTMENT IN CALCUTTA

© 1979 Elliot Tokson

Published by Fawcett Gold Medal Books, a unit of CBS Publications, the Consumer Publishing Division of CBS Inc.

ISBN 0-449-14131-4

Printed in the United States of America

10 9 8 7 6 5 4 3 2 1

1

Alec Cavender stepped into the early sun away from the crude stall he had been leaning against. He washed the dust from his throat with the rest of his cold tea, handed the thick, stained cup back to the tea peddler, and lifted his eyes. There was something to look at finally.

Across the unpaved street was the great black prison. Inside, a black flag had been run up its staff and was just clearing the top of the wall. It was no larger than a gentleman's handkerchief. Before it reached the top of the staff, the roll of a drum or two floated from the prison yard over the half-empty market stalls. The drum roll barely rose above the jabber of Hindu and Moslem workers and peddlers streaming over the road between the dark wall and Cavender.

Cavender saw the flag and heard the roll because he was looking and listening for them. No one else paid them any attention.

The flag fluttered at the top of the staff for little more than a minute, the drumming ceased, and the flag dropped quickly out of sight.

The execution on the other side of the wall was over. Someone had been hanged.

Cavender's face darkened. It was a battered, rather leathery face, but not a coarse one. The long nose that had been badly broken and badly set still retained a touch of the aquiline grace it once had. And the long horizontal dimple in his left cheek never lost its appeal even when he clenched his jaw, as he was doing now, and the dimple looked more like a scar. His eyes, normally a warm and moody gray, were now hidden in the shade of his Panama pulled low over his brow.

He had seen two hangings in his long career, both in the North-West Frontier, when deserters, Indian or English, were quickly dispatched to keep the troops disciplined. At one of them he had been in charge himself.

He remembered those days when he could disguise himself as a native and pass among them—fluent in their language and their customs and able to enter their dens and brothels. The hanging affair was only one of the nasty jobs his superiors had found him so skillful at.

The hanging across the way brought the memories back in a wave of nostalgia, the rotten parts only faintly in his feelings. But he wasn't back in India to revive memories.

When the black flag dropped, he did not change his position. His dark gray eyes did not shift their focus. He pulled the wide-brimmed Panama lower over his forehead to shade the whole lower half of his face. He waited patiently. It was something he had learned to do over twenty-five years. Patience was from Allah, the Arabs said, hurry was from hell. Cavender believed it.

Nearly an hour later a white flag, just as small as the black flag, was drawn to the top of the same staff. That's what Cavender was waiting for.

It was the white flag that had brought him on private inquiry business ten thousand miles from Brussels to this dusty, crowded, market-lined street outside the massive stone prison of Calcutta.

It was a beautiful day in December, 1913, the kind that come in India only during the pre-monsoon weeks in winter. It was the time that Cavender had savored most during his army service in India long ago. And now, older, more seasoned, heavier, working as a private agent out of Belgium, he was back in India after years of absence, enjoying it again.

For more than an hour before the black flag went up he had stood patiently in the shade of the peddlers' stalls stretching up and down the road near the prison. He was built for standing over long periods of time. In his body and face he had lost some of the angles of his youth, but

6

his legs were strong. He was of medium height, his shoulders thick and sloping under the ecru tailored suit he wore buttoned tightly across the heavy chest. The coat was cut loose in the waist so that the small Mauser pistol he carried there would not bulge the fine cloth.

Calmly he had waited for the white flag. Being British and having spent years in British services, he trusted British devotion to tradition. A condemned man was hanged under a black flag. A time-server was released under a white one.

As the white flag rose, Cavender turned his attention to the small iron-clad door set deep into the stone wall across the way. The view was now blocked by the steady flow of natives moving in both directions. The congestion had grown worse in the last hour. He changed his position until he could see the door clearly.

In a few minutes B. D. McLaughlin would step through the door. B. D.—Brendan Daniel. He was called Bull-dog by his fellow officers of the army, and Black Dog by his closest friends. And that was because he loved dogs and always kept one, usually a bull terrier. That was long ago. Now he would be just McLaughlin, an old Irish ex-soldier, dishonorably drummed out of Her Majesty's Indian Expeditionary Forces in '97. It would be difficult calling him mister.

Thinking about the man, Cavender lit a long, dark Suerdieck and moved back into the shade of another stall, waiting for the farewells to be said beyond that iron-clad door. And after sixteen years there would have to be some of those.

Sixteen years ago Cavender had known McLaughlin for a short period in '97 on the North-West Frontier during the tribal uprisings. The Irishman had already been serving for years in the Guides Infantry when Cavender met him in the field fighting the Afghans.

McLaughlin was a Guides Major then, and Cavender, fifteen years younger, was a subaltern in the 31st Punjab Infantry, leading a Sikh company into the battle. It was in the bloody Mohmand Valley, Cavender recollected.

7

That's where their units had joined in the hardest fighting of the punitive expedition that year.

Not since then had Cavender returned to India, until now. He found his memory repeatedly and sharply jarred by the sights and sounds and smells of the native hordes of the city. He recalled the bazaars and the brothels—and since yesterday, especially the brothels—of the Indian towns of the North-West. Up there he and McLaughlin had been thrown together on that field of battle, and afterwards they had occasionally met on a polo field in Peshawar, usually on opposite sides.

These less-bloody games always ended over a decanter or two of the best whisky the "scouts" could locate. But the two men had not become very close. By temperament they were too far apart. McLaughlin was given to excesses of all kinds, Cavender to severe self-restraint. The confirmed *bon vivant* and the young ascetic. It was not until long after they had parted that Cavender grew to understand how good the pleasures of life could be, and how necessary. McLaughlin had been way ahead of him.

Now, through a curious chain of circumstances, they were being brought together again outside the old dark prison where McLaughlin had spent the last sixteen years of his life. And Cavender, who had come to help him through the next few weeks, would have to greet him, instead, with some unexpectedly bad news.

2

There had not been bad news, really, until yesterday. That was when the woman Rose McLaughlin had told Cavender about McLaughlin's other daughter. It was in the morning and Rose was drinking her tea across from him in his hotel room when she suddenly looked up at him sharply.

"He's got another daughter, you know!" she blurted out.

Cavender cocked an eyebrow at her and fixed her with a gray stare.

"I've kept it to myself because I thought it would muck things up for us on the way out here." She watched Cavender's deep gray eyes and caught the gleam.

"Nothing surprises me," Cavender finally replied with a dry, warm smile. "Not very much."

The young woman rose from the table, came around, and slipped into his arms. "You can find her, Alec." She kissed him on his cheek, right on the dimple. He rubbed her breast through her dress until she pushed him away. She looked at his brown silk tie and stroked it with her fingers. He did not answer her. She stood up again and walked to a window.

She was short and her hips were heavy and her breasts slightly too large for her height. She was dark-skinned and brown-eyed. When she spoke she showed a perfect clean-toothed mouth. Her lips were strikingly red. Her hair was straight and shiny and the color of dark wheat.

Having broached the subject, Rose went on with a rush. "A Moslem girl, or a Moslem mother, anyway. Legitimate or not, he never said. He mentioned her a bit in his letters and then finally got round to saying he would like to find her and take her out. Sure now, what do you think of that?"

Cavender knit his brows together loosely, forming shallow lines in his forehead. The dimple she had kissed was deeper. His eyes stared moodily at the side profile of her face, almost blocked by the thick wheaten hair. Then his face broke again into a half smile, half smirk at the mouth. His large white teeth showed evenly.

"India isn't the biggest place in the world, but it's damn well the most crowded," he said, as though that were the last word on the matter.

Rose spun to face him. Her face was a plea.

"Oh, but, Alec, I've seen her! Sure, it's her I think I've seen."

She had been at the prison yesterday just to see where McLaughlin was kept, still afraid to make the first visit. The Indian girl, about seventeen, had been outside, too, loitering aimlessly. On a wild chance Rose had called her name—"Farashah." The girl had seemed startled and left the area suddenly. Rose had followed her.

"She went to a house near the river, Alec, a . . . bad house. You know the kind I mean."

"Brothel, Rose, a brothel. Every city in the world has got at least one. Even Dublin."

She reddened under her dark skin and looked at the floor.

"Listen," said Cavender. "Calcutta is worse than most. Where life is cheap—and it's damn cheap here—flesh is going to be cheaper. Don't go feeling badly for her if that's what you're thinking of doing."

She looked hurt. He went over and lifted her face with a large gentle hand under her chin. She was beautiful, all right. She would never be pretty, but she was beautiful. There was too much passion in her face that did not go well with her coyness. It was uncommon for an Irish girl, but she was Irish, he was sure of that. Irish through and through.

He looked at her pleading eyes, thought about Mc-Laughlin getting out the next day, and shrugged. "I *could* go and take a look if you can describe where the house is she went to."

Rose could. And early in the evening Cavender went there. That was only fifteen hours ago.

3

The house was in the western city on a small lane off Kidderpore Road near the Hooghly River. The air was cool and damp here and the foghorns from the heavy river traffic floated continuously over the district. Along the lane a single unbroken low wall fronted a whole cluster of bungalows, giving an impression of a single structure. There was a single entrance and no windows on the street side he could see.

A lone light glowed dimly at the front entrance and two men were lounging near the door.

Cavender walked up toward them, throwing his head first over one shoulder and then over the other as though he were nervous about being seen. One of the men stopped him. He was a short, powerful Bengali wearing a black turban. He studied Cavender briefly under the light.

"English, sahib?"

Cavender nodded and grunted.

"You are new here, sahib. Inside—only children. You like?"

A chill crept over the back of Cavender's neck. A child bordello; the joy-children of Siva. He knew about them, and he knew about the perfumed European gentlemen who came out here to hunt tiger and never failed to visit the children. Of course, there were children to be had in Europe, but not with such easy access as here. The Indians allowed it, their traditions fostered it, and the British, who could have suppressed it, respected tradition. There was a time when Cavender would not have blinked at the thought of the practice, but time had softened him in some ways, as it had hardened him in others.

He looked at the two small chunky guards. "I . . . I . . ." He fidgeted and looked around nervously and wrung his hands as though he had suddenly been caught in an embarrassment. Then he stammered softly. "Yes . . . Yes . . . But . . . not too young, do you think? I'm really not like—"

"Oh, sahib," said the Bengali reassuringly, "we understand. It is perfectly all right. No shame, sahib, no shame. A female is a female. You can find older girl inside, or younger girl. All the same. All here to please. The gods consent. Go in."

He swung the door inward and Cavender entered, bowing slightly to both. The door closed behind him. He was in a small windowless room furnished with low settees along all the walls. Two doorless openings showed dark hallways leading into blackness. A man in Western clothes and wearing a monocle sat there fidgeting with his hat as Cavender had pretended to do a moment ago. He avoided looking at Cavender. Cavender remained standing.

Some time passed. The odor of cheap heavy perfume filled the air, mingled with an occasional waft of sweating human bodies. The air had nowhere to go and grew stale and thick. It was as though the odor was in the walls. It was familiar to Cavender. He had smelled it before, and often, when he had to frequent the bordellos and saloons of Peshawar years earlier doing those quiet, unpleasant jobs the Colonial Office found for him, with the consent of the Army. The smell was not easy to forget. It never changed. It wasn't pleasant and it wasn't unpleasant. It was unlike anything else. He guessed it did not matter whether the girls were children or women. In the fleshpot the scents were all the same.

As he was thinking about the odors, delicately light tapping footsteps came out of the darkness of one of the hallways, and a tall, small-boned, fragile Chinese woman tip-tapped into the room on tiny high-heeled silver slippers. She bowed to Cavender and then walked to the other man, bent and whispered to him. Her silver slippers

12

flashed from under her gown. The man rose, pale-faced and pinch-mouthed, and with his hat held in front of him over his heart, he followed her timidly into the darkness, keeping his eyes straight ahead.

Cavender heard a door open down the corridor somewhere to the left. A soft ruffle of voices soared into the passageway and then was suddenly cut off. Five minutes later the Chinese woman returned. She smiled and bowed again. Before she could speak, the front door opened and two men came in noisily. They greeted the woman in German and sat down, glowering openly at Cavender. Germans liked to be first.

"This way, please," the woman said to Cavender in good English. The sour looks from the Germans harshened. Cavender winked at them and followed the click-clack of the silver slippers into the darkness.

Near the end of the hall, the woman opened a door. A murmur of voices flowed out into the darkness and then died slowly as she stepped inside. Cavender stayed close behind her. The scent in the room struck his nostrils. It was a big, well-lighted separate wing of the bungalow jutting toward the rear. There were rows of small beds along the three walls like an army barracks. Standing or lounging all over the place was a small army of young girls, wearing colorful saris and no veils. A quiet sea of childish faces turned up toward the door where Cavender and the Chinese woman stood.

"Your choice, sahib," the woman said, offering him the roomful with an extended hand, palm up, slender fingers partially curled. With the same hand she beckoned to a girl nearby who rushed forward and stood, head bowed, before them. The woman raised the girl's head gently. She was not older than ten or eleven.

Cavender stepped back as though he were judging the girl and her sisters, but a single careful sweep of the room was enough. There was no girl even near Farashah's age in there.

He pretended a little embarrassment. "Not here, madam," he muttered into her ear. "In private, please."

The woman nodded to the girls, the murmuring and

13

shuffling began, and she led him out, down the hall, and through a rear door into the night air. From here Cavender could see that the bungalows were separate units connected by a clever network of partially open courtyards. The brothel had been carefully made into a honeycomb of fleshpots spread out over a large area. The woman crossed a small court to the next bungalow and brought him to an empty room. There she asked him his preference.

"I have a delicate brown-skinned girl, eleven years of age, or an Oriental child just a few months older, very doll-like. I have trained each of these girls myself. Or would you prefer a girl of your own race? There are several here, Caucasians, lovely but a little coarse."

Cavender winced inside. He remembered a slave market on Nosy Be, off the coast of Madagascar, that he had gone to on another case three years ago. He had been looking for a girl then, too, and had found her. That had not turned out too well.

"Sahib?" asked the Chinese woman.

Cavender said, "Are they all experienced? I don't want anyone too new at this, you understand."

"The Indian girl, a Deccan child, has been here nearly a year. The others almost as long."

"Good," said Cavender. "I would like all three."

"Ahhh," said the woman, her face lighting up in a smile. Her teeth were tiny and perfect.

"But there's something else," said Cavender. "An older girl, seventeen, eighteen. I would like someone like that, also."

The woman's penciled eyebrows perched high for a moment in thin arches. She hesitated and then answered carefully. "We have had a few of that age here occasionally. But our visitors generally prefer the others. I will send you one. She will please you."

She bowed and started for the door.

"How much will all this cost?" Cavender asked.

The Chinese woman studied him before answering. Cavender could see her guessing what he would stand for. She said, "Fifty pounds."

14

"Forty," said Cavender. "Ten apiece." His instinct to bargain was not just for the part he played. Money was something he did not throw away carelessly.

"Accepted," she said quickly. She put out her hand.

Cavender counted out twenty pounds. "The rest later," he said.

Her lips pouted but she said nothing. She nodded her head toward the door and again he trod silently after her along dim halls lighted by oil lanterns, across courts from one bungalow to another. Once a door opened as he passed and a man came out. Behind him in a dimly lighted room a girl lounged near a bed. She turned away when she saw Cavender. She was holding money in her hand.

The man disappeared down the hall.

The Chinese woman on mincing steps went inside and partly closed the door. She spoke softly to the girl, kissed her on the cheek, and took the money. The girl was naked, thin, and pathetically, seemed not unhappy. She saw Cavender again and twisted her body a little and smiled and waved a hand.

Cavender waved back but the muscles in his face were bunched. He had to force himself to remember where he was. This was India. The child in there, instead of starving to death in the streets, was probably doing better where she was, eating every day, getting some care, some praise, even some medicine when it was needed. It was good business to keep the girls well and looking well.

In a room he was finally brought to in the same bungalow, Cavender found another young girl with no clothes on, just like the one he had seen, the same slimness from youth, not hunger, the same slight breasts and hairless body, the same meaningless smile.

He sat on the edge of the bed and waited. The girl came and stood nearby unashamed. Soon the dainty clicking footsteps returned. The Chinese woman ushered two other young girls in, closed the door, and clicked away. As soon as the door closed, the new girls dropped their saris on the floor and went over to the first girl and whispered and giggled. Brown, white, and yellow, as though he had ordered a la carte in a restaurant. And none of them over twelve. Three charmers, smiles full of knowledge and no fear.

Cavender continued to sit doing nothing, waiting for the fourth one, the one he really wanted to see. Finally, he couldn't stand it any longer. The girls were beginning to wiggle tauntingly.

"Jesus Christ!" he muttered angrily through his teeth. He picked up their saris and threw them at their legs and said in Hindi, "Get dressed and be quick about it and then sit on the bed and be quiet. Quick."

The little prostitutes looked startled. Then, realizing he was serious, they squealed to each other, got their bodies covered and onto the bed. There was a knock on the door.

"Come," said Cavender.

The girl there was in her mid-teens, northern Indian, light, smooth-skinned, dark hair, dark eyes, pretty.

"Farashah?" asked Cavender.

The girl blinked and looked mystified.

"Are you Farashah?" he repeated.

The girl nodded her head—*no*. Cavender had to remember they did that the opposite way in India.

"Where is she?"

"Gone," said the girl, shrugging her shoulders. "There was a girl here—I don't know her name. But not Farashah." She spoke matter-of-factly. "Some men came, took her away. Two, three hours ago, maybe later."

"What men?"

"Chinese men."

"Did they take her to another place like this?"

She tilted her head to the side to study him. "Maybe, maybe no. Ask Madam Yen-Choo."

"Show me the room the girl was using," Cavender said. He moved toward the door.

The girl did not move at all. She smiled. "For what, sahib? Am I not fine enough for you? See. Am I not nicer than she?"

Like the two younger girls before her, she dropped her sari to the floor. The three young girls giggled and chattered. The body that was bared was not the undeveloped

16

one of a child. It was fine and round and satiny. The limbs were long and graceful.

God, if he hadn't paid for her, he could have wasted a half hour right there—after he kicked the children out. But he did not like why she would be doing it with him. He had been with prostitutes before, but not often and only when the need was great. He remembered a mountain brothel in a Yemenite city on a long trek with an Arab guide. He had had the need then. Now he had not, and the older he got the more he wanted from a woman than just her body. He couldn't get that from this youngster.

"Get dressed," he said to her. The little girls behind began to giggle louder. One taunted him that he was not a man. They were afraid he would tell the Chinese woman they had not pleased him. They began to complain.

"Show me Farashah's room," Cavender said again. He started to open the door. The girl fixed her sari and appeared about to cooperate. Suddenly she shoved the door open and began yelling. The three young children set up a howl. Doors flew open up and down the hall. A few men came tumbling out of their rooms pulling on their clothes, cursing. Lights went out. Lights went on. There was some screaming from young children and more curses from men. Small white bodies and brown bodies flashed into and out of rooms.

Cavender tossed the Indian girl aside and began to move quickly down the hall, trying doors, throwing open the unlocked ones and forcing the others. The locks were flimsy. If someone was in the room, he called out "Farashah," and then ducked out if there was no response. Once someone threw something at him that shattered against the wall next to his head. A cheap perfumed smell washed over him.

He crossed from one bungalow to another. The ruckus spread along with him like a straw fire. He kept opening doors and finding only young children and a few customers. Then he found the two Germans who had scowled at him before. There were young brown boys in the room with them but no girls. When the Germans saw Cavender they broke from some kind of brown huddle and in a

17

flurry of white and pink flesh pinned him against the wall. But they weren't strong and they weren't in shape. Without much effort he worked his Mauser out of its holster, wriggled it up between his body and the naked body of one of the Germans, and pushed the muzzle hard under his chin. When the man realized what it was digging into his flesh, he went slack and fell back with his hands raised above his head. His friend followed his cue.

Cavender apologized for the interruption and left them standing with their hands raised and their pink and white round bodies looking rather ridiculous under the white light. The brown boys in the room were all crouching shyly to hide themselves.

There was shouting in the hall from both directions. Two doors down Cavender came upon the man with a monocle, with a girl astride him. They did not even stop when he burst in. The man looked up over the small naked back hunched over him, and in German said, "Please leave us alone now."

Shaking his head, Cavender backed out and someone began to pummel his back. He ducked to one side and turned. It was Madame Yen-Choo, throwing her small fists at his head. Her face was twisted into an angry grimace. He caught her wrists and pinned her against the wall. Under her kimono he could feel her hard small body writhing against his. It was an erotic feeling.

"Where is she?" he said roughly.

"Who?" she asked. The writhing decreased.

Cavender thought he'd play it rougher. He put his hand around her throat and squeezed. She squirmed against him and then went soft.

"The girl that should have been here tonight. Farashah. No one special to you, no one you should be hiding. Just someone's daughter."

The woman twisted her head against the wall and screamed and hurled some words at Cavender in Chinese. She tried to kick him in the shins. He avoided her sharp-toed slippers by pushing his legs between hers.

Heavy steps came pounding down toward them.

Cavender backed away fast enough to catch the first

18

Bengali guard in his arms and spin him hard into the wall. He threw a fist straight up into the Bengali's throat, hurting him just enough as the second Bengali jumped on his back. He spun around on one foot and struck at the Bengali's stomach with his right elbow, pulling an arm lock free from his neck with his left hand. The Bengali smashed into the woman, who groaned and went down in a small heap.

For a moment Cavender was free. The two squat Bengalis were shoulder to shoulder opposite him. The passage to the street was behind him. In the glow of the corridor lights, Cavender could see their faces. They were surprised enough to study him before deciding what to do next. The woman on the floor moved and started to sit up. She was between Cavender and her guards. She groaned.

The Bengalis started to come slower for Cavender. He did not want to shoot them, but he drew his Mauser pistol and held it straight out and high so they could see it clearly. They stopped and cursed him in Hindi.

In their language, Cavender asked, "Where is the girl Farashah?"

The woman spoke from the floor. "Leave them be. They know nothing. I know nothing. We had a girl here, older. She is gone. She went out twice and never came back the second time. It happens. A girl is taken, kidnapped, now and then, here and there, never to come back. She will be replaced the same way. She is probably at work right now in some other place in Calcutta. But you will never find her."

"Where?" asked Cavender. "Would you take a guess? A name?"

Madame Yen-Choo sat gracefully against the wall and said nothing. Cavender fished out a twenty-pound note from his trouser pocket and tossed it crumpled into her lap.

"Well?"

"No," she said. "There are too many would want her for their houses and could take her. You would need the police to find her—but I do not think you will want the police."

19

She started to rise and the guards moved to help her. She waved them curtly away. "Or, if you knew someone important in the city, like a rajah with enough connections . . . But by yourself, never."

The odd thing about that remark, Cavender was thinking as he bent down to retrieve the twenty-pound note from the fist of Madame Yen-Choo, who had not earned it, was that he did know a rajah, the prince of a small state north of Calcutta, a man who might be able to help.

But Cavender had had no time, and he was not in India to ferret a girl out of some sweaty brothel.

He was here for that white flag, fluttering lazily in the morning breeze. The white flag that was just now beginning to creep down its pole toward the ground inside the walls of the prison.

4

The small door Cavender was watching swung inward and a figure in the shadows ducked low, filled the doorway, and then stepped out into the sun and straightened up.

Cavender knew him at once. He was tall and wide and a little stooped. His face was lanternlike, long and square, his hair white, short and thick. He wore an old cotton suit, drab gray and ill-fitting, a shirt, and no tie. Indian sandals were on his feet. He carried a small burlap bag tied with coarse hemp.

Cavender himself was wearing his customary warm-climate clothing: the ivory-colored linen suit, light shirt, dark silk tie, brown-and-white English leathers, and a wide-brimmed Panama straw. He wanted to look as *pukka sahib* as he could, especially since he carried Belgian papers. In India being British was a marked advantage.

Each man was a far cry from the soldier he had been at their last meeting, in creased shorts, pressed shirts, gleaming leathers, and pith helmets. They had shaken hands, said good-bye, and parted—never expecting to meet again. But here they were, thirty feet apart and about to begin a long and perhaps risky journey together back to Dublin—if Cavender could persuade him to leave a daughter behind in a brothel.

Whatever happened, as he looked at the tall Irishman he could already feel a stronger concern for him than he professionally should. There were still signs in the way he moved that an old glory in him had not completely faded. He took three or four long strides away from the prison door and stopped, as though it was not easy to leave sixteen years there behind him. Then he moved forward and stopped again and began to search up and down the street expectantly. He could have been looking for Farashah, or anybody. Cavender could see him deliberately breathing in the air as though it differed from the air on the other side of the wall. He could see him inhaling the sights and sounds of freedom. Cavender savored it with him for a moment.

He started to cross the heavy foot traffic toward the older man. Suddenly, a gray-bearded, turbaned Sikh stepped out of the flow of the crowd to McLaughlin's side, seized him by the arm, and began to talk to him intensely. Cavender worked his way through the throngs and stuck close to the prison wall, twenty feet away.

The Sikh spoke with his braceleted hand on his curved sword, his left hand on McLaughlin's arm. Cavender's right hand was curled around the butt of his Mauser. McLaughlin listened to the Sikh, shook his head, yes, then nodded, no, then shook yes again. Cavender determined the yeses and noes from the expressions on the Irishman's face. McLaughlin spoke some words calmly and continued to search around, not paying full attention to the Indian. A puzzled, worried look appeared in his face. Cavender kept back out of sight. The girl he was probably looking for was not going to appear.

Finally McLaughlin removed the Sikh's hand from his arm, said something harshly, and started to walk up toward Cavender's position, still searching for somebody. The Sikh stared after him and then shouted words Cavender could hear:

"It must be so, McLaughlin. It must be so."

The words were crisp and sharp and as intent as the Indian's face.

The aging Irishman shrugged his shoulders without stopping or turning, and shook his head.

The Sikh swiveled around on one foot, stepped into the flow of traffic, and was swept out of sight down the road.

Almost at once McLaughlin seemed to make up his mind, gave up looking around and headed down the road in the direction the Sikh had gone. Carvender went after him.

Overtaking the tall white-haired man, Cavender said in a low voice, "Hello, Major."

McLaughlin straightened and turned slowly as though stabbed by a thin dagger. Close up, his skin was rough, red, and deeply furrowed across the forehead and down the cheek lines. The red was not from the sun but from his naturally florid disposition. His eyes were still piercing bright blue.

The blue eyes flickered for a moment and then grew brighter with recognition. "Son of a dog, I am; is it Cavender?" Then came the deep, throaty Gaelic growl that hadn't changed. "Ahrrrr, yes, man it is Cavender! I'll be damned, it is!"

He gripped both Cavender's hands and shook them hard. His face broke into the lines of a great smile. The keen spirit in his voice was still there, and so was the strength in his arms and fingers. Cavender smiled back.

"Who would have hoped it even? I heard years ago you had left the service, gone in for yourself. Grapevine news. And an old acquaintance of ours—Jimmy Harrison, a colonel now, you'd better know it—passed through a year or two back and said hello. Mentioned you were in

22

Brussels. That's how I came to put your name in that letter. But I never hoped to see you show up here like this. What a lucky shot on the wing that was!"

The tall Irishman cast an arm around Cavender's thick shoulders.

"You look good," said Cavender, just to show he could say something before McLaughlin could continue. He let McLaughlin run on. Sixteen years in jail bought him that. And Cavender knew anyway there was no stopping an Irishman bent on talking. The news about the girl could wait.

"You look dandy yourself, Alec. Heavier then I remember in your tunic, maybe. Not so sharp in the bone line there"—he traced a long bony finger along Cavender's cheek and jawline—"and that nose never mended right, did it. Army surgeons, what? But"—here he squeezed Cavender's upper arms—"not fat. Not fat. In shape you are, I can feel that. And so am I. Feel that." He offered Cavender a hard bicep to feel. "Not bad at sixty-one, and sixteen years in prison."

"It's good to see you like this, Major," said Cavender breaking into a light smile. "How did you manage?" The men were walking side by side now as the street widened and they found room.

"I've no complaints about the treatment they gave me, my boy. They had my record in there and they treated me well. Better than a lot of the other bloody poor bastards in there." His face grew more serious and his large head nodded with his words. "But I shouldn't've been put in at all. I did my duty—as I saw it. And speaking of the army, let's not have any more of that 'Major' shit, no more of it, d'ye hear. Call me by name—McLaughlin will please me."

From the side he was looking steadily at Cavendar as they maneuvered their way through the traffic. "A little gray you've gotten, haven't you. And look at my white top."

Cavender laughed. "If we could we'd move backwards like crabs," he said, "and grow younger."

"That we would," agreed McLaughlin, laughing, "that

23

we would. And that calls for a drink. We managed some good things in the hole but good whisky wasn't one of them often enough."

"There's a bar at the hotel," Cavender suggested. "It'll suit you."

"Good enough," said McLaughlin cheerfully.

As they walked through the dusty, crowded streets among the turbaned and robed natives, McLaughlin swallowed in the sights of men and women rushing around in the business of living. He stared unashamedly into the unveiled faces of Englishwomen out on shopping sprees without their husbands. He followed their heavily corseted bodies into and out of taxis and horse-drawn tongas. They were easy to spot under their parasols. Then he watched the native women swinging loosely under thin robes, their rolling hips faintly but definitely showing.

"Look there, my boy," he said, pointing to a young Indian woman carrying a load on her shoulder that exaggerated the circular swing of her hip. "I'll pluck one of those young brown berries any day of the year before I'd touch one of our own potato-and-beef eaters." He made a deep animal growl in his throat as though he were plucking one right then.

They walked faster. But soon McLaughlin began to stop at different stalls to buy melon chunks, grilled mutton on sticks, cooked vegetables rolled inside crusty dough. He licked his fingers. Cavender joined him and they savored the street foods.

"This riles a man's thirst," said McLaughlin, finishing a stick of mutton and sucking his fingers clean. "There's got to be a nearer pub. What do you say?"

Cavender agreed.

Before they had gone fifty yards, they saw a flurry of excitement break out in a small square at the intersection of two roads. At first there were some shouts, then a great hum of voices. People scattered away from one end of the square, stopped, swarmed back and formed a solid knot around something at the far end. A strange hush fell over the crowd.

Cavender and McLaughlin swung into the square and

moved around the outer edge of the mob. Two native Indian policemen pushed into the crowd from the other end and shouted orders. People dispersed. Cavender and McLaughlin angled forward for a closer look.

In a clearing near a crumbling plastered wall lay the nearly decapitated body of a Hindu thug, darkening the ground under it. The flies had already caught the scent and were beginning to swarm. Standing a few feet away was the gray-bearded Sikh Cavender had seen accosting McLaughlin at the prison. The ivory handle of a dagger grew out of the front of the Sikh's left shoulder. In his right hand, braceleted by the steel bangle, was his short curved sword, streaked with blood.

5

No one moved to help the gray-bearded Sikh. The deep scowl on his face stopped anyone from coming closer. The two policemen were forcing onlookers to move back. When they reached Cavender and McLaughlin, they nodded politely, passed them by as though they had rights no one else had, and went on scattering the natives.

Soon the two "sahibs" were apart from the Indian mob. The Sikh recognized McLaughlin at once. The scowl on his face deepened. He raised his left hand, grasped the handle of the dagger in his shoulder, and with one straight thrusting movement drew it out of his body as though without effort or pain. His eyes never left McLaughlin's face as he tossed the dagger halfway between them. Cavender had seen other bigger men pass out from similar wounds. The Sikh hardly wavered.

"It was the Greek," he said distinctly. Then he turned

and started to move away toward a side street. One of the Indian policemen approached him unthreateningly and took him into custody without resistance. Three more policemen, Anglo-Indians this time, came running up to help their native colleagues.

Cavender touched McLaughlin's sleeve. "It's that time to get out of here before they take us along."

Without another word, McLaughlin followed Cavender out of the square and through the streets until they spotted a small place whose bar was already open. The bar was dark and empty. For Cavender it was a little early to drink, but he knew McLaughlin would want company. They ordered their whiskies neat. The waiter went away.

Cavender said, "The Sikh was talking to you." He made it sound almost like a question.

McLaughlin kept his eyes toward the bar as though he was watching the man there reaching for some glasses. He said, "You didn't see him jump me right outside the prison door?"

"No," Cavender lied. "I almost missed you, too."

"You might say he knows me," snorted McLaughlin. "You'd have to say he said that to me."

"Who's the Greek?" asked Cavender.

Before McLaughlin could answer, the waiter returned with two glasses and a bottle. He poured the whisky to a third of the glasses.

"Leave the bottle," said McLaughlin. When the man went away again, McLaughlin raised his glass.

"To success in recovering the book," he said, "and to the IRB."

Cavender went along with that, although he didn't know what book he meant and only vaguely recalled any IRB. "To success."

Cavender sipped at his drink. McLaughlin swallowed his whole and coughed only once. The Irishman filled his glass again.

Cavender repeated his question. "Who's the Greek?"

"There is no Greek I know about," answered McLaughlin soberly. "That's a funny one. There's a Russian, though, hanging around, who's been after me, even been

26

to see me once for a few minutes in the hole. Making me some damn crazy offers for what he thinks I've got, he has."

"Thinks?"

"No, you're right. What I have got. The book."

He picked up the second glass and stared at the brown liquid for a while, swishing it around. Then he pointed the glass at Cavender in a little salute and emptied it. He filled the glass again halfway. This time he quietly savored the full taste of the whisky in small sips, rinsing his mouth each time before he swallowed.

Cavender sipped at his drink slowly.

After three or four sips, McLaughlin said, "It's good of you to come out here, Alec. I never really thought they would find you or, if they did, you'd be willing to come, being English and an ex-damn-good-soldier and all that."

"I don't know who 'they' are, but she found me, all right—that daughter of yours—and she wouldn't take 'no' for an answer. I remembered you had been married in Ireland, but I didn't know about Rose."

McLaughlin looked up a little strangely. Cavender thought it might be the whisky. McLaughlin smiled.

"Ahrrrr, so it was Rose did the persuading, was it? My own daughter. And what did she tell you?" He replenished his glass again and sipped at it, continuing to look at Cavender over the rim.

The subject had now changed, Cavender sensed that, but he was willing to let the story of the book come out the way McLaughlin wanted it to in his own time. He offered McLaughlin a Suerdieck, and the two men sat silently, puffing at their cigars.

Cavender said, "She told me what she knew. You were finishing your time and getting out. You needed protection. You had something valuable, she didn't know what it was or how valuable it was or who would want to take it away from you." Cavender took an envelope from his pocket. "She gave me this letter from you, asking that she hire someone you could trust to come out here to meet you. My name is mentioned on the back of the first sheet. Remember?"

He handed two sheets of paper across to McLaughlin, who peered at them in the dim light and handed them back.

Cavender asked, "It's a book, I take it, connected with what happened in Peshawar, huh?"

"Taxila," corrected McLaughlin, naming a much smaller town on the North-West Frontier. "You might say it is."

"I never had the whole story about what happened to you back there," said Cavender. He finished his first whisky and let McLaughlin pour him another. He didn't touch it. "In '98 I went to the Sudan with Kitchener. That's when I heard of your trouble. Grapevine stuff, too. Some Sikhs were killed up there, something had disappeared. You had gone to prison. Some of your men were cashiered. I never got all of it. It sounded messy. When the Sudan affair ended, it was South Africa next, and the Boers. Then I left the service, spent some time with Scotland Yard, and finally out of everything, onto my own. I lost you completely."

"Just as well," muttered McLaughlin.

Cavender asked, "What sort of book is it, McLaughlin?"

McLaughlin stared at Cavender squarely in the face. He wasn't drunk, but he wasn't sober either. Cavender watched him finish his third large drink. He pushed his chair away and wiped his mouth with the back of his hand. He laughed.

"Time enough for all that later, Alec. But right now, do you think you've enough cash in your wallet to get me a suit like what you're wearing? I've had enough of this sack they've given me." He tugged at the lapel of the cheap suit.

Cavender nodded. "Anything you want, McLaughlin."

"There are a few other things. A pair of good leather boots, even if they're English."

Cavender paid the bill, and they went out into the bright sunlight.

"And a gun, Alec. I'll be wanting the biggest pistol I can get in Calcutta." He stood there blinking in the strong light. "You know, my boy, it's been sixteen years since

I've wrapped my hand around a woman's teat or the butt of a Webley. And I'm over sixty now and I'm a little afraid of getting a woman. But a gun—I can't be waiting to get my hand again around the butt of the biggest Webley-Green I can find."

6

Webleys were around in plenty. But in the two sporting stores they passed on the way to Cavender's hotel, there were no Webley-Greens, the favorite of British officers who could afford to buy one. McLaughlin, however, was more than satisfied to find a heavy four-barreled Lancaster in the big-game .577 caliber. "That'll stop a tiger if it'll stop a man," he chortled, handling the weapon. In his hand the heavy pistol didn't look so big. There were two twenty-round boxes of cartridges on a shelf. McLaughlin took them.

"Are we going tiger hunting?" Cavender quipped. They were not going to fight the Afghans again, where the Lancaster would be useful.

"You never know what you can run into in India," replied McLaughlin, searching through a pile of old holsters. "You were long enough here to learn that, my boy. Ah, this will do perfectly." He pushed the pistol into a long black leather holster. "Made for each other."

Cavender thought about what was up in his hotel room waiting for McLaughlin. Maybe there *were* things made for each other.

On the same street as the sporting shop was an Anglo-Indian tailor shop. McLaughlin chose a ready-made "fifty" suit, one that was half finished and could be tailored to a customer's needs very quickly. It was a silk-lined linen, like Cavender's, in a darker tan. He bought a woolen suit, too, heavier and suitable for a Dublin winter. Stocked, said the tailor, for Englishmen going home.

A few doors away he found a pair of light boots, a few shirts. He turned down the ties. Cavender kept digging out his wallet.

McLaughlin put an arm around his shoulder as they headed again toward his hotel on a side street off Upper Chitpur. "You'll get it all back, and more, my boy, you will. I promise you. Keep your records straight."

"There's the place," said Cavender, pointing to a modest, narrow-front, four-story building. "But before we go up, what do you say to another drink? Spending money like that is dry work."

"You *are* a man after my own heart, Alec, and a reader of minds, too," said the Irishman, turning in through a small door next to the hotel.

It was not another drink Cavender wanted, but the answers to some questions before he took the Irishman upstairs. And there was still the problem of Farashah nagging him. Any of it would go better over whisky. He chose the seat facing the entrance and eased himself down behind the small table. A trim waiter glided over. They ordered whiskies again.

Cavender asked the first question before the drinks arrived.

"What did the Sikh want outside the prison?"

"The same thing the Russian's after. The book. Ready to pay for it, he is. Everybody is ready to pay for it. Except that the Sikh is what you'd expect from a Sikh. You lived with them. He was tough with me, tougher than the Russian. The heathen made a threat, he did. He and his society figure the book belongs to them, to India. That's rot, that last part. But they don't intend letting it off the subcontinent."

The whiskies arrived in two cut crystal glasses. Neither man touched the drinks, as though drinking would end the talk. Maybe Cavender was wrong about the whisky.

He held up his fingers and counted on them. "A Russian,

some Sikhs, an unknown Greek, and who knows who else. Your daughter wasn't wrong, McLaughlin. You do seem to need protection."

McLaughlin slid his hand inside his jacket. Cavender could see him caressing the butt of the big gun, which he had insisted on wearing immediately.

"Me, needing protection, ahrrr," he snorted. Then he grew sober. There was a pause. "Maybe I do—but only if it came from someone like you I can trust. When I was in the hole I thought I would be needing some help when I got out. You're still young, Alec, and you're still British. I'm getting old, and I'm Irish. And since they kicked me out of the army, I'm Irish straight through. Do you know what I mean, lad? It's a sad change from those days, isn't it, when a man could protect himself with this and feel safe." He drew out the Lancaster and laid it on the table.

Cavender placed his hand over the gun and pushed it toward the Irishman. "Put it away now," he said quietly. "It's really not that bad. I'm not nursemaiding you." He lifted his glass. "To those days, McLaughlin, what do you say? You were mentioned, I think, twice in the dispatches. I only made it once. Winston Churchill wrote you up once —saving some of your sepoys, wasn't it? To the old times we thought would never end."

They drank. Cavender drank his straight down. It was late enough in the day for that now.

"Those dispatches," mused McLaughlin, licking a few drops from his lips. "They helped in prison some. Meant something to the guards. Churchill, was it? He's grown in government, hasn't he? The other one was from a *Times* man. Used to know the name. I remember that day. Forty-six I was, and crazy like a youngster with his first mount. Had to get my men moving and dashed across my own front right before the enemy and made the entire line giving that order. They shot the hell out of poor Devlin. Ah, that was the horse, that one. He made it before he finally dropped. I finished him myself, buried him myself, too, after the bloodshed."

He thought about something for a while. His face had lost some of its vigor.

"If you've got a bed for me upstairs, I'd like to be lying down for an hour."

Cavender nodded, then spoke casually. "You were looking for someone when I reached you this morning. Anybody besides me? Or should I know about that?"

McLaughlin cocked his head at Cavender. His bright blue eyes were watery. His breath was heavy and strong from the drinking. The whisky was finally having its effect. He was looking weary. His pistol was still lying on the table. He slipped it back under his coat and started to get up.

"I thought there maybe would be a girl there, an Indian girl waiting for me. Farashah, a little butterfly."

The name sounded strange across the table. Cavender decided to say nothing. There was something else on his mind.

"Sit down for another minute," he said.

McLaughlin, who was leaning across the table on his outstretched arms, settled back in his chair.

Cavender said, "There are a couple of surprises for you upstairs. I'm supposed to keep them surprises, but I don't like surprises myself. Now wait a minute—it's not to do with the Indian girl. It's your daughter Rose. She didn't just hire me to come out here. She persuaded me to let her come along."

He waited long enough to let that sink in.

McLaughlin blinked his eyes a few times.

Cavender said, "She's up there waiting for you right now."

The words had no other visible effect on McLaughlin than those eye-blinks. He rose to his feet only slightly unsteady. Cavender got up.

"Rose, is it?" McLaughlin said distinctly. "Now ain't that the nicest! To come all the way out here to see her dear dad, did she! I hope the other surprise I've got coming will be better than this one. Because I don't have a daughter named Rose. I've got an Indian girl. But I don't have an Irish daughter at all."

Cavender replied, "Yes, I know. I was pretty certain of that. Let's go up there and find out who she really is."

32

7

As they approached Cavender's rooms, two sharp barks broke from behind the door, followed by a steady low growl.

"Huh!" grunted McLaughlin.

Cavender shrugged.

McLaughlin's grim face brightened. "By Christ, I don't know who that gel is in there, but that bark belongs only to a bull terrier!"

The door opened before Cavender knocked. The short, stocky woman with the beautiful face stood there with one hand holding the door, the other by her side.

"Come in, please," she said, looking at McLaughlin and not at Cavender. She stepped aside.

But blocking the doorway was a young, heavy shovel-mouthed bull terrier. Its head held high, its narrow eyes beadily studied the two men. The long rat tail hung motionless. It was solid white. It stood like a snow statue that no one dared move.

With a growl of his own, McLaughlin fell to his knees, whispering words to the dog, letting him sniff the hairy back of each hand. He slipped his fingers along the side of the head, rubbing, stroking, tracing the head line, massaging the ear. The tail moved and waved a fraction.

Cavender removed his hat and watched the man and dog.

"Look at that," said McLaughlin as the tail fanned the air. "They didn't call me Bull-dog for my love of horses, you remember." He got to his feet. The dog came over, sniffed at Cavender, who had cared for him nearly a month, and then trotted back to McLaughlin's side. The dog knew who had claimed him, whom he really belonged to.

Cavender stepped inside and closed the door behind him.

The woman faced both men placidly. Her face was innocent and open. It was a disarming face that said she was guiltless of anything Cavender was thinking. She said:

"You know, of course, that I'm not Rose McLaughlin. It's Rose O'Connell. I'm sorry, Mr. Cavender, that I had to lie. I thought it was the only way to make you come out here."

He raised an eyebrow at her use of his last name.

"Don't apologize," he replied without scorn. "I didn't believe much of it. I believed less than what turned out to be true. At least you got 'Rose' right. Now you can tell us both the rest of it. This is Mr. McLaughlin."

The hand Rose offered McLaughlin was not delicate, but it was shapely. And when she said "Mr. McLaughlin," she said it the way it was meant to be said, in a rich Irish lilt. She flashed him a warm smile saying it. Cavender had seen the same flashing smile often on the long journey from Brussels to Calcutta.

They were in a small sitting room furnished with a few rattan chairs and a small divan with a rattan back. There was a table near the windows. On the far wall were two doors leading to separate bedrooms. Cavender could see McLaughlin looking at the bedrooms and working on the relationship between Rose and him.

McLaughlin nodded to Rose without speaking. She sat on the divan. Cavender and McLaughlin drew their chairs opposite her. The dog sat near McLaughlin's feet and then dropped heavily to the floor, resting his head on his crossed paws. He turned his eyes up toward McLaughlin.

Rose addressed Cavender. "Seeing how you didn't believe what I told you, why did you agree to take me?"

Cavender did not have to think about that. "I don't expect clients to be completely truthful," he said, "not right away. As long as they're not asking me to be funny. You weren't, and your money was adequate." He could have added that what she looked like was another reason, but he didn't. She already knew that. On the long trip aboard the P&O liner, she had been easy and indulgent. It had been like a murky honeymoon, making love to a woman who was his client and who claimed to be the daughter of an old acquaintance.

"I see," said Rose, without smiling.

"Well, how about it? Who are you?"

Rose folded her hands calmly on her lap. She talked to both men.

"I was sent to Mr. Cavender by people in Dublin. Sure you know what's happening there. It's a bit of a mess and getting messier every day. Ulster wants union with England, and Dublin wants independence. The Irish Republican Brotherhood in Dublin is growing. They need funds. They need arms. The Orangemen are forming an armed militia. So, the IRB is, too. They're the ones you're working for, Mr. Cavender. They want Mr. McLaughlin safely out of India because he wrote to them—isn't that right, Mr. McLaughlin? He's offered them some kind of rare treasure if they could help him get it out of India. The letter I showed you was real, except I rewrote it under their orders to leave them out of it and make it personal. It was the Council felt that you would be the best person to get in and out of India without stirring up a lot of British dander about Mr. McLaughlin's Irish connections. They're feeling you can get him out with whatever he has—some kind of manuscript, is that it?—although I didn't tell you that. Am I correct, Mr. McLaughlin?"

McLaughlin grinned at Cavender as if to say, What the hell! He said, "She's right about that, all right. That was the letter I wrote. Copied, but pretty much mine. Putting your name in it was some lucky shot."

"We're hardly home yet, to be thinking of being lucky," said Cavender. He was thinking of the Indian girl.

Rose said, "We used the daughter story because no one knew how you'd feel working for Irish nationalists, your being British, an ex-soldier, a Scotland Yard man. They asked some people about you, you see."

The dog lifted his head and rested it on McLaughlin's

knee. Cavender thought about McLaughlin's remark that some things were made for each other. There was some strange proof of that right there.

He asked, "What about the dog? I know you kept a terrier on the frontier, but how did the Council know that? And why take the trouble to bring one way out here? —And he was a little trouble, nursemaiding him on the boat and since we've been here. Once I got him out here I didn't trust the wallahs with him."

McLaughlin stroked the dog's head. "I didn't ask them right out to send one. That was a surprise. But I did write them more than that one letter you saw. I told them what I missed most. And a dog like this could come in handy any time. I think I said that once. Look at that chest and that jawline." He held the dog's head up.

"Just like that," said Cavender skeptically. "You wrote letters to Dublin, to a gang of Irish nationalists offering to get them money, telling them about a rare book, about yourself, the dog. And the prison people winked their eyes."

McLaughlin shook his head and laughed. "No. They never saw the letters. It took me years, but I made my own mail route. It was slow but I got the cooperation of some of the Tommies to set up my own post office. For the last five or six years nothing I wrote or got was seen by anyone. I made more than a few pounds, too, from those who could afford it."

Rose got up and went to the side of McLaughlin. She laid a hand on his shoulder. The old Irishman who hadn't touched a woman in many years reddened. He turned his head to look up at her profile inches away from his eyes.

Rose spoke. "You've had these few minutes to think about it, Mr. Cavender. You know who your real employers are. Are you still with us? Whatever Mr. McLaughlin has got is going to an Irish fund. And that fund is working for Irish independence—home rule, you see."

In Cavender's left cheek beneath his eye, the long horizontal dimple, with the peculiar quality of looking like a long scar or a bloodless cut when he grimaced or set his jaw, was deepened now just a shade. He could control it by parting his teeth a bit, but most of the time he did not bother. He did not bother now. Rose had raised a question of loyalties.

"I don't work for causes or against them. If the money is good and"—here he subtly caught Rose's eye for an instant—"some other benefits possible, I'll take the job. I've read my Kipling but I've read my Swift, too. If the Irish can get out from under, good luck to them." He looked at McLaughlin. "Now, if we can find out just what it is you've got and where it is and how much it's worth, perhaps we can lay out some plans."

"Not that fast, Alec, my lad. I've got a funny feeling that there's something left to tell me. You're a detective, and you've got the face for it. It doesn't give away much when it counts. But Miss O'Connell's not that good at it. And I've got to know one thing before we start looking for any book. Where's my Indian girl, my Farashah? She's mentioned in those letters, too."

Rose inhaled sharply. She said, "Oh, Alec."

8

They caught an express train for the north early the next morning. There was nothing else that would do. McLaughlin would not budge unless they made this one try to find the girl. An exchange of telegrams the night before had assured Cavender that his old rajah friend with the numberless connections in Calcutta would welcome his visit.

Rose had protested weakly that the needs of the IRB were urgent and that they would be wasting time. The girl might turn up on her own as she had before. The manuscript was their object.

McLaughlin shook his white head. "They've waited a long time. They'll wait a few days more, my lass. Don't be forgetting it's a gift they're getting."

Cavender and McLaughlin boarded the train alone. Cavender carried his leather pouch with his Broomhandle Mauser and its accoutrements in it. McLaughlin led Basil on a short leash. Rose had refused to go, but just before the train pulled out from Howrah Station she appeared on the platform with some luggage and found them comfortably settled in their compartment. She joined the party without explaining her change of plans.

By noon Cavender was shaking the rajah's hand on the open platform of the small station in the Bengal province a hundred miles above Calcutta. He was a short and wiry man in his fifties, brown-skinned, well educated. He wore simple white silk, a modestly jeweled turban, a long red waist sash, and a short silver-hilted sword tucked into it. There were four mounted servants behind him and two other sturdy ponies.

Their greeting was warm and brief as it had been between them in the past. That had been during a native disturbance when the rajah had cooperated with the British, and Cavender had been among the few young officers sent in to handle the problem. They had taken to each other.

Introductions were made. They, too, were brief. The rajah greeted Rose warmly, holding her hand in both of his. His expression changed as he met McLaughlin. He smiled quickly and welcomed him with the same warmth he had showed Rose, but not before Cavender detected an odd uneasiness appear in his manner and then as quickly disappear.

He spoke then to Cavender. "You seek a favor, Cavender. That is well what friends are for. But will it wait an hour, my friend?"

"It will wait an hour," said Cavender.

The rajah took Cavender by the arm and led him toward the two ponies. When they were a few feet away from McLaughlin and Rose, he said, "McLaughlin is your friend from the army days?"

"Friend and present employer, you might say," answered Cavender. "I'm here now about him."

For a moment the rajah was serious. Then his face softened into an easy smile. He shook his head. "Good. Your friends are welcome to come with us. My men will give up their horses. Miss O'Connell, however, may be prudent not to join us. I am not offering you a pleasant affair this noon. But having you along is already making it better."

He mounted his horse easily. Cavender got into a white duster and had some difficulty as his pony shied. McLaughlin had a way with horses, as he did with dogs, and had none. Rose elected to go along. She rode badly but stayed in the saddle.

The terrain was flat and covered with high, coarse grass and scattered forests of meems, mangoes, and pepuls growing down from the low hills to the north. The trail was dry and dusty, ready for the winter monsoons.

They rode to witness the killing of an old bull elephant. The rajah explained: "He ran amuck last week. From 'must,' I know it. The villagers don't understand. He destroyed a village and some people were hurt. He will recover, but the villagers don't understand. They have demanded his death. The British commissioner has agreed. They have run the elephant out today."

He turned to Cavender, who rode at his side. "He has served me well for years. I will go there to see him die." After a silence he said, "We two rode him together, Cavender, on the tiger hunt, before you left India. Can you remember?"

Cavender nodded. "And his mahout can do nothing with him now?"

"The man is away. I have sent for him but he cannot be back for one day, two days. The villagers will not wait."

Later, near a grove of mangoes, they sighted a mob of people gathered at the far end. They were jeering and shuffling and gesticulating.

The elephant was standing on the near side of the grove in the shade. He was an old magnificent bull, indifferent to the shouted insults hurled at him, strong, still awesome in his fading glory. He had one yellow tusk whole and one broken and rubbed smooth at the break. His eyes were tiny, red, his hide leathery and scarred where tigers had got to him.

As Cavender and the rajah came up, he began to pace four or five steps in one direction parallel to the grove, stopped, and paced back, shaking his massive head and throwing his trunk up into the air. At the end of each stroll he trumpeted to the sky, then he snorted heavily and eyed the natives around him who were penning him there with the racket of their hundred raucous voices and knocking sticks.

The assistant commissioner sent for the job was a young Englishman who had showed up with an old .44 Henry rifle. He approached the rajah sheepishly, apologized for what he was going to do, and admitted he had never killed an elephant before. The rajah shook his head and offered him no help.

The crowd began to call angrily to the Englishman to get on with it. Cavender thought they wanted to make a fool of him. McLaughlin remained quiet and observant. Rose was strangely excited. Her face had a faint flush, her eyes were intent on the elephant, her hands were clenched at her waist. The rajah walked toward the bull and called out, "Tumba, Tumba." At the sound of his name the elephant stopped pacing, eyed the small prince, swayed menacingly toward him. The rajah was motionless. The great beast reared up threateningly. He trumpeted. Then he came down onto all fours and shook his head and began to pace before the trees again.

Cavender started over to tell the young policeman that his Henry could not do the job right. Before he reached his side, a huge clod of earth sailed out of the crowd and powdered the elephant on the broad expanse of his trunk. For a moment the great beast appeared puzzled. Then, seeming to discover where his assailant was, he broke into a wild charge against one bunch of villagers who had grown bold enough to crowd him on the right. In a frantic scramble the natives fell over each other to get away.

Some men made it into the grove. Others fled down a road screaming.

One half-naked, brown-skinned man slipped on wet grass and went down. In a gray blur the elephant was above him, bringing down one leg with his full weight onto the bare back of the man. The man's body was mashed into the mud, his skin peeled from his back like a skinned animal's, his arms and legs stretching out above the surface of the ground.

The policeman was working the lever of his rifle, and the bullets were popping small sprays of dust from the elephant's side. They did nothing to slow him down. When the elephant finished with the native, he lumbered back to the tree grove and trumpeted. The policeman continued to fire. The elephant finally seemed confused. He stopped moving and stood like a statue.

Cavender shouted over the sound of the firing, "You're going to make it bloody damn long with that thing."

The English officer stopped shooting and came up. "You're right, sir," said the young man. "I'd ask you to try it except it would ruin me with those fookin' blasted heathen."

The villagers were jeering louder, and the heckling was getting malicious.

The officer turned his back on the natives and sent a runner over to the house of a plantation owner and had a heavy Rigby rifle brought back. The owner did not come himself but sent the gun and five shells.

Cavender decided to tell the policeman where to place the shot, but the man waved him away.

"Let me save face with those rotten cowards," he snapped, throwing a bitter look at the crowd of howling natives.

The first two head shots knocked the old bull off his feet. But he rose almost immediately and stared off into the distance. The last three shots put him down again. He trumpeted once from the ground and lay there, breathing hoarsely, but he did not die. Reddish foam flowed from his mouth. His left eye now seemed to be staring directly at Cavender and the rajah, standing next to him.

The policeman was cursing softly. He lay the empty Rigby on the ground, picked up his Henry repeater again, loaded it to its capacity again, and walked closer to the elephant. He began to fire round after round into the great beast, searching for the source of life buried deep inside his body.

The rajah had tears in his eyes when Cavender looked at him. McLaughlin had not moved except to comfort Basil, who was whimpering softly at the smell of death. Rose was trembling and pale next to him.

Cavender's face was grim, his dark gray eyes narrowed, his forehead furrowed, the long dimple now looking like a wicked scar. Almost imperceptibly, a hand touched his arm, then slid down to his wrist and held it.

"Can you stop this, my friend?" The rajah was shaken. The tears on his cheek had dried but his eyes still glistened. "It is foul. The old who have served well deserve a cleaner death. But I will not do it myself to save that fool."

The policeman stopped firing. The breathing of the great elephant had not changed. The small red eye was still fixed on Cavender and the rajah.

Cavender started to remove the big Mauser Broomhandle pistol from his pouch, then remembered McLaughlin's four-barreled Lancaster and asked for it. He checked the chambers and the location of the firing pin to see which of the four barrels would fire next. He walked quickly to the elephant, remembering what he had learned when he had hunted with the rajah. The villagers fell quiet. Only the friends and relatives of the dead man continued their wailing.

The great elephant stirred. He tried vainly to lift his head. There was pity in Cavender's touch as he laid his hand on the leathery flap of the elephant's ear. He stretched the ear out and forward and down. Two inches back from the ear hole and a hand's width down, he pointed the Lancaster, holding the pistol away from the head. He fired. A taste of bile rose from his stomach into his mouth.

When the roar of the .577 died, the heart of the elephant died with it. Cavender felt sickened. Something

42

noble had perished. He looked over at the rajah. The Indian lifted his hand slightly in a small salute of approval. The villagers cheered and rushed forward. Before Cavender reached the rajah, they had descended on the elephant with their knives and were busy dismantling the carcass.

McLaughlin took his pistol back and went over to talk with the two servants standing with their ponies. Rose was shaken and ashy-looking. She avoided Cavender's eyes and walked quickly toward McLaughlin. The policeman was down among the natives.

The rajah held Cavender apart from his friends. "Now, my friend, you may ask what you will. No favor is too large. The old bull died with heart. May we all do as well. He was older than you or I. And at the end he knew it was a feeling hand and a good heart that finished him."

Cavender took that for what it was worth and how it was meant. The Hindu knew more than he did about such things. The rajah listened as Cavender told him what he wanted. He told the story briefly.

The rajah mused afterwards, "A girl. A young girl named Farashah. A butterfly. It may be impossible to find her. It is Calcutta. But maybe not."

The rajah had friends everywhere, relatives, servants. The circle of these people spread to Calcutta and beyond. A few telegrams and some telephone calls would send fifty or more men into the brothel system of the city.

"If a girl named Farashah is working in Calcutta this night, my people will turn her up this night."

Cavender mounted a pony. The rajah turned back from his own horse, hesitated, and then touched Cavender's leg. He looked up.

"There is another thing, Cavender. It bothers me that I must say this." He glanced over to where Rose and McLaughlin were mounting their ponies. "This man McLaughlin. He is called Bull-dog, too?"

Cavender shot a glance at the Irishman and then brought his eyes back onto the rajah's face. He shook his head—yes.

The rajah said, "Be careful, then, my friend. In the

bazaars there has been talk of the man McLaughlin with the name of the dog. There is talk of the Guardians with his name."

"The Guardians?" asked Cavender. "Who are they?"

"Ah, I do not know who they are," said the rajah. "I do not know what they guard. They are from the North-West and they have business with this man. They are Sikhs. I know nothing more. And I know this only by chance through the gossip of my servants."

As the party rode away from the scene of the killing, McLaughlin fell behind. Cavender went back to join him. The big old Irishman had stopped and was sitting slouched in his saddle, staring broodingly at the great carcass under the knives of the natives.

"How did you feel?" he asked Cavender, without taking his eyes from the dead elephant.

"Sad. Pretty rotten."

"It's worse with an animal, isn't it. Much worse."

Cavender nodded.

McLaughlin wheeled his horse around slowly and started away. "For a minute I felt that the old bull was me," he said.

They stayed to dinner with the rajah and caught a night express back to the city to wait for his word.

9

The wait was not long and the news was bad. There was no girl called Farashah in the brothels of Calcutta. The message was brought by the rajah's man in Calcutta, with the rajah's regrets. The search had been thorough, but the butterfly was not to be found.

44

McLaughlin had just gone out for a walk with Basil, and Rose was in her bedroom, when Cavender spoke to the Hindu. When the man left, Cavender went in and told her. She was lying on the bed. She propped her head up on her elbow.

"I wish we hadn't gone there. We wouldn't have wasted this time and we wouldn't have seen that bloody awful thing with the elephant. Sure, you're not going to let him keep looking for the girl, are you?"

"If the rajah can't find her," he assured her, "we can't either, not without spending a year here. McLaughlin's no fool."

"I'm glad to hear you say that. It's time we got after what we've come here for." She turned onto her back and watched Cavender looking at her. She smiled. "When will he be back?"

Cavender shrugged. He reached down and stroked her thick honey hair.

"All right," she said. "Let's."

When McLaughlin returned and read the note the Hindu had left, he crumpled it and threw it onto the floor.

"Blast it, Alec. For nothing it all was."

"We could have been mistaken," said Cavender.

"Yes," said Rose. "I could have been wrong about everything."

McLaughlin growled, "Ahrrr."

Cavender said, "All right. We've done what we've could. Now it's time we talked about the book, McLaughlin. Isn't it?"

Before McLaughlin could answer, Basil jumped to his feet and growled. McLaughlin laid his hand on the dog's head. In the silence they could hear a footstep outside the door. Then came a light knock.

Rose frowned at the interruption. McLaughlin remained blank, but he moved his hand inside his coat. Cavender motioned for them to stay where they were and went to the door.

The fat face of the man filling the doorway was strangely youngish. Under thirty, Cavender would say. It was nearly a blue face. Along the cheeks and where the jawline should have been there was hair under the skin that no amount of shaving could ever remove. The eyes were dark thin slits in the puffy flesh, the skin where the hair didn't grow was dark, smooth, and oily. His hair was black, slick, and plastered to his head. Beads of sweat made him gleam darkly.

And he was fat. He was fat everywhere, in the face, in the neck, in the globelike body bulging his suit. He was fat in the fingers.

"I am Achilles Stathopolous," the man said. His mouth was small and delicate, his voice high and mellow. "The bookseller of Athens."

Cavender stepped aside and the fat Greek glided by him into the center of the room. He bowed slightly to Rose and extended his hand to McLaughlin. That's when Cavender noticed that his fingers were much longer than they first seemed. McLaughlin's big Lancaster, which had appeared moderate-sized in his hand, would have looked rather small in the hand now being extended. His other hand, with a large gold ring on it that didn't look large, clutched a hat. He wore a starched white suit that rode up into the air in the back when he bowed.

"You are Mr. McLaughlin, I'm certain," purred Stathopolous. "And these people? They are interested in the . . . the manuscript, also?"

"Manuscript?" pretended McLaughlin. "What manuscript are you talking about? Who are you?"

"My name is Achilles Stathopolous, the Athenian bookseller," the Greek repeated, unperturbed. "You did not receive my letter in . . . your recent abode?" The word "prison" seemed to embarrass him. "I sent you a letter through an employee there and paid him to see you received it. That was after my efforts to visit you personally two weeks ago proved futile. The letter seems to have failed, too. May I sit down?" He had no trace of foreignness in his speech.

He went to the divan, drew a large handkerchief from inside his suit coat, sat down, and mopped his face and neck. The room was not hot, and the overhead fan was not moving. Keeping his handkerchief to his neck, Statho-

46

polous continued. "I sent my name in to see you on a visiting day, but they said you would not see me. I do not know why. That was too bad, Mr. McLaughlin. Had you seen me then, we could have speeded things up quite a bit. Now there has been trouble and there will be delays, I'm afraid."

"What trouble?" interrupted Cavender. "Do you mean trouble with the Sikh?"

"Who are these people?" asked Stathopolous in a slightly complaining tone as though they had suddenly intruded. "Must they be here while we talk?"

"I'm afraid we must," said Cavender mockingly. "My name is Cavender and this is Miss O'Connell. We're both old friends of Mr. McLaughlin, working together for mutual interests, you might say. If you have to talk with him, you'll have to talk with us."

"I see how it is," said the Greek resignedly. "And you already know about the Sikhs, then?" His eyes were no longer slits but open like round pennies. He put his handkerchief away and laid his fat hands palm down on his thighs. His eyes became slits again. "The trouble I spoke of? No, I do not mean the Sikhs. But the trouble can wait for the moment. Let us get to the first business at hand."

McLaughlin sat down again. The bull terrier lay next to him. Rose sat on the small space left on the divan and turned halfway to watch the Greek. Cavender took the remaining chair.

"The Taxila manuscript," announced Stathopolous when everyone was settled. "I want it, Mr. McLaughlin, and I'm prepared to offer you more, much more than either one of these 'friends' of yours can. I assure you of that."

"These people are not interested in buying anything I've got," said McLaughlin gruffly, standing up. "I don't know why they bothered to introduce themselves to you. I've no business with you I can think of, Mr. Stathalous. So if you've got more to say, say it quickly and leave us be."

"Stathopolous, please," corrected the Greek quietly.

"Let's hear what Mr. Stapolous knows about the Taxila

manuscript first," suggested Cavender. "It might be interesting."

"Please, Stathopolous," corrected the Greek unperturbed. He spelled his name out slowly.

"All right, Mr. Stathopolous," growled McLaughlin. He sat down again. Cavender lounged against the wall.

The fat man eased out a long silver-and-black-enamel cigarette case, removed an oval-shaped brown cigarette, and accepted a light from Cavender. Cavender smoked a Suerdieck. Rose had not spoken a word in the Greek's presence but seemed to observe everything said and done. Cavender thought she was good and composed.

The room filled with smoke quickly, each smoker giving off a different scent. Cavender said, "Now, as you were saying . . ."

"Mr. McLaughlin has told you what the scrolls are, I take it."

"Let's hear you tell it," Cavender insisted.

McLaughlin leaned back and glanced at Cavender from the side. Cavender shrugged. McLaughlin said, "Go ahead, man."

"This is foolish," said the fat Greek with a sigh, "but if you insist. The Taxila scrolls, as Mr. McLaughlin well knows, are an old copy of the *Iliad*, Homer's *Iliad*. How much of that great epic they actually contain only McLaughlin knows—and the people they were taken—the people who possessed them earlier. But even if the scrolls hold only a portion of that great book, they may be old enough, perhaps the oldest extant copy to be of great interest to collectors and libraries."

Cavender's face remained unchanged except for a slight narrowing of his eyes. He had once worked on a case involving counterfeiting rare manuscripts at the Bibliothèque in Paris. It had taken him less than three weeks to tag which of the library's three curators was creating near-perfect duplicates of some rare books and upsetting the book markets of Europe. But during that time he had learned something of the value of a book. Old manuscripts could range in worth from very little—a few hundred pounds—to phenomenal sums bookmen would not even

48

mention, depending on the age, the condition, the significance of the piece, and even on its history of earlier owners.

When he asked, "How great of an interest?" he was not asking in total ignorance.

"I'm prepared to offer you fifteen thousand pounds, if they are the Taxila scrolls. You see, Mr. Cavender—and I talk to you because it seems apparent now that you are a kind of agent for Mr. McLaughlin—I have been in the rare-book world since I was taken into a bookshop at age fourteen. For seventeen years I have been dealing with books of this nature. I've handled a Gutenburg Bible, A Shakespeare first folio, a Caxton Chaucer. If the Taxila scrolls really contain an early *Iliad*, they would be worth a thousand pounds a hundred years, if they are older than ten centuries. I've chosen fifteen centuries as a likely number."

Here the Greek turned to McLaughlin. His voice remained high and calm.

"What do you say, Mr. McLaughlin? Fifteen thousand pounds, and more, perhaps, if they are as old as they might very well be. That's almost a thousand pounds for every year you've paid for them."

McLaughlin laughed out loud beratingly. The weariness that had been showing in his face before was gone. "I'm sorry, Mr. Stathopolous, you've come to Calcutta for nothing. The scrolls, if I really had them, and I don't, would not be for sale. You see, my good man, while I was in prison"—the fat Greek blinked his eyes at the word—"I made a private covenant, I did, with God. I promised that if He let me survive my term in good health, I would turn those scrolls over to a cause good enough for His approval. If I could ever get my hands on them again, that is. And if I ever do get my hands on them, you can be bloody sure it's fulfilling my part of the bargain I'll be doing. He's fulfilled His."

He struck himself lightly on the chest several times. There was no talk about a daughter. The girl seemed to have vanished from everyone's thoughts. "If anybody gets the Taxila *Iliad* it will be my own Irish friends, it will.

For the freedom of all good Irishmen and Ireland herself. Believe it, Mr. Stathopolous, on your way back to Athens. And if I were you, I'd be getting my ticket right away. The Sikh you tried to kill the other day didn't get killed. And he knows who it was put the knife into him."

"What about a Sikh? What Sikh?" asked Rose, speaking for the first time.

"Do not worry about any Sikh, my dear young lady," said Stathopolous, moving his eyes over Rose's face and body as he extinguished his cigarette in a glass ashtray at his elbow. His face never lost its composure. If there was disappointment somewhere deep within his flesh, his appearance remained optimistically Buddha-like and his voice confident. "Could I at least arrange to see the scrolls? If the businessman in me can't be gratified at the moment, at least let the booklover be—for a few moments. Certainly that is not asking too much."

A long silver ash hung on the end of Cavender's cigar. He carefully carried the cigar to the ashtray, walking in front of the Greek.

"Forget the scrolls, Mr. Stathopolous," he said, looking down at the top of the sleek head. "They're not here."

Stathopolous looked slowly from Rose to McLaughlin and up at Cavender. He pushed himself to his feet with some exertion, but Cavender had the feeling he was not so slow, not so lethargic as he seemed. He was obese, but he was young.

Cavender stepped in front of him, blocking the door, as he fixed his hat to his head. "I'm sure you're not going to leave," he said, "without telling us more about the trouble you mentioned before, the trouble we're facing because you didn't get to see McLaughlin in prison."

"Of course, the trouble," purred the Greek. "You mean the trouble I am going to save you from." He paused, adjusted his hat again. His voice, softer and higher, acquired a tone of self-satisfaction. "Yes, that's correct. To show Mr. McLaughlin there my good faith and concern for his well-being, I'm going to help him out of this trouble."

He reached into the breast pocket of his jacket, took out

50

a long envelope, dropped it on the divan where he had been sitting.

"You look like an intelligent man, Mr. Cavender. Certainly when you understand what I am doing here, you will reason with Mr. McLaughlin to do business with a man you can trust. I will be at the Birmingham Royal when you want me. Good-bye, Miss O'Connell." He bowed. His coattail rode up into the air. Somewhere in the folds of fat on the young Greek's face, Cavender saw what seemed like the traces of a smile. Cavender moved aside. Stathopolous opened the door, stepped out, and half turned his massive frame.

"That"—he pointed a fat finger toward the envelope on the divan—"concerns Mr. McLaughlin's daughter. You've been looking for her, I hear. I am certain that that will interest you."

He closed the door. In the few moments during which no one in the room moved, there were no footsteps heard outside. But when Cavender opened the door to check the hall, Mr. Stathopolous was gone.

10

McLaughlin's face looked haggard. In his hand was a note and a small brass key that looked familiar. His voice was almost spiritless, but his accent would not let the tones go completely dead.

"What's going on, Alec? It's got mucked up, the whole thing. I never really thought she would turn up, but when you said she might be in Calcutta right now, I felt like a father. Saw her last when she was four years old. Now this bloody book is muckin' her all up."

Cavender took the note. It was written in English in a clear but tiny hand that made Cavender bring it close to his eyes. It said:

> Mr. McLaughlin.
>
> The Russian is holding your daughter. No doubt you'll be hearing from him soon, with an offer to trade—the manuscript for the girl.
>
> I know where he is keeping her. I know Borodin. Nothing will stop him. Without my assistance you'll never find her alive, without losing the scrolls.
>
> To show my good will, I offer you back your daughter.
>
> Use the key enclosed. Room 417 in your own hotel. The information you want is there. You will have to deal with me now.
>
> Hotel Birmingham Royal.
>
> ACHILLES STATHOPOLOUS

Cavender weighed the key in his palm. It was like the one he had in his pocket to his own room. "Let's go," he said.

Rose stayed with the dog. 417 was on the floor above them. They took the stairs, with Cavender leading the way.

Up in the room they found another Sikh, like the cousin of the one who had been outside the prison and later attacked in the square. For a second Cavender thought he was the same man. He was pretty much the same age, gray-bearded, dressed exactly like the first Sikh, wearing the same steel bracelet on his right wrist that all Sikhs wear to remind them not to steal. But this man was paler.

He was lying face up on the floor with a long gaping wound across his throat. The cut had been made by an expert, starting low on one side and coming up close under the ear on the other. The dead man's short curved sword was still in its hanger tucked in his waistband.

From the condition of the body and the pool of blood, Cavender judged the Sikh had been killed in the past seven or eight hours. He, McLaughlin, and Rose had probably been pulling into Howrah Station when it happened.

On the breast of the dead man was a small sheet of paper. The handwriting on it was in the same niggardly small script of the Greek. Cavender squinted until the words grew clear.

> *Your daughter is being held in a duk bungalow in Blackburn Lane, number range 68–72. Uncertain. You will have to find the exact place yourself. Her guards are two Chinese matrons. Yet I advise caution.*
>
> *Borodin will stop at nothing. The man beneath this note is another Sikh who was troublesome to the Russian. This is his work, not mine.*

There was no signature this time.

Cavender handed McLaughlin the note.

"I think you'd better tell me everything you know about the Russian."

On the way down McLaughlin told what he knew. The man was Count Sergei Borodin. He had visited McLaughlin once perhaps ten years ago in the hole, offering to buy the Taxila Homer. He was an internationally known book collector, at least that's what he claimed. He was an athlete, an auto racer, motorcyclist. He had become an aeroplane pilot; in Russia flying had become very popular.

"He told you all this during that one visit?" asked Cavender. He stepped off the elevator into the small lobby.

"No," said McLaughlin. "But there's no figuring a man. Since that visit he's been sending me a letter every year. Around the time of Saint Patrick's Day. And each time he's made the same offer—some great bit of money he's offering—and he's told me some of those things about himself. Where he was, what he was doing. Thought he would cheer me up, he did. Saint Paddy's Day reminded him that I existed. And he tried again. Now this. As if I didn't hate those Russian bastards anyway. I'll break his bloody neck if I ever see him."

As they went out into the street to look for a taxicab, Cavender asked, "Did you think there was this kind of nastiness in him?"

"How do you tell?" McLaughlin asked.

11

Blackburn Lane wasn't easy to find or to reach. Cavender and McLaughlin rickshawed over to Harrison Road, where the city was awash with people, animals, carts, machines, taxis, and hundreds of other rickshaws. It hadn't changed since Cavender was last there years ago except, he thought, to have gotten busier, noisier, and smellier.

As he passed the crowds he recognized members of dozens of sects, religions, castes—Jains, Parsees, Gurkhas, Pathans, Brahmins, warriors, peasants, Buddhists, Bengalis. He felt a small pleasure identifying each type immediately. And he hadn't forgotten how to avoid the untouchables.

There was vitality and excitement in the streets in the late afternoon air. Cavender felt stimulated and at the same time tranquil. But that feeling didn't last long. No one they asked had heard of Blackburn Lane. They avoided asking the police. Cavender began to stop taxis. Finally the fifth driver said that Blackburn was somewhere down in the Chinese quarter. And he knew where. But even that didn't make it much easier.

It was nearly dark before they could cross the great city to the Chinese district. The crowds in the streets, the jammed market places, the strangled squares kept their speed to a crawl. And the city's hundreds of roving white cows seemed to be on every street, forcing them to frequent halts where they had to wait patiently until the animals moved. The driver angrily pounded at his horn and shouted out the window, but he could do nothing else. The great bony humped cows took their own slow time. And time passed.

"The dark may be better for us anyway," said Cavender, as he watched McLaughlin growing more nervous and impatient. "If there's trouble I'd rather not have it in broad daylight."

Gruffly, McLaughlin muttered, "Y're right." But he did not stop clenching and unclenching his hands as the minutes slipped away.

The sun had already gone when Cavender began to observe more Chinese on the streets than Hindus and Moslems. In a few more minutes pigtails and skullcaps were everywhere and the turban and fez had disappeared.

"We are here, sahibs," said the Hindu driver.

Blackburn Lane was one of a maze of similar narrow lanes cutting in parallel lines or at right angles to each other through tangled acres of low-roofed, screened-in bungalows. The *duks* were all monotonously shacklike, put together of gray boards and tarpaper, built almost touching each other on all sides except along the road front. The driver admitted he was lucky to know the lane only because there was a popular Chinese opium house and brothel on it where he dropped fares occasionally.

There were low fences in front of the *duks* with the small numbers on them required by the police. Cavender stopped the taxi in the forties block and asked the driver to wait with his engine running. He took out a ten-rupee note, tore it in half, and gave the driver one piece.

"We may have to leave in a hurry," he said to McLaughlin. "I don't want to be running around blind in these dark streets looking for a way out."

The street was badly lighted by widely spaced electric arc lights that cast small circles of light around their own poles. Little was really visible except by its darker shadow among fainter shadows. The lane was crowded with the shapes of people. They loitered in the road, against the fronts of bungalows, on the small porches, wherever there was one, even in between the shacks if there was room. Faces were pale blurs.

Everyone Cavender got close enough to see was Chinese. He felt the heads turning as he and McLaughlin intruded in their town. At least in two places three or four forms leaned out through windows and women's voices, softly laughing, called their invitations.

The air was pungent with the odor of pork and vegetables cooking in ginger sauces, and at one place, next door to where women called them, a thick, sickening odor of opium smoke hung over them like a cloud. They walked through it for almost two minutes. They walked slowly to avoid causing a stir. They behaved like sahib sightseers.

As Cavender passed each bungalow he searched for a number. Some of the shacks had no numbers he could find, others had small white figures painted on small posts close to the road. He found a 64 but no 66, 68, or 70. He kept walking. He found a 74.

Three Chinese drifted over and jostled Cavender. McLaughlin, three feet behind, strode up fast and placed a hand on the chest of the closest one. Cavender grabbed one of the others by the right arm, spun him around, and swung his thick forearm around the man's throat. The other two Chinese fled into the darkness.

The Chinese in Cavender's grasp squirmed and clawed, but he could reach nothing. Cavender spoke first in English.

"Which one is seventy, where they're holding an Indian girl?"

The Chinese did not answer.

Cavender asked again in English, then in Urdu. He increased the pressure against the Chinese's larynx. The man's head bobbed slightly. Cavender relaxed his grip.

"That *duk*, that *duk*," screeched the Chinese, pointing to a shadow of a bungalow a few yards behind them.

"How many in there?" demanded Cavender in Urdu.

The Chinese shook his head. "Don't know. Don't know." He held up two fingers and a thumb and then a third finger.

56

Cavender released him. He disappeared into the dark after his friends.

There was a solitary light on at one end of the bungalow the Chinese had pointed out. It cast a pale glow through two screened openings in the room. The rest of the bungalow was pitch dark.

"Come on," said Cavender softly, coming up close to the Irishman. "On streets like this everybody knows everything going on. I believe that Chinaman. That's the place."

He walked back down the street, watching the bungalow and listening to McLaughlin breathing heavily behind him. He saw two shapes moving in the lighted room.

He stopped and waited until McLaughlin was at his side. "Stathopolous was wrong. They don't look like women to me. We'll take this a little more carefully."

"It'll be time we're wasting," muttered the big McLaughlin. "And we've wasted enough already. We could shoot our way in and out of there before those bloody Chinese know what's hit 'em."

McLaughlin moved forward into the outer rays of an arc light. Cavender caught a glimpse of the pistol in his hand. He laid a hand on McLaughlin's arm.

"We won't take any chances, but let's do this without guns, if we can, and keep the police out of it. Did you see more than two in there?"

"Two's enough and damned be the police. Those coolies have got my girl in there."

Cavender gripped his arm tighter. "We'll do it my way or you'll go in there alone and get her killed and go back to prison likely."

McLaughlin cursed softly and went silent.

"I'll go round the rear. Give me some time to get there. Then count fifty and start pounding on the front door. When you start, I'll come in the back door and take them. You got that? A simple frontal diversion. And don't use that cannon unless you really have to."

"All right, Alec, this time we'll be doing it your way."

It was not hard for Cavender to get around the side of the *duk*. The light from the end room reached out far enough to keep him from tumbling over refuse or stepping into holes. He had to squeeze by several men standing in a circle smoking. Once in the back he recalled how Indian bungalows were generally laid out—a flat side in the rear with a two- or three-step rise to a doorway in the center. Usually there was only a screen hanging there without the door.

He found the stairs and rear entrance. But instead of a free-swinging screen closure, a fairly rigid rattan door blocked the entrance. He crept up the steps. There was no handle of any kind on the door. He laid a hand on it and pushed gently. It moved about an inch and then held, locked by some kind of latch on the inside.

He reached inside his coat and drew his small pocket Mauser. In 7.65 caliber it was hardly a man-stopper, but he had practiced with it enough to hit what he aimed at. And he had found from experience that where you put the bullet was more important than the bullet itself.

With gun in hand, he laid his ear against the door. There were some voices coming from the left side of the bungalow.

Then McLaughlin started to bang on the front door. The voices inside grew excited. There was the sound of naked rushing feet. Cavender hit the bamboo door hard. Something broke and it opened about a foot and then held fast again.

A loud crash came from the front of the bungalow, followed by some excited gabbling in Chinese. Cavender went up against the bamboo again. This time the door opened wide enough to get an arm and leg inside and push aside a table that was blocking his way. Then he was in a small dark room. Across the room was an opening covered by strings of beads.

It took Cavender less than a second to get himself across the room through the curtain of beads. But during that time there came a man's high-pitched scream followed by the shuddering roar of a heavy pistol shot. Silence. Then came the clear thudding sound of a body hitting a hard floor.

The room Cavender had burst into was lighted from a Chinese flame lantern hanging on an interior wall. Several low settees were spread around and there were a few thin rugs scattered crazily on the floor. A black table was turned over on its side. Ivory mah-jongg pieces were strewn around the room. The board was half hidden under a body sprawled on the floor. The upturned face was that of an old Chinese. The eyes were open, the long thin Oriental moustache touched the floor. A black skull cap remained undisturbed on the thin scalp.

Aside from the curtained entrance where Cavender was standing, there were two other doorways side by side in the adjacent wall to his right. The doors to both were open. In the farther door stood McLaughlin, holding his Lancaster pistol on a second Chinese across the room. That man, too, was no longer young. He glared wildly at McLaughlin, uttering over and over, "Double-cross, double-cross, no shoot, no shoot."

In a scrawny hand he held a thin Chinese dirk with a wavy blade. As Cavender paused, the blade twinkled through the air. The Chinese's arm had not moved. The knife was thrown underhand by a hard snap of the wrist.

Standing in the next doorway was a Chinese woman, her hand to her mouth. She screamed just as the knife was thrown. McLaughlin twisted his head away toward her and the knife thudded into the wall a few inches from his neck.

Everything happened so fast that the curtain of beads behind Cavender was still rustling noisily where he had burst through them.

Cavender saw the anger tighten in McLaughlin's face. In an unexcited voice he was able to say, "McLaughlin, there's no need to squeeze that trigger now. He's got nothing—"

The explosion seemed to buckle the walls outward, and buried Cavender's last words. The Chinese knife-thrower appeared to be lifted into the air backwards by an invisible force. His feet came off the ground his arms stretched out as in an embrace. He dropped onto the settee directly behind him and fell to one side. His feet flopped back onto the floor. His torso lay stretched out heaving.

"God damn it, McLaughlin," Cavender muttered between his teeth. "Is that what you did in Taxila? It was senseless."

The woman had stopped screaming and was gone. Cavender stopped thinking about McLaughlin and ran through the doorway she had been frozen in. He felt his way down a dark hall into a room at the end.

There were noises in the room. Someone was sobbing. Someone else was breathing hard. Cavender pointed his Mauser at the sound of heavy breathing. He used his left hand to fish out a long sulfur match from a small pocket.

Holding the match as far from his body as he could stretch his arm, he struck his thumbnail across its head. The match flared up, smoked, and burned evenly. It threw plenty of light on a Chinese woman cowering in a corner. Her knees were drawn up in front of her, her arms wrapped around them. She sobbed into her legs.

Over the sight of his pistol, sitting on a low settee, was a woman wearing the Moslem veil of purdah. Her sari was white like her veil. She was breathing hard. The veil trembled under her breath. Her eyes were staring straight at Cavender.

"Farashah?" It was McLaughlin calling to the girl from behind Cavender. "Is that you, my girl? Is it Farashah? My Butterfly?"

"Father?" The voice was tremulous.

The match burned close to Cavender's fingers. He lit another one and put his pistol away.

"It's me, Farashah, McLaughlin. Can you remember? Can you remember I carried you on my shoulders when you were four?"

Cavender didn't know what else a man could say at a moment like this. It was as good as anything else.

The girl rose. She seemed very small in the pale glow of the match. She walked slowly toward Cavender and the man she called father. She kept her head bowed and stopped a few feet away. "I don't remember very much, except what mother told me before she died." Her English was clear and nicely schooled. There was little uncertainty in her tone. She seemed unafraid.

"I think you'd better save the rest of it for later,"

interrupted Cavender. "If we can avoid the police, we should—and sooner or later they'll be around, even down here."

He shook the match out and led the way back down the hall to the front of the bungalow. He found the front door swinging open on one broken hinge.

The street in both directions had become almost deserted. The gunshots had sent the local residents to cover. Cavender thought they were more afraid of meeting up with the police in an inquiry than they were of stopping stray bullets. These were the people found in the slum quarters of every big city who saw nothing, heard nothing, knew nothing. Cavender counted on them to keep McLaughlin and himself out of the metropolitan jail.

Up the street, the taxicab was perfectly visible under a sputtering street light because the crowds were gone. Cavender headed for it at a fast walk. McLaughlin and the girl were close behind.

They passed a rickshaw whose wallah was standing motionless inside the traces.

"Mr. McLaughlin, sir," came a voice from within the rickshaw. It was a high purring voice.

Cavender stopped. "Take the girl to the taxi," he said to McLaughlin. "I'll handle Stathopolous." He walked to the rickshaw.

"You came for the show?" he asked without sarcasm.

"I did not expect you would have had to shoot women, Mr. Cavender," said Stathopolous, gripping the side of the rickshaw to draw his corpulence forward.

"Hah," Cavender snorted, "those weren't women in there. You were misinformed."

"Ah, I am sorry," said the Greek with a sigh. "I had some men following the Russian. They followed him here and reported that there were only women in there, the undependable dogs. But what can one really expect from these people? No matter. The affair seems to have turned out well. You've got the girl. Now I think it only fair you urge Mr. McLaughlin to deal with me in the matter of the manuscripts. He owes me at least the right to examine them and to take my bid. He wants to contribute to some

Irish fund; my money will do just as much for Irish freedom as the scrolls. Tell him that. Tell him I know how to receive gratitude with grace, will you?"

"I'll do that, Mr. Stathopolous, I'll do just that. And it was the Russian behind this, you say? Where is he now?"

"He was behind it all the way, Mr. Cavender, all the way. He seems refined, but beware of his refinement. I cannot tell you his whereabouts at the moment. He has disappeared. But my incompetent men are looking. You know my hotel. Come to see me later tonight. Hours are not important. I think we should talk alone, and I may have more things to tell you." He leaned back into the darkness of the rickshaw.

"I'll try," said Cavender.

Stathopolous called to his wallah and was carried off silently down the empty lane. Under a streetlight Cavender looked at his watch. It was not yet nine o'clock. It was just three days since he had walked into the brothel on Kidderpore, and he was already beginning to feel tired.

12

Three policemen were waiting stiffly in the hotel room when Cavender walked in. McLaughlin and his daughter were behind him. Rose got up from her chair and walked over to Cavender. Basil was not in sight.

"Hello," she said to McLaughlin. She looked at the girl in the veil and said nothing. Then to Cavender she said, "They've been here for half an hour. Sure someone's been killed in the hotel. They're here to see him." She tilted her head toward the Irishman.

The policeman in charge was English. The other two were light-skinned Hindus.

"My name is Lieutenant Bentley, Calcutta Metropolitan," said the Englishman. He was in his mid-twenties, handsome, tanned dark, clean-shaven, and immaculate. His white shirt sparkled, his tan shorts were sharply creased, his white leather straps and holster were freshly creamed and spotless.

"Alec Cavender," said Cavender, taking the hand extended to him. "British, but residing in Brussels. This is Major Brendan McLaughlin. And his daughter."

The officer shook McLaughlin's hand and nodded to the girl. The Indians remained motionless, their arms crossed on their chests. Their eyes shifted to take in the Moslem girl. They, too, appeared clean and smartly dressed. There was a healthy male smell in the air, coming, Cavender thought, from coconut oil rubbed into their skins.

"I'm sorry about this, sir," said Bentley, talking to McLaughlin. His pith helmet was in his hands but he was not embarrassed or sorry. "There are a few questions I would like to ask you. A man has been found dead on the next floor almost directly above this room. Murdered, I'm afraid. He's a Sikh, Mr. McLaughlin."

Cavender noticed the "mister." Bentley kept his eyes on McLaughlin, waiting for a response. He got none. "Mr. McLaughlin, we know why you were sent to prison, sir."

Farashah moved closer to her father, who put an arm around her. They had talked in the taxi a little, and those few words had quickly drawn her to her father. Cavender had noticed it and mused about such daughterly ways.

"I'm sorry, miss, but I've got to do this." Bentley was trying too hard to be sorry. Cavender didn't believe he was. He looked efficient and somewhat ambitious.

"Now don't you be shy, young officer," McLaughlin said cheerfully. "You've got your duty."

Basil barked from the bedroom. McLaughlin opened the door and let the bull terrier follow him into the room.

"That's a fine bull terrier you've got there, sir," said Bentley. He patted Basil on the head. He straightened up from stroking the dog. "Well, anyway, there was talk at the central station house yesterday about you, your release. We didn't have any records handy about the trial, so there was just talk. Someone said four Sikhs were killed during the rising by a squad of regulars you were leading on a raid up there in the North-West Frontier—I've never been there myself. Said the raid was unauthorized. You went in for it."

"That's right, my boy," said McLaughlin. "For sixteen years. But sure now, there was some question, you know, about that 'unauthorized' bit. Will you ask your questions."

"When we got the report about the murdered Sikh upstairs, I had to check all the rooms in the hotel and when I came in here I found your prison bag in there. Pure coincidence, yesterday's talk and this. This lady here, Miss O'Connell, was reluctant to say much about anything. Your name was on the inside—and here you are. Down at the station they're going to want to know if this killing has anything to do with the killings in Taxila, is that where it was? Or whether your showing up here was just bad coincidence for you."

"I think that this can be settled right here, Lieutenant Bentley," said Cavender, handing the police officer his credentials and identification, including his discharge from the army and his release from Scotland Yard.

"When was the Sikh killed?" he asked.

"I'm not a coroner," replied Bentley, "and we haven't got one over yet, but I'd say some time last night or early this morning."

"Good. If you can make sure of that, then Mr. McLaughlin had nothing to do with it. Since his release two days ago he's been with me, not long enough away to do any killing. And we weren't even in Calcutta until after eight this morning, and not in the hotel until nine P.M. or later. Miss O'Connell can vouch for that." Rose nodded her head. "You can check the ticket agents and porters at Howrah—and talk to Rajah Kan Sind in Bengal if you want or to the assistant police commissioner up there. Never got his name."

Bentley brightened up and got out a notebook. He wrote rapidly as Cavender repeated some details.

"I'm glad to have this," Bentley said, waving the notebook when Cavender was through. "You won't be leaving the city, I presume, until these people can be contacted. It would be even more helpful if you gave your word to remain here in this hotel."

"If that's an order, son," said Cavender, injecting some annoyance into the words, "I'll have to call someone over your head. You'd be putting us all under house arrest."

"No, no, sir, I don't intend that, Mr. Cavender," said the lieutenant, reddening. "But if Mr. McLaughlin could make himself readily available until—say, noon tomorrow —that shouldn't inconvenience any of you. If I could have your word, Mr. Cavender. Otherwise I'll have to leave one of my men downstairs."

McLaughlin dropped onto the divan and rubbed the bull terrier. "Seeing how things are, that will be fine with me. It has been a long day, it has, and my bones are weary. I'll be going to bed as soon as things quiet down around here, and I'll be sleeping in the morning, just to feel what it's like. If you need me, you'll find me right here."

Farashah edged over to stand by her father. Rose watched her curiously for a moment and then led the policemen to the door.

"I'm glad it's worked out this way," said Lieutenant Bentley, returning Rose's smile and blushing a little. He said good night.

Cavender went outside into the hall with him. The Indians went down the hall to ring for the lift.

"Lieutenant, that was good about the prison bag. But you already knew McLaughlin was in this hotel. He's been followed since he got out, hasn't he?"

Bentley was not experienced enough to control the flinch near his eyes. Cavender said, "I thought so."

"You spotted him?"

"Uh-uh," said Cavender, shaking his head. "Just a guess. Then you know damn well we were out of the city when whatever happened happened."

This time the young officer reddened in anger. "You're

very smart, Mr. Cavender. But you know as well as I do that following him was necessary. When he killed those Sikhs in '97, something disappeared that a lot of people are interested in seeing reappear. Our government people, for one. You probably know exactly what it is. We don't, yet. But we will. And whatever it is, McLaughlin will not get it out of India. Even with your help."

"I expect not," said Cavender. "Not now." He went back into the room.

13

McLaughlin, Rose, and Farashah were talking about the kidnapping when he returned. He listened as Farashah finished her tale. Her bright, darkly mascaraed eyes shone through the veil slits. Her voice was soft and fragile. Her story was what Cavender expected. He took the summary from McLaughlin. Two men—Chinese. A motorcar. No one to help her.

"Where did you say you were picked up?" asked Cavender.

"Ahrrr, hell, Alec, what does it matter?" complained McLaughlin.

"It matters," said Cavender. He repeated the question.

"On Kidderpore Road," replied the girl, dropping her eyes to the floor.

"Was there a man there named Borodin? Borodin? Someone with an accent, not Chinese?"

"No," she said. Then hesitantly, she said, "They spoke only Chinese but someone may have said that name. Borodin . . . Bor . . . o . . . din. I think they did."

McLaughlin took her hand gently in his.

"That's all over, Farashah. Now listen, my g.... your own true father, you my own daughter. I'd like t.. you to give up this purdah, to come out from under the veil, to come out for good and all. I have the right to ask this. Will you do it for your father? C'mon, girl, it's your face I'd like to see now."

As though she had been waiting for someone to ask her, Farashah reached up quickly, fumbled for a moment with a hidden catch, and then let the veil fall away. Cavender's eyebrows drew slightly together, pushing his forehead up into lines. Older Moslem women, he knew, would sooner be beaten than unveil before a strange man in circumstances like this. Even Moslem prostitutes kept themselves under the veil until the very last minute when they were with customers, and then as soon as they were finished went back under.

The face that was revealed now distracted Cavender. She was Eurasian, all right, but there was very little of the European in her. She was beautiful, brown-skinned, and dark-eyed, obviously taking most of her characteristics from her mother and very little from McLaughlin. For one thing her teeth were good, white and even, and nothing like an Irishman's. For another, her skin was smooth and soft and unblemished. McLaughlin had given her, perhaps, the fine line of his nose. That was all Cavender could see between them.

"Now there's a sight for you. Will you look at that." Beaming, McLaughlin leaned forward and awkwardly kissed her cheek. "You'll not be wearing that thing anymore, do you hear? Not as long as we're together and you're my daughter and half-Irish. Hey!"

The girl dropped her head and shook it "yes" and raised it. Her eyes shifted from her father to Cavender and then settled on Rose, as if she were the easiest to face unveiled.

After a few moments of awkward silence, Cavender said:

"McLaughlin, I think it's time we put some cards on the table face up. The whole business is getting more complicated by the hour. You've got a stubborn Greek who wants the scrolls—and says he's willing to pay, although we haven't seen his money yet. There's a Russian out there who likes to play dirty games. There are some Sikhs somewhere in the picture and we don't know what they're prepared to do. And now there's this Lieutenant Bentley, who tells me you're a subject of some interest to the government."

"They'll find out I had nothing to do with up there," said McLaughlin, pointing to the ceiling with his thumb.

"They know it already," said Cavender. "They have a shadow on you. I took a guess and Bentley didn't know how to handle it. He admitted there was someone following you. Probably all the way to Bengal. I think we were lucky and lost him on the way to Blackburn. This *is* the toughest city in the world to follow anyone except on foot. Get into a taxi and good-bye. But if that shadow did stick to us all the way to the bungalow, Bentley's going to be right back here soon. And even if he didn't, that shooting is going to get to the police soon enough and they could make some of those coolies talk. What I'm getting at is that if we're going to recover those scrolls, we've got to do it now and get out as fast as we can. Where are they?"

McLaughlin scratched his white head as though that helped him think. He rose, stretched, and said, "Right. I'll take you to them tomorrow, Alec. We'll all go. Don't worry about them. They're safe enough. All I'll say now is that they're not too close by where anybody but me can get their hands on them. What I need right now is some sleep." He called the bull terrier to his side. "Which bedroom?"

"No," said Cavender flatly. The dimple in his left cheek deepened to look more like a small cut. "That's not good enough. It's time someone else knew where they are. You want to get them to your Irish friends. You made your deal. I've made mine. With the same people, it seems. They're paying me to get them there. I'm going to do that. And the way people around here are getting cut up and shot down, it would be a lot smarter if two of us knew what we were doing."

McLaughlin studied Rose for a while, but as though he was thinking of other things. She sat with her hands folded on one knee that was crossed over her other leg. The position showed the full line of her leg to her hip. She looked back at him. There appeared a faint smile at the corner of her mouth. Cavender thought of living sixteen years without a woman. He was wondering whether Rose was thinking the same thing and sympathizing with the Irishman.

Rose spoke first, speaking softly: "If he doesn't trust us enough yet to tell us, Mr. Cavender, then I don't think we should coax him. We'll just have to trust him." She walked over to one of the bedrooms. Cavender couldn't decide whether there was a little more obvious swing to her hips than usual. "Your daughter Farashah can share this room with me. There are two beds in it. If Mr. Cavender doesn't mind using the divan tonight, you could use the other room. Do you mind, Mr. Cavender?"

Cavender thought, What the hell! and nodded his head. Sixteen years without a woman for a man like McLaughlin! He could see this coming on the train back from the north. Rose had taken to the big Irishman. If she wanted to visit him during the night, why not. Cavender would lose nothing.

McLaughlin was saying good night to Farashah while Rose was finding the girl a spare nightdress. Cavender checked his heavy gold Dent. It was ten-thirty.

"Everybody staying put for the rest of the night?" Cavender asked. Everybody was. "Good. I'm going out for a while."

"Alec, my boy. It pains me to ask, but do you have fifty quid? I'll be up earlier in the morning than you, from long practice, you know, I'll be picking up my suit and feeling like a human being again. I'll need to buy a few other things as well. It looks like you'll be getting to bed late and there's little sense in my waking you early."

Cavender counted out ten five-pound notes. "Remember what you told Bentley."

"Oh, the hell with him," McLaughlin chortled. "I'll be out with Basil for a walk. If I've got a shadow the three of us will have an exercise."

As Cavender walked down the hall to the lift, McLaughlin came halfway through the door.

"You're going to look for the Russian?"

"No," said Cavender, swinging open the gate. "I'm going to see the Greek. I don't like him. But all we've done on this trip is talk about money. It's time we saw some, hard and in hand."

14

Everyone was asleep when Cavender let himself into his hotel suite. Basil met him at the door, growled a little, then trotted back into the room where McLaughlin was sleeping. Cavender peered in. The Irishman, wearing only his drawers, was stretched out on his back, snoring lightly. Basil climbed onto the bed carefully. It was a maneuver gentle enough not to disturb McLaughlin. Cavender marveled at it, shook his head, and blew his breath out through pursed lips.

Then for a moment he listened at the door of the other bedroom. One of the girls was moaning softly in her sleep. He took off his clothes in the sitting room and lay down on the divan and smoked a cigar. He got up once to clean and reload his Mauser pistol and once to use the bathroom. When he returned to the divan the second time, Rose was there. When he kissed her he thought he could smell a faint familiar aroma like something good that had gone a little stale. He put the thought away and was very gentle with her. They spoke little and enjoyed each other.

When they were through and he was smoking a Suerdieck and she a Gaulois, she said, speaking softly:

"What happened tonight? Did you see him? The Greek?"

"Yes. There was a lot of talk, rambling, evasive. He

wasn't bubbling with any information. He showed me some money and even let me take this."

He held up a single five-hundred-pound note. She took it and snapped it twice. He said, "He thinks I belong to him now. He even hinted I might take the manuscript away from McLaughlin and make myself a lot of money." He took the note back. "It nearly broke his heart to let this go. But he did. I think the scrolls are going to be worth something to your people, if we can get them out of India—that is, if we can get McLaughlin to dig them up. Stathopolous casually threatened to turn him in to the police for the trouble in the Chinese quarter."

"Oh, do you think he will?"

"Well," said Cavender, "he sat there in his fancy rooms in a silk gown with big half-moons of sweat under his arms and talked about big guns and little guns. He's got a point. McLaughlin carries a big gun and the shooting out there was with a big gun. But—do I think he'll go to the police? No. He's in this thing a hell of a lot deeper than we think."

Cavender got up to find an ashtray and brought it back to the divan. Rose's cigarette glowed in the dark as she drew on it.

"After we talked he came down into the street with me when I left, almost as though he was afraid I wouldn't give him his five hundred pounds worth of loyalty. Here's the good part. There were a couple of Sikhs waiting for us— or for him. And he was lucky. They tried to strangle him. But he's much tougher than he looks. And he's not as slow as he acts. When I was upstairs with him he got a telephone call."

Rose got up. "Excuse me for a minute," she said, and went into the bathroom. When she returned, she asked, "What about the telephone call?"

"The telephone rang. It was next to me and he was sitting across from it. He thought I was going to pick up and he nearly tripped over himself to get to it before I did. But he moved very fast."

"Did you hear who it was?" Rose asked softly.

"No," he said. He leaned over to drop an ash onto the

ashtray on her side and his arm brushed against her breast. She drew back.

"What happened outside?" she asked.

Cavender leaned back against a pillow. "He was lucky they weren't using their swords or his head would be in a gutter right now. I think they're blaming the killing upstairs on him, not the Russian. I frightened them off with a pistol shot, a little too high to hurt anyone."

"Why?" Rose asked, lighting another cigarette.

"I don't know. I'm not sure just yet who should be getting shot."

"Who do you think is behind all this, Alec?"

He dropped an ash and brushed it off the light bedcover. He tried to see Rose's face in the glow of her cigarette.

"Who knows?" he answered. "I haven't met the Russian yet. But I will—pretty soon."

When Rose left his side, he lay for a long while unable to fall asleep.

15

People were moving around trying to be quiet when Cavender opened his eyes. It was a gloomy morning. A table had been set up where McLaughlin, Rose, and Farashah were eating breakfast. Someone had thrown a sheet over Cavender.

"You're a deep sleeper, my boy," said McLaughlin cheerfully. "We've saved you some breakfast, if you hurry. It's cold, but it's good."

It was eight-thirty. A cool damp breeze came in through

the open windows. Cavender said good morning and went into his bedroom to dress in fresh clothes. The suit he came out in was a slightly darker ivory than the one he had worn.

At the table Farashah seemed more docile, Rose a little tight in her feelings, and McLaughlin calmer and relaxed. Cavender ate cold eggs and warm lamb chops and listened to McLaughlin and his daughter try to piece together some memories of the girl's childhood. No one mentioned the Greek.

Farashah seemed to remember very little from the days before McLaughlin had left for good. When McLaughlin prodded, she began to recall the incidents he described and she smiled and said she remembered those good times together. Then she spoke more about her recent life and some about her mother. About those things McLaughlin did not press her. Cavender listened with some interest.

A little before nine-thirty, McLaughlin put on his cheap prison coat. "I'll be drifting down to that tailor shop to pick up my new clothes and a few other things. You finish your breakfast"—Cavender was having his tea—"and don't worry about the police."

"I won't. I'm not exactly your nursemaid," said Cavender. He put his cup down. "But I was sent out here to look after you. Be careful and watch for those Sikhs. I had another little run-in with them last night."

As McLaughlin opened the door, Cavender asked, "You're not thinking of picking up the scrolls by yourself, are you?"

"Now, do you think I'm completely mad, Alec? To get you to come way the hell out here and then shoot off on my own! Think a little better of me, my boy. I'll be back in an hour and we'll work out a definite plan together." He grinned at Farashah. "Good-bye, my beautiful girl." He had not even questioned Cavender once about the Greek.

Farashah smiled at him. As soon as he was gone, she went into her bedroom and back under the veil and spoke with no one.

At ten-thirty Lieutenant Bentley called.

"It's all right about McLaughlin, sir," he said to Cavender. "Everything checks out as you said it would. But I think I ought to caution you. I have good feelings toward you, Mr. Cavender, *and* toward Mr. McLaughlin, in spite of what he may have done. Your records on the frontier are enviable. It was my hope that I might have done something like that. But . . . I want to tell you that there are inspectors here who hope to trap both of you with something incriminating. It would be feathers in their caps if they could reopen McLaughlin's case and then close it completely. I'm telling you this as a friend."

"Very decent of you," replied Cavender. "I'll keep them in mind, but there won't be anything to close because there isn't anything to open. We're just going to say good-bye to old India and go home in a week or two."

"I'm glad to hear that, sir," said Lieutenant Bentley. "And good luck." He hung up.

"I'll bet you are," said Cavender to the dead line. He replaced the receiver. Bentley was young and ambitious. Cavender knew the type well enough from his two years with the Yard. Right now the lieutenant was probably sitting smugly in his office imagining Cavender in some kind of panic heading across the city to a mysterious Hindu treasure. Downstairs there would be a man waiting to follow him. Someone was probably close behind McLaughlin right now.

He asked Rose to order up another pot of tea. He spent the next hour smoking and resting. Rose puttered around anxiously. She listened for footsteps in the hallway and then disappeared into the room to talk with Farashah and then came back. Cavender let her alone.

At eleven-thirty a message was brought to Cavender by a Hindu boy wearing a white turban, shirt, and tight pantaloons. The message was not unexpected. Cavender was hoping it would come when McLaughlin was not around. The boy stood waiting in the hall while Cavender read it. Rose came up behind him. He reached for a small pencil in his pocket and finished reading the note without her seeing it.

It was an invitation for Cavender and McLaughlin to

74

dine with the Count Sergei Borodin and the countess in the
public dining room of the Empress-Gresham in one hour.

16

Rose complained when he told her he was going out alone
again.

He circled her shoulders with a thick arm. He cupped
her chin with his other hand and gave her a light kiss on
her lips.

"You're not going to be left out, little Rose, not at all.
When we get to Dublin, I'll see that you hand the
manuscript over to your friends with your own hands.
That's a promise. Did I tell you how good it was last night?
It was very good."

The girl's cheeks flushed and she drew away angrily.
"Oh . . . you . . . you . . . old bastard," she cried.
"Go ahead, but last night was the last time."

On his way down in the lift, Cavender was thinking
how relative everything was. White-haired McLaughlin
would not stop calling him "boy." And Rose, in her
twenties, had the joy of calling him "old."

Downstairs the lobby was empty. He stepped outside.
A small dark man in Western clothes loitered across the
street in front of a store. Cavender checked his Dent,
looked up at the third floor of his hotel, and then ducked
back inside. At the rear of the lobby he found a narrow
passageway leading to an alley next to the hotel. He took
it. When he reached the end, he watched the small dark
man cross the street for the hotel entrance. As soon as he
disappeared Cavender ran for an empty rickshaw passing
by. He took precautions and changed his rickshaw twice,

reversing directions. Finally he found a taxicab, which was slower than the rickshaws. He walked the last quarter of mile to the Russian's hotel. The small dark man was nowhere in sight.

The Empress-Gresham was the finest hotel in Calcutta. The structure seemed to grow endlessly out of marble of every shade of white. It looked as though it had been designed for a maharajah whose elephants would be using its stairs, hallways, ballrooms, and even its lift. Everything had been designed on the grandest scale and in the costliest fashion. Gilt, damask, silver, crystal were everywhere—on the walls, the ceilings, the tables. The floors were carpeted in Persian. There were statues and working fountains everywhere. Servants were spotlessly dressed in gold-buttoned white uniforms with scarlet turbans, some distinguished by white ostrich feathers as marks of rank.

In the dining room dozens of Anglo-Indians were being served by dozens of Indian servants. Gilt-edged carts covered with silver serving dishes were pushed slowly from table to table. Overhead ten-foot wooden-bladed fans kept the air moving. Toward either end of the dining room great punkahs swung from the ceiling, sweeping the stale air away as four young half-naked wallahs pulled on their ropes to keep them moving. The high windows in the room were raised outward to let the air circulate. Fine lace window hangings moved in the breeze, helping to keep the sun and flies out and letting the air in. The diners looked comfortable, content, and prosperous.

A maître d'hôtel whose turban supported three ostrich feathers took Cavender's name and led him across a black marble floor toward several tables on the edge of the courtyard gardens. It was a choice location. As they made their way easily among the tables, Cavender singled out the man he took to be the Russian. Seated, he appeared to be of medium height and slim build. He looked up and sat back when he caught sight of Cavender approaching behind the head waiter.

His head was a perfect pear shape, from a broad skull covered with smooth, short white hair to a manicured short white beard. His small ears were close to his head, his eyebrows were frosted, his nose was long and strong, and his eyes soft gray. His forehead was wide and smooth.

The count rose gracefully from his chair. He wore a dark cutaway suit. A white, high collar set off a dark nubby-silk tie. There was aristocracy in every line of his body and every crease of his clothing. There was intelligence and self-assuredness in his face. Cavender anticipated a warm dry handshake. He got it.

"Mr. Cavender, please sit down," the count said, still gripping Cavender's hand with his right and offering him the seat across the table with his left. He was shorter than Cavender had guessed. He was in his fifties, lithe and trim.

"The countess will join us later. She is as interested as I am in this acquisition. Perhaps more. Will you join me in lunch." His accent sounded more French than Russian.

Cavender ordered the poached trout, white boiled potatoes, and two paratas. He drank gin and tonic.

The count continued to eat. He talked between mouthfuls. "I expected to see Major McLaughlin with you. I hoped for some personal dealings. I saw him once, you know."

"I'll have to do for now," said Cavender.

"Yes, I see. Ah, well, my inquiries have led me to consider you the major's agent. Is that correct?"

"Partly," said Cavender. "I'm here to assist him in any way I can. That means to accompany him to Dublin in any way he wants."

"He's conveyed to you, I am sure, my interest in the Taxila manuscript?" asked Borodin.

Cavender nodded. "I know that you've been in touch with him for ten years. But your tactics to get him to deal with you are all wrong. You don't understand Irishmen. Threatening his daughter's life, holding her as a hostage, rough stuff like that was hardly intelligent."

The count was frowning. He started to speak. Cavender talked over his words, tightening his voice to make his anger convincing, but keeping his tones down. Nearby diners heard nothing.

"Don't interrupt me. McLaughlin got out a few days

ago and a lot of nasty things have been happening. We're both losing patience. I'm not here now to mediate any transaction between the two of you. But if you think you can use me in some way to help you, you're going to have to give me something. Some information, first. I don't think I have very much at all. And if I continue to feel I'm in the dark, then those scrolls are going to wind up some place where no one will touch them for a long time. Or they'll stay right where they are."

A waiter set his fish in front of him. Another brought the potatoes. A third brought his vegetables rolled in thin pancakes. Softening his voice, he asked the third waiter for a white wine. Then he relaxed to enjoy the fish and listen to Count Borodin's reply.

Count Borodin paused to fix a cigarette to a small black onyx cigarette holder. He lit it and blew smoke from his nose in fine streams. He had never lost his composure. Cavender thought of Stathopolous, who seldom lost his, and he wondered if it was an interest in books that did it. When the count spoke he spoke with a quiet assurance.

"Just what kind of information were you asking about?"

Cavender was about to answer when a very pretty woman in her late twenties walked up to the table. Count Borodin rose, held her hand to his lips, and then introduced Cavender to her.

"My dear, this is Mr. Cavender, Major McLaughlin's associate. My wife, sir."

"Mr. Cavender." She held out an ungloved hand. Cavender, already standing, took it. Her voice was throaty, her accent Russian, heavy.

"The count is a very fortunate man, Countess," said Cavender, meaning it.

"Thank you," she said, drawing off her other glove as an act of undressing. She sat on the far side of the table between the two men, her back to the gardens, her chair slanted to face Cavender on the angle. Her eyes were glistening black, and her hair, shiny black also, was pulled back tight from her face. The hair style made her high cheekbones nicely prominent and gave a touch of a slant to her eyes. The unusual polish of her white skin was

78

emphasized by one round black beauty mark on her left cheek. The flaw was exactly where Cavender's dimple helped lighten the coarseness of his own face.

She wore a simple, expensive white lace dress that hung straight to her shoes, and only one jewel. That made her unique among the many glittering dowagers around her. But it *was* a very large, very yellow diamond on the first finger of her right hand.

As she studied the menu she said something to her husband in Russian that Cavender knew had nothing to do with food. She waved the menu once or twice in slight pretense that it did. Borodin's eyebrows went up a trifle, his lips pursed momentarily, he looked quizzically at Cavender, but he said nothing. He beckoned to a waiter and ordered a crabmeat salad for his wife.

"Would you say you have the major's trust, Mr. Cavender?" asked Borodin, fixing another cigarette to his holder.

"I don't know how much trust a man can offer who's just finished sixteen years in prison. Especially when he thinks he didn't deserve that sentence. I would say he trusts me as much as he does any man. That doesn't mean he's been baring his soul to me."

The count murmured thoughtfully, "What kind of information were you asking about?"

"First," said Cavender flatly, "how much are the scrolls worth to you?"

Without raising an eyebrow, Count Borodin said, "Mr. Cavender, if the scrolls are what I take them to be, I would be embarrassed to offer anything less than fifty thousand pounds sterling. As a starting figure, you understand."

That deepened the dimple in Cavender's cheek and brightened his eyes. "Stathopolous's first figure was a lot lower," he said. "But I saw his money."

"You'll see mine, too, I assure you. That Greek mountain of flesh is a fool, for once." Borodin laughed softly and slapped the table. "What do you think of that, my dear?" he asked, reaching over and placing his hand on hers.

"Vhat a fool, Sergei, isn't he? If this is all true." And she emitted a small laugh, too. She could not pronounce her w's.

"Now," said Cavender, "when you tell me what we're after, that will make three of us laughing at the Greek."

Just then a waiter showed up with the countess's crabmeat salad.

17

"Well, my dear," asked the count, not bothering to hide his question in Russian, "we do need Mr. Cavender now, do we not? What is your opinion?"

The countess fixed a cigarette in an ivory holder twice as long as her husband's and, closing her eyes briefly, nodded her head once. She said softly, "Why, yes, I suppose." She didn't seem to like Cavender.

While the count talked, the countess smoked and picked at the crabmeat. Cavender smoked thoughtfully. The dining room continued to empty. The place grew quiet enough so they could hear the fans and the great punkahs worked by the young wallahs.

"We are here in India, Mr. Cavender, you, Miss O'Connell, I, my wife, Stathopolous, and yes, even Major McLaughlin himself, and who knows who else time will turn up—all because of some old bits of . . . paper? . . . leather? We do not even know what they are, and except for the major himself, we are not even certain that they are any more than fragments or scraps. We are hoping they will turn out to be well-preserved scrolls, legible and complete. And that is only a hope. So much of life turns on hopes. But that is not the point. To the point then.

"Consider what we hope we have, Mr. Cavender. An ancient copy of Homer's *Iliad*. A great Western epic, an epic whose influence for more than twenty-five hundred years has been profound on Western values and thought, on Western language, on Western literature. Now consider this: India, in spite of the British raj, has been a most un-Western world, a world of the East, Hindu, Moslem, Buddhist. Before the eighteenth century her contact with the West had been almost nonexistent.

"Well, then, ask a question, Mr. Cavender, if you will." Cavender did not have to think long. He was already asking the question of himself. "How did the old manuscript get to India at all?"

"Not simply to India, Mr. Cavender, but to a remote city in the North-West Frontier far distant from any cultural center like Bombay or Delhi. That *is* the question. Where did it come from? Who brought it in? When?"

The grand dining room had emptied. Cavender was alone with Borodin and his wife and the four wallahs mindlessly pulling on their ropes to move the air around. All but a few waiters had gone. Borodin beckoned one and ordered a cold champagne. When the waiter left, he reached into his inside pocket and took out a neatly folded sheet of paper. He unfolded it, smoothed it out carefully on the table, and passed it over to Cavender.

It was a page that had been cut from a book. The print was small. At the top were the words *Plutarch's Lives*. Penciled in next to this title were the words "Dryden's Translation." A third of the way down from the top, a short passage was underlined in faded black ink.

He was naturally a great lover of all kinds of learning and reading, and Onesicritus informs us that he constantly laid Homer's *Iliads,* according to the copy corrected by Aristotle, called the casket copy, with his dagger under his pillow, declaring that he esteemed it a perfect portable treasure of military virtue and knowledge. When he was in upper Asia, being destituted of other books, he ordered Harpolus to send him some.

The last line of this passage was doubly underlined.

Cavender scanned the rest of the page for the name of the man who had loved Homer so much. But he already knew it before he found it at the bottom. He looked up at Count Borodin. The dimple in his cheek had deepened into a crevice, his brows were pushed up, and dark lines crossed his forehead. His eyes seemed more deeply sunk than before. His lips pursed in an expression of half-belief.

"That's absolutely right, Mr. Cavender," said Borodin quietly. "Alexander the Great. The conqueror himself took those scrolls into India. Plutarch says there he traveled no place without his Homer. Add a little history and you have it."

"You add the history," said Cavender.

"Alexander invaded India in 326 B.C. He came in the only way possible—through the northwest passage from Afghanistan. He penetrated the Hindu Kush and broke through the Khyber Pass. At times he was opposed but at times he wasn't. The people of Taxila welcomed him and an Indian general named Porus became his friend after the two had met on the field of battle."

"And all this is historical?" questioned Cavender.

"Indisputably."

Count Borodin fished into a small watch pocket with two fingers and drew out a large imperfect silver coin. He dropped it into Cavender's hand. "There's nothing legendary about that, Mr. Cavender." There on one side was the handsome curly head of a man, and on the other, a scene of battle.

Borodin continued: "He did not stay long. Less than a year. It was more like a raid into the Punjab than an invasion. When he withdrew, he bequeathed gifts of his esteem to Porus, who by then had been made governor of Taxila. He gave him arms, and busts of himself. He had silver coins struck with his portrait on one side—that is Alexander you are looking at now—and a picture of Porus on an elephant facing him on horseback, on the other side."

The coin was heavy and roughly made. Cavender rotated it between his thumb and forefinger, weighing its heaviness, thinking of its history.

"A tetradrachm, Mr. Cavender," said Borodin.

Cavender felt a small thrill in his hand. It reminded him that the violence and nastiness in his life had not deadened his basic romanticism. He offered to hand the coin back. Borodin did not take it.

"There are others like this in the great museums. It is quite real." Borodin watched Cavender's eyes. "Would you like that one, Mr. Cavender?"

"Not just yet," said Cavender. He pushed the coin across the table.

"Perhaps as a token of my gratitude in the near future?"

Cavender let that go. He said, "What you have is a theory. Alexander the Great brought his Homer into the Punjab on a raid and left it there. How do you prove that McLaughlin's manuscript is the one Alexander owned?"

The countess smiled knowingly, again a bit patronizingly, at Cavender. Cavender winked back at her.

The waiter showed up with a bottle of iced champagne, uncorked it, and left.

Borodin smiled. "The proof is exactly what is going to make this manuscript so valuable. You see, Mr. Cavender, a man who loves a book with the passion Alexander had can not refrain from leaving his commentaries on that book. And Alexander did leave his. Now where would a man of his impulse and learning—he was a private student of Aristotle, you know—where would such a man leave his remarks? Where else, sir, but in the very margins of the scrolls as he read and reread them."

Count Borodin paused to drink a half-glass of champagne.

"Yes, Mr. Cavender, you can knit your brows again. What I am saying is true. I have done my research. In his own handwriting, in the margins of the text, Alexander scrawled his views and noted his favorite passages. Just think for a moment—Alexander's remarks, in his own handwriting, on Achilles, on Ulysses, on Helen of Troy, on Hector! The tapestry of history will not be changed, but how enriched!"

Cavender snorted. "You haven't seen the scrolls. You were talking of hopes."

"No, I have not seen them. If I had, they would never have left my hands. But I am just as certain what it is they contain. Come now, do you believe it?"

"That the scrolls have remained in Taxila for over two thousand years and are still extant?" He made a face and shrugged. "Credo quia absurdum est."

"Exactly," sighed Borodin. "Of course, the survival of the scrolls was no miracle of chance. It was the miracle of human devotion and Indian fatalism. No one knows who the early caretakers of the scrolls were, but for the last five or six hundred years there has been a small caste of men in Taxila called the 'Nehang.'"

Borodin pondered the word again. "The Nehang. It means the 'guardians of the scroll.'"

Cavender's brow was furrowed. He recalled the remark the rajah had made warning him about the danger to McLaughlin. He had heard of the "guardians," too.

The count was still talking. "It has been said that day and night the scrolls have been attended at least by one guardian in the manner of the Jews, who keep a light burning endlessly above their own sacred scrolls."

"And the 'guardians' are all Sikhs?" Cavender asked.

"Ah, then," smiled the count. "You do know more than you claimed. The 'guardians' were converted to Sikhism in the seventeenth century. Their worship of the warrior was perfectly harmonious with the image of Alexander. As centuries passed, the aura surrounding the scrolls and their guardians grew. The town supported these men and if a guardian died without leaving a son to take his place, the other guardians elected an outsider to take his place.

"But time brought other changes. What the scrolls actually contained was gradually forgotten. They were never read, probably never unrolled. And, written in ancient Greek, they probably could not have been read if they were opened. That's what I'm hoping has preserved them in good condition. The only thing remembered was that they had been connected somehow with Alexander. But by the beginning of this century, although the Nehang continued to exist and to guard the treasure, the chain of knowledge had grown so weak that even Alexander's connection with the scrolls passed from their memory. All that was remembered was that the scrolls had something to do with the Greeks who had come to the Punjab thousands of years ago."

Count Borodin poured some more champagne. Cavender and the countess joined him. The count raised his glass.

"To the end of my story, Mr. Cavender. I hope you are not bored. And to the recovery of the scrolls."

Cavender touched his glass to the count's, extended to him over the table. He turned to find the countess holding her glass out to his. He touched it and they drank together.

"Enter Brendan Daniel McLaughlin. Somehow the major got wind of the scrolls, heard of their Greek connection, and got bitten with an interest. Then when luck put him in charge of a raid on a building belonging to the Sikh Nehang, the temptation was too great for him. Something, perhaps, snapped in his mind. Curiosity? Greed? Who knows? He went into the building to search for contraband weapons, saw where the scrolls were being kept, killed the guardians—perhaps they attacked him first— and went off with the scrolls.

"The rest, except for where he went and what he did with them before his arrest, is court history to be found in any newspaper of that time."

Cavender finished his champagne. "It's a great story, Count Borodin, and worth telling. But if you haven't seen the scrolls yourself, and even if you had, how can you be certain the scrolls are authentic?"

"Mr. Cavender is the skeptic, no?" quipped the countess. "Questions and doubts. You are not a happy man."

Cavender smiled. "Nor a disappointed man, Countess. Someone once said that when a man expects to get what he wants badly instead of what he is likely to get, the disappointment is going to be much greater when he fails."

"But the greater risk of disappointment is part of the excitement," said Borodin. "I *have* to believe that the scrolls are authentic, that Alexander's handwriting will be there. And I expect more, Mr. Cavender. The Plutarch passage mentions that the copy of the *Iliad* in question had been corrected by Aristotle himself. I expect also to find Aristotle's own hand on the manuscript."

Count Borodin stood up.

"You understand now why I am offering the sum I mentioned before. As for you, a twenty-percent commission fee if you deliver the manuscript to me, legally and properly. And an Alexander coin as a small bonus." Borodin held the coin in his hand and pushed it back into his watch pocket.

Cavender got up. "McLaughlin has his own plans for the scrolls."

"Something called the IRB. Yes, I know," said Borodin, helping his wife from her chair. "You will earn your commission by persuading Major McLaughlin to accept my offer."

As he started to walk away, he said, "May I hear from you as soon as you present it to the major? With your advice favoring it, I trust."

Cavender stalled as he had with Stathopolous. Everybody seemed to think that all they needed to do was wave the promise of money and he was theirs. He said flatly, "I'll talk to McLaughlin, of course. The money may appeal to him. But I'd like to see some of it before I do."

"You shall," the count said. He dropped an envelope on the table next to Cavender's hand and led his wife toward the mammoth lift just outside the dining room where elephants could be hauled to the upper floors if they had to be. Inside the envelope Cavender counted five five-hundred-pound notes, English sterling. That made him take the count seriously. He headed for the grand portals and a taxi ride back through the swarming streets of Calcutta.

At his hotel there was no sign of the small dark man.

Upstairs, he found McLaughlin out. Farashah was out, too. The bull terrier was gone. Rose was in her bedroom on the bed, tied hand and foot with strips torn from the bedsheets and gagged with a stocking.

18

Rose shook her head and made sounds with her tongue moving around her mouth. Her brown eyes smoldered. Presently she was able to talk.

"The blackguard! He came up quite jolly in his new suit. I told him you had got a message and gone out and that the policeman Bentley had called saying he was in the clear. He talked to his daughter for a while in Indian. When I was pinning my hair he came up behind me and put his arms around me. I thought he was going to get funny, but then he had my arms pinned to my side and his sweet little daughter was wrapping that sheet around my legs. He was apologizing all the while he was tying me up. And he was sorry to stuff a dirty stocking in my mouth. The blackguard! I near choked to death."

"Pack your things," Cavender ordered, "and throw mine into my case. We may have to leave in a hurry. I'll take this with me now." He slipped his leather pouch over his shoulder. It was packed with his big Mauser, a silencer for his smaller Mauser, and some extra clothing. "I'll be back soon. Stick here. If I have to move fast, I'll move without you if you're not here."

He stopped first at the desk downstairs and asked if there were any messages. A clerk he had got to know during the last two weeks gave him a piece of paper folded twice. It read:

Thanks for the help, Alec, and the money. I think I should be capable of doing it on my own from here. Too many people into this thing for me. I think I'll disappear for a while. My little Farashah and I will handle the rest.

I'm not running out on you, my boy. See you in Dublin with the scrolls. You'll get what you were promised. The IRB will live up to its word. We Irish always do. But if something does go wrong Rose should be some consolation. I slept light last night. You're lucky. When I wrestled with her getting the bonds on she fought enough to give me a little rod on, my first with a woman in a long time. I envy you, my boy.

But watch out. She's a shelalegh.

Sorry I had to filch from her purse. Earnings these past years have been poor. Your fifty pounds didn't go far enough.

BLACK DOG

And don't worry about Basil. He's where he wants to be.

Cavender asked the young Hindu clerk if McLaughlin had taken a rickshaw or a taxi. The clerk had not noticed.

Outside, Cavender spent fifteen minutes talking to the wallahs and the taxi drivers on the street. He learned nothing. He hired the last taxi driver he questioned to take him to the Howrah Station across the Hooghly River. He had been across a few days earlier, almost awed by the masses of people covering the massive webbed structure of the Howrah Bridge. But today, under a low leaden sky threatening to wash the land away soon, the thousands of those same Indians scurrying over the river seemed almost paltry. Cavender rolled the window up and concentrated on the job.

If McLaughlin was leaving Calcutta, unless he was going to sea, and Cavender doubted that, there was only one sensible way to go. By train. There weren't many trains in India and they didn't run often or on schedule— they had been lucky to catch the express to the north the other day—but there was plenty of track going every- where. And sooner or later there would be a train to take you wherever you wanted to go. Roads were few—and those few so dependent on good weather that they were more often impassable than not. The British and the natives alike used the train. And in Calcutta, the station was the Howrah, large, rambling, old, and dirty.

A young handsome Indian clerk wrote down the proposed schedules and destinations of the trains leaving for the next four days and handed the sheet to Cavender.

None were leaving that afternoon and only one had left for the north that morning. McLaughlin was still in Calcutta. All trains for the rest of the week were running in the morning, except one. One train was leaving the following afternoon at about four for the south along the coast. Two, on the morning after, were heading for the northwest and southwest. A northbound train and two westbound trains were due to leave on the third morning. And another southbound train and a northeast train bound for Burma were scheduled for the fourth day. Beyond that the schedule was indefinite.

At another window Cavender purchased separate detailed maps of the several train routes of the Indian rail system. He went to a tea shop in the station and sat down and spent ten minutes studying the train routes along with the time schedules. He drank tea and smoked a cigar.

At the end of ten minutes the hunch he had was still not strong enough to take too much of a chance on. He went back to the ticket window and bought a first-class compartment for two people on the southbound train leaving the following afternoon and a first-class compartment on the northbound train for the day after.

It was three-thirty when Cavender climbed back into a taxi. The sky was beginning to lighten to a paler gray. It took twenty minutes to cross the four-hundred-yard span of the Hooghly Bridge and nearly another hour to make it along the Strand Road South around the great Maidan Gardens, crossing Kidderpore Road, with its brief memory of Madame Yen-Choo and her girls, and then onto Alipore Road to the National Library.

There in the reference room he spent the next hour, until almost closing time, poring over all the newpapers he could get covering the late winter of 1897 through the spring of '98 when McLaughlin's trial ended and he went away to the Calcutta gaol.

He found what he wanted. McLaughlin had been arrested just outside of Howrah Station when he was spotted by military officers who were in the vicinity looking for someone else. He was empty-handed. He had gotten off a train from the south, its last major stop having been Bhubaneswar.

Cavender checked one of the maps he had bought and traced his finger along the coast from Calcutta to Bhubaneswar a distance of a hundred and fifty miles. With a pencil he drew a circle around Bhubaneswar and the neighboring coastal towns of Puri and Konarak.

Something then began to nag at the back of his mind. He got up and stared out of the windows toward the zoological gardens across Alipore Road and tried to remember. Nothing came to him. He went back to the newspapers.

The courtroom had been crowded with local Sikhs who came to see the British do justice on an Englishman who had killed Sikhs. There was no mention of a missing manuscript, and the Sikhs from Taxila had only said the murdered men were "guardians of the scroll."

When McLaughlin was questioned about what he had done and where he had gone after the raid, he remained mute. His defense throughout the trial remained steadfastly the same. He had received spoken orders to raid the Sikh building to search for hidden arms and arrest anyone possessing any knowledge of weapons in the building. He had followed these instructions and been resisted by several Sikhs who threatened him and his squad with their swords. Shooting broke out and the Sikhs had been killed. Now the Anglo-Indian government was using him as a scapegoat to whitewash English officialdom for the attack because there had been a savage outcry from the residents of the city. McLaughlin claimed the trial was to pacify the natives.

There was nothing else of interest to Cavender. He walked over to the windows again and looked at the lightening sky. Across the street the zoo elephants were being led into their houses. The big striped cats were drowsing on rock perches just visible over a high wall.

The nagging in Cavender's mind continued.

He left the building and walked east on Alipore looking for a taxi. He stopped to watch a big four-wheeled military wagon rumble by, drawn by four magnificent Percheron horses. It was a heavy goods wagon fully loaded to above its high sides. The horses were something to watch. Their muscles were taut, their coats glistening, their harnesses ringing in unison.

Suddenly, Cavender, having turned his head to follow the horses, became aware of the sun as it broke through the overcast and shone directly into his face from its shallow angle. The nagging in his mind stopped. His face tightened and his eyes narrowed and brightened.

The elephants, the cats, the horses, and now the sun all flowed together into a fixed image to jar his memory. McLaughlin was heading south, and Cavender was pretty certain where.

19

Cavender came close to not making it, although he had twenty-two hours until his train was to leave. It was chance and his own weakness for women that did it.

From the library his rickshaw wallah took him through the sprawling Maidan park that saved Calcutta from being an ant colony. They passed the trapezoidal racetrack, the ponderous Fort William in the distance, the polo fields and cricket grounds. Some were in use, others were vacant. It was a green world set in a white world going dirty.

When they emerged at the eastern end of the Maidan, the wallah trotted down the narrow lane to avoid the heavier traffic on the main streets. They entered a tiny, almost secluded square bounded on four sides by high tenement buildings. Only the single lane entered the square at one side and left it on the other. Aside from a lone taxicab off to the right side of the square, there was no other vehicle there except Cavender's rickshaw.

In a corner of the left side of the square as they entered, a large fire was burning on the cobblestones. The heat struck Cavender's face, carrying with it the sweet odor of burning flesh, reminding Cavender of another fire that had destroyed the bodies of people he had liked. He immediately recognized the signs of a Hindu funeral.

A small crowd of mourners was gathered around the pyre in a semicircle about twenty feet from the flames. Among the women there was a lot of wailing, shuffling, swaying, arm-waving. The men stood stolidly by and stared blankly into the crackling blaze. Deep in the heart of the fire could be seen a heavily wrapped figure in the early stages of combustion. The winding sheets had burned partly away and the exposed parts of the body had begun to blacken.

Cavender's attention was caught by something else that brought a stark grimness into his face.

On the far side of the pyre he saw a small knot of women struggling wildly among themselves. Hair-raising screams rose above the blistering crackle of the fire, mingled with cries of what seemed like joy. He leaned forward and stood up in the rickshaw for a clearer view.

Three women were dragging a fourth toward the flame. The fourth woman fought desperately against her captors. She had dug her naked feet into the rough cobblestones and was bent like a hairpin, buttocks out away from the fire, twisting and turning her body as two of the women dragged her by the arms and the third held her around the waist and pushed from behind. The woman's sari had nearly been torn from her body and hung in tatters around her legs. Her face was distorted in terror. The faces of her three tormentors grinned in a kind of crazed ecstasy. Two younger, slender women fought against the three older, stronger ones, trying to free the fourth but doing badly.

Suttee!

Hindu widow-burning. He remembered the legend. The goddess Sati had killed herself over the rumored death of her husband. Sati—"true wife"—became *suttee*.

The British had not completely stamped out the practice. The belief lingered. A dead man's wife had no right to live beyond him. Among the Hindus there was no place for the widow. As his corpse burned, the widow was expected to burn herself with him. No infidelities then. If a man possessed more than one wife, all of them would die. He had heard of one rajah in the nineteenth century whose pyre was built to provide ample room for his forty widows to hurl themselves together into the funeral fire. The tradition was dying, but dying hard.

Cavender's wallah had stopped a few yards away and left the traces of the rickshaw to join the five or six men who were watching the scene unmoved.

Grimly fascinated in spite of himself, Cavender watched also. He had seen suttee before but never like this. On those few other occasions among the Sikhs in the North-West, the widows had been older and worn, had leaped willingly into the fire to join their husbands. The suicides had been embraced with eagerness and applauded by the relatives of both people.

This was different. There was no suicide here. It was going to be murder. Hindu custom sanctioned it, but British law and the will of the widow called it murder.

As Cavender hesitated, the widow was losing her struggle. By inches the three older women were drawing her closer to the flames. Driven by forces that sank deep into their ancient pasts, they shouted encouragements to the widow, they chanted the Hindi words for "brother" and "son" and "husband." The dead man was all three to those four women. With their feet and their bodies the older three fought off the attempts of the younger women to help the widow.

The widow's struggles weakened. Her feet, bleeding now, slipped over the stones in her own blood. Her screams and pleas were fainter, her body had begun to slacken. The circle of people had broken to clear a way to the fire.

There was a sandy dryness in Cavender's mouth. His gorge rose to choke him. His face was drawn tight. The muscles in his jowls bulged, the dimple in his left cheek looked like a gash. The commitment to his job struck across his mind. Yet there was time for that. If there had been no time he might have turned away, left the woman to the fate her own people devised for her.

A close friend of his once remarked that Cavender had a chivalrous complex, that he would rather save a woman than sleep with her. Cavender would have denied it, but not vehemently. Someone else remarked then that he would save her *in order to* sleep with her. In any case, the impulse sometimes brought him trouble he could have avoided easily.

He had been standing there idle for less than a minute as the scene, its meaning, its horror flashed through his mind, along with the thought of what had brought him to India.

When he finally moved, it might have seemed to a witness that he moved on impulse. He did not. He knew clearly what the choices were and he acted deliberately. The leather pouch he carried went out of the way, under his arm, around behind his back.

He jumped from the rickshaw, seized the traces, and, pushing the light carriage in front of him, drove it across a line of people by the fire and through the open space on the other side. People fell back shouting in bewilderment. He ran the rickshaw straight into the two women holding the widow by the arms, knocking them aside to the cobblestone but missing the widow herself. People were stunned. A loud groan went up from the spectators. Cavender counted heavily on the shock. He did not want to use his pistol.

At one point he came so close to the fire that its blast seemed to scorch his face. He thought his suit was about to burst into flames. He moved faster than anyone could expect a big man like him to move. His legs were good, the best part of him, and he had never let the rest of himself go to flab. Before anyone had recovered he had run around the overturned rickshaw and wrested the widow from the grasp of the third woman.

The half-naked widow threw her arms around his neck in desperation and almost ruined everything. For a moment he was encumbered. The third woman had wrapped herself around his legs. He could not move. Across the way several men had begun to stir and were hurling angry words at him. He was safe for a minute or two but the air was filled with grief and anger and frustration that would soon break down their reluctance to attack a Westerner. He had to get out fast if he intended to save anyone and himself.

He pushed the widow aside, bent, and clipped the third woman on the side of her jaw. She was the second woman he had struck with his fist in a few days.

Supporting the widow around the waist he hurried her stumbling across the small square toward the idle taxicab. Someone inside the cab had opened the rear door and was yelling in English for him.

Cavender felt people close on his heels and reached for his pistol. Then he saw they were the two young women who had been on the widow's side.

The widow climbed into the taxi. A man who had been in the rear seat had climbed out the other side. He was an older man, a Hindu wearing a Western business suit. He slammed the door on his side and Cavender could hear him say, "Get out. Get out."

He turned and pushed the two younger women in beside the widow and started in after them. The driver was shouting for him to hurry. The Hindu businessman had begun to walk briskly up the lane to safety somewhere.

Before Cavender could get in, strong hands tore at his jacket. Something hard struck his head, knocking his hat into the lap of the nearest woman. He heard something tear. Somebody punched him in the back. He spun around swinging. He connected with one man who had a heavy club in his hand. He caught him in his windpipe and the man fell to his knees choking. Two other men ripped at

95

Cavender with their bare hands. They were older and weaker and slighter than he was but they could delay him until younger, stronger men made up their minds to join them. Cavender seized one of them by the arms and tossed him aside like an oversized doll. He kicked the second man in the groin and made him vomit. A fourth man stood back and cursed and threatened and shook his fist impotently.

The three women who had tried to immolate the widow were in the middle of the square on their knees, their bodies prostrate toward the taxi, wailing and pounding the cobblestones with their fists.

More men, Cavender's wallah among them, had got nerve up to move threateningly toward him. Cavender backed up and jumped into the rear seat, pulling the door closed after him and falling on top of the women.

The driver threw the clutch and the taxicab jolted forward and sped out of the square into the narrow lane ahead. The Hindu businessman who had given up his cab was nowhere in sight.

For a few moments nobody spoke. Only sobs of joy poured from the three women hugging each other and weeping. The two younger women did what they could to cover the nakedness of the widow with their own saris. Cavender averted his eyes as well as he could. They gave him an address a dozen blocks away on Bentinck Street. They would be safe there, one woman said. Once the dead man's funereal fire died, the widow could not be touched.

When the sobbing quieted the gratitude came. The words were profuse and mixed with expressions of concern for his condition. His head was slightly bloody, his jacket torn at the shoulder seams, his trousers stained with vomit. He was their savior, their Rama, their prince. Soft hands caressed his arms, his face, touched his head. They would tend his hurts, mend his garments, succor him.

Cavender might have felt foolish if he had not been in India before and learned what the meaning of *dharma* was, doing the right thing, securing the future of one's soul. The women had a debt to pay. They would not leave the taxicab without him. Their gratitude had to be properly expressed.

The taxi driver stopped before a small dwelling, little more than a two-story hovel, in Bentinck Street and looked back at Cavender with envy.

The widow continued to plead that she would be sinful if she allowed him to depart without this little care she offered. Her sisters would suffer the same guilt.

Cavender looked at his clothing, smelled the vomit, touched his head delicately. He looked at the anxious faces of the three women, tearful, not terribly bad looking, not exactly beautiful, pleading. He made a face at the taxi driver.

The driver said, "Be kind, sahib, and do not be a fool."

Cavender reminded himself that he had never been unwilling to mix pleasure with business, if there was time.

"Well?" asked the driver, a bit impatiently.

"Yes, well," said Cavender, patting the arm of the woman next to him. And then under his breath, "What the hell!"

20

The room the three women brought him to on the bottom floor was large and neat and divided into three separate areas that could be closed off by thin cloths hanging from strings strung a foot or so over Cavender's head. There was a small bed in one area and floor bedding in the other two. An old woman and two small children were sitting on the floor on the mats. When the old woman saw the three younger women, she burst into tears and flung herself around the neck of the widow. She listened to the story of the woman's rescue and took Cavender's hand and kissed it. She thanked him for saving her daughter's life. She herself had never been threatened by suttee. No one in her husband's family expected it.

"My daughters know the meaning of gratitude, sahib. Were I younger I would show you gratitude myself. But accept their kindness in whatever way they choose to show it. From me, accept my words of thanks. It is good you have broken this terrible thing."

Without another word, dry-eyed and smiling, she left with the children.

At once the three women went about working out their gratitude, doing the right thing. The widow first found another sari to wear over what Cavender had noticed was a fine figure. She did not draw the curtain to put it on. Then she instructed her younger sisters in their tasks.

Cavender was asked to remove his clothes. The request was natural and the widow made it unashamedly. Without complaint he slipped off his trousers and his coat. The women said nothing about the pistol he laid on the table, nor did they inquire what his leather pouch contained. He removed his shirt and tie simply because he felt foolish wearing them with his underpants. There were several titters over the massy curled hair covering his deep chest and belly from his neck down into his underpants. The Hindu women were unused to seeing so much hair on their men.

One of the sisters began to sponge his trousers from a bucket of clear water while the second worked with needle and thread on the split seams of his jacket. The widow bathed his head wound with cool water, dried him, and touched the sore spot with a mild antiseptic. Her hands were gentle and efficient. When she finished she set herself busy at a stove and soon the odor of meat, frying rice, and simmering sauces stirred his appetite. At that moment a stranger would have viewed the scene as that of a husband and his three wives, save for Cavender's rudely European look. Cavender smoked a cigar and enjoyed the princely treatment.

98

By the time the food was ready, his trousers had been cleaned and ironed dry, his coat mended, his Panama sponged. His body was relaxed, his imagination beginning to concoct a fantasy.

Dinner was consumed with little conversation and only silent expressions of continuing gratefulness. He was served and tended to as only Eastern women could do it. But during the meal he found it next to impossible to read the looks of any of the women. No one avoided his eyes, and although their glances were warm and open, they told him nothing. He expected that the gratitude had its limits.

When they finished he reached for his Panama and said good-bye. He started for the door.

That did it. The widow rushed after him and seized his hand. "Sahib, you do not like any of us? You have saved my life and you ask of me, of my sisters, nothing more than what you have had. This night our beds are empty. Do you not wish to be with one of us?"

Cavender stared at the widow and the upturned faces of her sisters. Smooth brown skin, clear eyes, clean black shiny hair, red mouths, long necks, small bosoms. This was the invitation. The taxi driver knew it would come.

Cavender thought of Rose waiting for him. He thought of a woman in Brussels. Then he thought of himself. For years he had followed a principle—ever since he had given up a rigidly ascetic code in his youth—a principle of never saying no to a woman who invited him to bed. It was an honor not to be thrown away lightly, no matter who the woman was. It was always something most women treasured most.

With a broad smile he tossed his Panama back onto a chair and sat down.

"You," he said to the widow. She smiled shyly at him for the first time.

"And you," he added, pointing to one of the sisters. She smiled, too. "And you," he pointed to the other.

The women all looked up, startled. Then they stared at each other. Soon they all broke into a laughter of embarrassment and led Cavender by the hand into the quarters where the bed stood. There they stood before him and asked him to choose who should be first. He shook his head.

"Choosing like this, I would lose two, my fine ladies, in gaining one. You choose among yourselves."

He pushed them back, drew the curtains, removed his clothes, and got on the bed.

It was the widow who came in first.

The Hindu loves the body for itself; it is the chief source of joy and the well of pleasure. Love is an enhancement but not essential. A Hindu woman gives herself fully from the soul when she gives.

If gratitude brought these women to Cavender's bed, it did not inhibit the pleasure they gave or received. Rose was fine. But these women were finer.

One at a time they visited Cavender. While he embraced one the other two were only a few feet away beyond the thin curtain listening to the sounds.

Just before dawn when they awoke him to make the circuit once again, he laughed, took the widow, and collapsed back into a deep sleep.

In the morning the widow made a frank and generous offer. The three sisters had met before he had risen, discussed their situation (and probably compared notes on him, he imagined) and were willing to accept him as husband to all three. If they had pleased him as he had pleased them, she said, the proposal would not be absurd.

Cavender said he was flattered. He did not even know their names, nor they his.

"A man must be insane," he said, "to refuse three such as you. But I am not free to accept. I have a memsahib and four children who wait for me. Had I none, you could not drive me away."

Nothing more had to be said. The women had fulfilled their obligations, he had accepted them graciously, and they parted.

Rose was both angry and relieved to see him.

"You couldn't resist the children, Alec. You bastard. You went back to the house on Kidderpore. I smell the little bitches on you. You ought to be ashamed."

Cavender laughed, chucked her under the chin, and

said, "Clean up your mind, lass, and finish packing if you will. We're going for a train ride tonight."

Howrah Station teemed. The great black engine he wanted was way up on track 3 being stoked, just beyond the roof line of the terminal. Thick funnels of black smoke spiraled toward the gray sky. Under the roof, hooked to the engine, stood twenty carriages. The first eighteen down from the engine were third and second class. The last two, closest to the station entrance, were first class. The third- and second-class carriages were covered with people, bodies leaning out of windows, jammed in aisles, bodies hanging on steps, standing on carriage linkings. The roofs of all the carriages, including the first-class carriages, bore hundreds of natives sitting or lying with their bundles beside them.

Cavender had seen it before. Trains were awash with bodies. Travel was cheap, and not a square foot where an Indian could find a toehold and something to hang onto was vacant. From the station entrance the carriages appeared decked out in white bunting. Little steel and wood was visible from the wheel-tops up.

They had to fight their way to board the first carriage. A gang of natives, some of them surly, had settled on the steps. Cavender said something sharply to them and the Indians began to move, several giving Rose and him some help with their bags.

Their compartment was roomy, clean, and comfortable. Cavender sent Rose to the rear platform to buy as much food as she could from the vendors who were shouting their goods there. Then he gave some coins to the Indians who had helped him.

He waited until he felt the train jar forward under his feet and, with Rose at his heels, he went up into the carriage in front of theirs. He tapped at the doors of the compartments, slid them open without waiting for a reply, unless they were locked, looked in, and apologized.

He found McLaughlin and his daughter and his bull terrier in the fifth compartment he knocked at. The door was unlatched. McLaughlin appeared to be kissing Farashah on the cheek and straightened up embarrassed.

101

21

"Well, ahhhhr, fancy that!" rumbled McLaughlin deep in his throat. Surprise did not prevent him from thrusting out his hand as though Cavender's sudden appearance was what he had expected. Basil stood up where he was sitting on a seat and wagged his tail.

Cavender took the hand but spoke sourly. "It's too late for me to let you try this on your own, McLaughlin. I'm in it up to here." He laid a finger under his chin. He rubbed Basil's head. "At least he's not unhappy to see us."

"Ahhhhr, Alec, believe me, man, I'm not sorry meself. It's that I thought I could finish it easier if I went alone. Attract a lot less attention. It's not you, Alec. Sit down, will you. You, too, Miss O'Connell." He smiled widely at Rose and his eyes seemed to twinkle. He talked to her. "And I thought it's less protection I'd need than I first thought, sitting in that cell these years, wondering what it would be like outside. It's not running out on the IRB I was thinking of, Miss O'Connell, you believe that, don't you. And it's sorry I am for having tied you up like that."

Rose's look was dark but not angry. "Yes, Mr. McLaughlin, I do believe you." She grasped his hand that he held out to her. He flushed. She avoided his look by turning to eye Farashah, who was sitting unveiled and silent through all this, head bowed. She had put a red dot on her forehead and had all the appearance of a high-caste Hindu instead of the Moslem she was.

McLaughlin reached into one of his bags and produced a quart of Irish whiskey. "Let's have a gargle," he offered Cavender. Cavender shook his head.

"We'll need a clear head in the next few hours. You were wrong about needing less protection. You've got company aboard this train."

The Irishman put the bottle to his mouth and took a long pull. He worked the cork into the bottle before he tilted his head at Cavender and said, "Company? You mean besides you?"

Cavender grunted. "There's a Sikh with us. Maybe two. I spotted one back there, on the rear step of the last carriage. They never hide the steel bangle. Middle-aged, like the others. He may have friends around somewhere else on the train. If they're with us when the scrolls come out it'll be worse than getting rid of them now."

Rose and Farashah sat quietly together on the same soft seat.

McLaughlin got to his feet. "Let's go back there and ask him to leave the train then," he suggested. "These things don't go too fast, not much faster than it's going now. I'd be betting he doesn't hurt himself very badly at all." He drew out his big pistol and weighed it in his hand.

Cavender spoke calmly, as though he didn't think McLaughlin was trigger-crazy. "No, not with that. Too often too permanent. I said we need some clear heads. There are Indians all over these two carriages. They'll howl up such a protest we'll have a riot on our hands. I'm not against a little trouble, but we've got to do something to make the others show their faces."

McLaughlin sounded a little disgusted. "You've gone soft, Alec, my lad, you have. This is the second time you've turned me down."

"You can think it if you like, McLaughlin, but there might be a better way. Let's find out."

A check with a native porter who passed by a few minutes later informed them that the train stopped briefly three times before it reached Bhubaneswar for a long stop. Two of the three stops were at small villages. The third was at a water station.

22

Later that night the train lurched to a stop next to a great water tank about a hundred and twenty-five miles south of Calcutta. Lights were burning up and down the track to illuminate almost the entire train. A long iron spout was swung over the engine's water tank.

Train porters waving lanterns went up and down the tank side of the train. From his window Cavender could see flocks of white-robed Indians leave the opposite side of the train and fade into the darkness like pale ghosts. Minutes later the pale figures drifted back and climbed aboard.

The Sikh left the train and stayed in the darkness. Cavender searched for another one but none appeared and no one joined the first one. Soon the porters waved their lanterns above their heads and began to shout to each other. The Sikh remained in the shadows twenty feet from McLaughlin's compartment.

With a few shrieks from its whistle, the train jerked into motion. The Sikh did not move. The front first-class carriage passed him, and then the second, Cavender's carriage, crept by. Still he remained motionless. When the train was fifteen or twenty yards beyond him and slowly picking up speed, the Sikh broke from the shadows and dashed down the track. Cavender lifted his window and saw the Sikh swing up onto the rear platform of the car.

Cavender went up to McLaughlin's compartment, spoke to him for a few minutes, and returned to his own. Rose was lying in one of the beds she had had a porter make up. She was half asleep, but she was watching everything Cavender did.

A half mile away from the lights of the water station, Cavender yanked the emergency-stop cord. Almost immediately every brake in the system locked every wheel. The train broke into a skid along the rails for another hundred yards, screaming badly and throwing streams of sparks out into the darkness along its whole length.

Cavender turned the lights off in the compartment and leaned out of his window. The commotion spread quickly along the tracks. Some Indians had been thrown from the train, others had been knocked down or crushed against each other. Everybody seemed to be shouting, but no one Cavender could see seemed to be hurt. The train had been moving less than twenty-five miles an hour when he had hit the cord. The porters came along with their lanterns, yelling for the passenger who had stopped the train.

No one knew anything. The porters continued their search for the trouble. The train sat for fifteen minutes, its engines steaming. Cavender did not move from his window.

Finally the porters gave up and an all-clear spread along the train. The porters signaled with their lanterns and called aloud, ordering everyone to board. The train moved forward slowly. From the darkness of his compartment Cavender looked up at the carriage in front.

A compartment door flew open and McLaughlin, carrying a bag, stepped down and hopped off, ran a few yards to catch his balance, and headed for the darkness. At the rear of the train a tall, turbaned form dropped off the side of the platform, trotted alongside the carriage, and went into the darkness.

At the same moment, McLaughlin, moving fast for a sixty-year-old man, came back out of the darkness toward the door of his compartment, which still swung open.

Cavender moved quickly. He ran to the end of his carriage, pulled the door back, and squeezed by three startled Indians to get onto the platform. The train was beginning to pick up a little speed.

The Sikh was already on the bottom step, grasping the

railing with one hand and drawing himself up. Cavender seized the handrailing next to him and, planting one foot against the Sikh's chest, pushed gradually to ease the man back onto the ground. The train was now moving at about twenty miles per hour.

Realizing he had been tricked, the Sikh acted swiftly. His right hand swept across his body below Cavender's foot and reappeared with his sword high in the air and began to describe an arc that would cut through Cavender's thigh. Cavender had seen *sutari* more than once. It was a skill peculiar to the Sikhs. He had seen the single-blow decapitation performed sacrificially on grown bulls. He had seen it in the field against the Afghans. The Sikh would take his leg off with no trouble.

He kicked short and savagely into the man's neck once and again into the face. He kicked upward toward the descending arm. The Sikh spun off the steps and swung outward. The arm holding the sword was flung back over the tracks. The Sikh absorbed the kicks and was slowly bringing his arm around, aiming the sword at Cavender's head. Cavender saw it coming. He chopped and kicked at the Sikh's grip on the rail while he raised his own to block the Sikh's. He dropped onto the platform and kicked out again. Something finally gave and the Sikh let go. With a fading cry he fell back onto the tracks into the darkness.

The train drew slowly away. For a moment Cavender thought he could see the man roll over and get to his knees, but this was only a trick of the light spilling back into the darkness from the train's rear lanterns. Cavender stood up and brushed his jacket and straightened his clothing. One trouser leg had caught up on his garter. He pulled it down. Then, deliberately, he faced the three Indians who had watched the fight.

All three were serf-caste Hindus. They glared back. The lanterns filled their faces with hollows and lines of hate and fear. Cavender felt each man's wish to kill him, if they had the courage. But they were not together and they were probably not armed. And there was always in every Hindu that deep bottom layer of respect for his British conqueror that inhibited his resistance. When an

106

Indian did express his hatred of the British, he usually did it indirectly or in large numbers, as the villagers had in the northern province over the execution of the bull elephant. By himself the Indian would do nothing. Except for the expected exceptions, like the Sikhs, whose courage was fundamental to their religion. If a Sikh hated, race meant nothing. He was dangerous to anyone.

The three natives on the platform would go on hating him but they were intimidated. They were not dangerous then. But they could be troublesome later when they reached a city or village.

He got out his wallet and handed each native a pound note. It was more money than they could make in a month. They looked up puzzled.

Cavender said, "That man needs help. A broken leg out here and he'll die badly. Give him assistance."

He picked up each man's bundle and pushed it into his chest. Then, by the arm, he brought them to the steps. "Go. God be with you. The Sikh will be grateful. Go."

One at a time the Hindus unhesitantly descended the three steps and dropped off the train, skillfully keeping to their feet. They had left the train like this before.

The train rattled on slowly through the darkness. Cavender lighted a Suerdieck and stood on the platform and smoked. The door opened behind him. McLaughlin came out and looked around.

"Gone, huh?" He smoked a cigarette.

"There was just one. He was very tough. We were lucky."

"Did you kill him?"

"I hope not. He was only trying to get back what he thinks is rightfully his. Can't blame him, can we?"

McLaughlin was serious. "We can't run a mission school while we're after their sacred treasure, bucko. If I'd wanted a psalm-singer I would never have asked for Alec Cavender."

"I haven't gone soft, Black Dog," said Cavender deliberately, using that name for the first time. "I've hired out to do a job, and I'll do the job, one way or another."

"I like to hear you say that, my lad. You've got the

107

heart for this kind of work, I can tell." He clapped an arm around Cavender's heavy shoulder, towering over him. They went back into the train that way. Before they parted at his compartment, McLaughlin, in a curious, throaty voice, said:

"You haven't asked where it is we're going. You know, then?"

"I already know."

McLaughlin bent to massage Basil's neck. The dog had come into the corridor from his compartment when Farashah opened the door. The girl stood half out of the compartment, leaning against the door looking anxiously down at McLaughlin.

Before Cavender turned to go back to his own compartment he said, "We're going to the Black Pagoda. Konarak. Remember, you described the place once to our mess sixteen years ago to get our minds off our own deaths. There had been a lot of killing that day. It was quite a description you gave. You had everybody's tongue hanging out."

McLaughlin laughed and slapped his thigh.

"I did do it that night, didn't I. You had the makings of a good officer then, and I see you've got 'em for a detective. Maybe you can tell me where the hell is the best place on this train for the pup to take a leak!"

23

The row was something Cavender was happy to have missed. He heard about it later. Basil had found his own place to go as McLaughlin was leading him through the carriages looking for one. The bull terrier decided to go on the robe of a sleeping Moslem, who woke up as he was finishing.

McLaughlin had almost had to use physical force to restrain the man from killing the dog on the spot. And then he had to drag the dog away to keep him from mauling the Moslem, who had threatened McLaughlin. It was the first time Basil had shown his teeth in anger. The entire carriage had been aroused, and when Basil and the Moslem had calmed down, everybody offered advice as to what settlements should be made. McLaughlin, giving his name to the man, publicly apologized. The Moslem, believing him to be British, basked in his victory. McLaughlin then paid him the price of a new robe, for the soiled one was now defiled and had to be destroyed. That satisfied everybody. Even McLaughlin. Basil had proven himself.

McLaughlin told the story over breakfast in a small restaurant in Bhubaneswar, and they all laughed. Afterwards, waiting for the omnibus to take them to Puri, the town closest to the temple at Konarak, the men strolled around the market and found no signs of any more Sikhs. The people here were smaller and darker, unbearded, and wore no turbans. Sikhs would have stood out anywhere.

The omnibus turned out to be a British Standard lorry with a long bed covered by a canvas top. The sides were open. Wooden benches were bolted to the floor from front to rear and four bamboo corner poles supported the dirty white canopy. The machine itself, including the wheels and tires, had been painted white.

As Cavender and McLaughlin headed toward the vehicle and the little crowd of people and animals around it, McLaughlin said, "How's that! There's the very Mussy Basil pissed on."

Cavender noticed a small Moslem talking vigorously to the driver, who was leaning against the open door of his cab. As they got closer he saw them coming, broke off his talk, and walked away. The driver, a chunky, light-skinned man in a skullcap, began at once to get his passengers aboard. He greeted Cavender and McLaughlin with a great smile that showed a brownish false tooth in the front, and then directed the traffic aboard his omnibus.

Thirty-six people crowded onto the benches. Cavender counted them. A few goats, a half-dozen chickens, and McLaughlin's dog rounded out the full live cargo. Cavender would not guess at the number of boxes, bags, crates, and suitcases that were crammed onto the chassis and tied under it. The omnibus appeared to sag under the weight. Cavender and McLaughlin found themselves seated near the driver. There was no partition between them. It was an open-air lorry.

Cavender's leather pouch was on his lap. His other bag was hidden somewhere among everybody else's. Rose and Farashah were on the opposite side of the lorry. As Cavender looked at them and thought of where they were going he thought of them, too, as impedimenta. He wished they were somewhere else.

The road to Puri was a dirt track. It was fifteen miles long and curved. The driver was careful and garrulous. He maneuvered the machine with such delicacy and knowledge of the road that not a chicken lost a feather and not a man lost his dignity. They swayed a lot but no one slipped from his seat.

The driver knew everyone on board, except Cavender's party. And he was soon joking with them over his shoulder about what the Black Pagoda could teach a couple of old English dogs. He knew, he said, without asking, that they had come for the sights of Konarak. And they had brought their own young women with them. The wisest decision.

"Learn and put into practice," he shouted over the noise of the engine. He grinned obscenely.

McLaughlin grinned back. "Learn probably nothing," he said, "but who knows? Is there anything new under the sun?"

They spoke Hindi. The conversation drifted along aimlessly.

Cavender joined in only when he had to. The girls sat without speaking. Farashah was not expected to. Rose did

110

not understand the talk. At one point when the talk had fallen off, the driver turned slightly so that he could see McLaughlin, and began anew.

"It is becoming quite an attraction, our Black Pagoda," he said. "More and more they have been coming since it has grown known. And with their ladies, too, like you. We have acquired this bus for it."

Cavender asked, "For how long have they been coming? We believed that few knew of the temple."

The driver tilted his head a bit and shifted into a lower gear to round a long slow curve. When the road straightened he said:

"For ten years at least. Before that few knew and no one came. But now they come."

McLaughlin had sobered. "How many have been coming?"

"Many, many," grinned the driver. "Last year, twenty, maybe. This year already ten. I have counted them myself. They are strange people, those who come. It shames them to have me watch them look at the *mithuna*. And so I go away to the beach."

"Are they permitted inside?" asked McLaughlin cautiously.

"There is no one to stop them, sahib, but few go in."

"Why not?"

"Ah, you must see for yourself. But inside does not matter. The *mithuna* are all that matters."

McLaughlin lit a cigarette. He asked, "Are there visitors there now?"

The driver nodded. "None this month. You are the first. And I will be pleased to be your guide."

"We'll spare ourselves the shame and go alone," said Cavender. "But we will pay to have the way from Puri drawn for us."

McLaughlin started to say something. But Cavender nudged him and he stopped. He talked about the weather. The morning was cool and gray. The wind was from the sea. The dry monsoons from the northeast would be blowing soon. But now there was always a chance for a good rain.

Four hours later the omnibus groaned and creaked its way into Puri. It was a town of a dozen scattered buildings and bungalows, one café, no hotel. Almost everyone farmed on the surrounding land and no one was in sight when the bus stopped in front of the café.

Before the passengers left the lorry, Cavender arranged to use a bungalow belonging to a young couple, who then went to somebody else's hut. He talked to another man about horses and then went to the bungalow he had rented.

It was a two-room shack with no doors or screens. Rose and Farashah took one room where there were two cots, and Cavender and McLaughlin settled for some mats in the other. Rose drew water from a well and boiled up tea on a small stove. Everyone stretched out and lay quietly sipping tea. The three smokers smoked. Farashah spent her time gazing at McLaughlin.

Sometime after two, Cavender said, "We've got the horses. Can we get to the temple and back before dark. I don't see waiting."

McLaughlin nodded. "If it doesn't rain we can."

The sky had grown heavier, with low clouds, and they could hear light thunder way to the north.

"Let's go," said Cavender. He was not an impatient man but he was beginning to feel more alone on this job than he had before.

The two horses he had found in the village were sound. But there was only one saddle available, an old British cavalry one.

"I'm afraid I'll be needing that, Alec, my lad. It's a long time I haven't been on a horse. And you're a bit younger to take the pounding."

Cavender did not believe him. It was true—on a saddle a man *could* ride a lot easier. But he could also ride a lot faster. He said "Fine," anyway and watched McLaughlin mount. The big Irishman had not forgotten much. He could still teach much younger men something about grace and style. He cantered the chestnut for a few minutes, waiting for Cavender to mount.

There was a way to do it without a saddle. And with

112

the Irishman watching he had to do it right. He was as good as McLaughlin was. Better. And it was important not to fumble a little thing like this and risk losing control in the affair or he'd be fighting McLaughlin all the way back to Dublin.

He held the reins loosely in one hand, grabbed a fistful of mane and with hidden effort pulled himself agilely up and on. He adjusted his curved leather pouch over his shoulder and trotted over to McLaughlin. He quickly settled into an easy rhythm, coordinating his body with the animal's. McLaughlin could not teach him too much about grace and style and the Irishman acknowledged his skill.

"You've been in practice, my boy, you've been in practice. That weight hasn't hurt you any."

"You'd never tell that you haven't," replied Cavender.

"Let's head for the bungalow," said McLaughlin when Cavender came up alongside him. "Basil's going along with us."

Cavender was not surprised. He knew all along that he had not been asked to bring the dog to McLaughlin for nothing. But he asked, "For the exercise? Or for his company?"

"You'll see," said McLaughlin with a wink.

"I guess I will," said Cavender.

But Cavender did not see anything that afternoon. He did hear something, though. They had started out along the narrow horse trail with the bull terrier following after them. McLaughlin took the lead.

They had gone about two miles when Cavender called to stop.

"Listen."

McLaughlin stopped. "I don't hear anything."

"There it is again." He heard a faint beating drone that came closer, and drifted away, then came closer and then drifted off again. "It's a kind of engine."

"I can't hear anything except the birds," said McLaughlin. "And this creaky old saddle, which ain't smelled the drop of oil this century."

"I don't hear it either, now," said Cavender.

"There's no place for any engine to fit around here," observed the Irishman. "Hey, look at that!"

A long ragged flash of lightning brightened up the entire sky. Rolling thunder swept across them seconds later, frightening the horses.

"What d'you think, Alec? You've got the skittier horse."

"I'll leave it up to you, McLaughlin. I can handle him."

As he spoke his horse gave a little side hop. Cavender straightened him up easily. But the inside of his thighs, taking the full weight of his body, were beginning to chafe under his wrinkled linen trousers. He was going to pay a good price for this trip.

The bull terrier ran by them up the trail. McLaughlin called him back. "I think we'd best be going back and start again tomorrow. We'll not be having two days running of rain this season of the year. And we need weather better than what's promising for carrying what we'll be carrying."

Before they reached the bungalow there was a heavy cloudburst that turned the dry land into a muddy mire. The horses loved it. Cavender was soaked through to his skin by the time he led his horse into a small shed behind the bungalow. He loved it as much as the horses. He peeled his clothes off in the shed and went out into the rain. McLaughlin was already there naked, washing his long, pale, gaunt gray-haired body.

"Like old times," said Cavender, and, like McLaughlin, with nothing but his hands and rain water, scrubbed at his own body, thick and dark-haired, his short neck and round muscular legs, and as much of his muscularly knotted back as he could reach. He massaged his scalp and the short graying hair, and he opened his mouth to let the fresh water pour in and out.

24

Cavender found a moment to talk to Rose alone. It was after they had eaten some of the food they had brought with them. The rain had lightened. McLaughlin had gone out to the bushes. Farashah was in the back washing in the rain. Cavender could see her slim brown body through the rear door. She kept a thin gown on, but it clung to her skin as though she wore nothing.

"Tonight," Cavender was saying, "when we go to sleep, move your cot so that you can keep an eye on McLaughlin through there." He pointed to the doorway between the rooms. "That's his mat. You can see it easily from in there. But it will be very dark, so you'll have to listen. If he moves, you wake me up. I don't want him slipping out of here and me chasing all over the province on bareback looking for him."

Rose looked at him askance.

"That's right. I don't trust him."

"Even with his daughter here? You don't trust anybody, is that it?"

"That's right," he said smartly and smiled. He took her chin in his hand. "Except you, my sweet. I'll watch the first part of the night." Then, changing the subject, he said, "You had an eyeful this afternoon, didn't you?" He grinned at her.

She reddened a shade. Her dark complexion showed color only high on her cheekbones near the corner of her eyes. "What do you mean?"

"You were standing right over there near that doorway, not quite back far enough to be unseen from outside.

115

You watched two grown naked men washing in the rain. Just as I'm watching Farashah out there now. Look at her."

Rose turned and stared through the doorway. Farashah was pulling the wet gown from her body.

Cavender said, "Isn't she lovely?"

Rose turned away and said strongly, "That doesn't interest me. At all."

"I didn't mean that it would," said Cavender. "But she is tempting. Fresh, firm, and untouched, I'd say. McLaughlin had some pretty nice things to say about you when you were out there. Oh, yes, you watched us and we had our turn watching you. We didn't mind and we didn't think you would. But watch out for McLaughlin. He got a little excited when you were out there. I didn't blame him."

Rose threw her head back and said, half-seriously, "You're turning out like the rest of them. We're here for Ireland and all you men think of is the jewels in your crotch. When will you wake me up?"

Cavender laughed. "I'll see you about midnight."

They went to sleep early. McLaughlin was the first asleep. The bull terrier was at his side. Cavender lay on his back and smoked. He could hear Rose and Farashah whispering. He crawled on all fours to the open doorway and listened.

They were talking about the train ride and the bus trip to Puri. Then Farashah said something about the journey to Calcutta. He could not catch what Rose said. They were on their cots four or five feet apart at the far end of the room. Their whispers dropped lower and he could understand very little. He listened for ten minutes until his knees began to ache. He heard something about money, something about McLaughlin, something about somebody else. It could have been Stathopolous, it could have been Cavender, it could have been no one.

He crawled back to his mat and lay there for another two hours listening to McLaughlin's heavy, steady breathing. The other room had grown quiet.

A little after midnight he struck a match and went in to wake Rose. He put his face close to hers and smelled nothing. He was annoyed. If something was going on between Rose and Farashah he wanted to know about it before he tripped over something. He called Rose awake and went back to his mat. He heard Rose go out the back way and come in a few minutes later.

In the dark he felt her lie down next to him. She had a thin nightdress on. That quickly came off.

"You hypocrite," he whispered to her.

"That I am," she admitted, and without a sound she made love to him twice in rapid succession, allowing him to be aggressive. Once they heard the dog stir when she failed to stifle a sound.

He thought he was finished for the night, although his marathon with the Hindu sisters had only increased his capacity and whetted his appetite; but when Rose aroused him a third time, he responded easily. This time, however, she wanted to do it all, from beginning to end. He remained passive and lay on his back and enjoyed it, wondering what this display of her passion was all about. Three times was more than Rose's usual, even during the first few nights they had spent together on the boat.

When they finished, she first and then he, she fell to his side breathing heavily. He was exhausted. He put his arms behind his head and muttered, "Good night, my sweet Rose. Three hours, two hours—wake me."

"Yes, my dear Alec. Good night."

She tiptoed back to her own room. He heard her climb back onto her cot. He stayed awake with great difficulty. His eyes wanted to close. His brain tended to slip into fuzziness. He forced himself to mull over some of the puzzles in this job. How did the Russian know so much about the scrolls, about McLaughlin, about McLaughlin's movements? How did the Greek turn up at the right places and right times? Did they both employ armies of shadows? Who had really arranged the kidnapping of the girl? And the murder of the Sikh and the attempted murder? One of them alone? Both of them separately?

And the money! There was plenty of money in the affair. Three thousand already in his pocket. Two thousand more and his expenses to come from the Irish Council.

What about Rose? Did the IRB know what they were sending when they sent Rose O'Connell? He wondered. When she walked into his office more than a month ago, she couldn't conceal her voluptuous mind or her body, even by pretending to be the loving daughter of a man long ago shut up in a prison. She was no Lucie Manette in a Dickens novel tearfully saving her father. In her eyes there was a shrewdness and in her solid body a sensuality that would interest almost any man. Her pretending to be innocent was never too convincing.

As he wondered about these things, Rose came softly back into the room. Cavender breathed louder and a little more regularly, like a man sleeping deeply.

"Alec?" The name came floating as softly as a goose feather. It barely tickled his ear. He did not move.

He heard her go to McLaughlin's side. She whispered some words that sounded like a cat's purr. McLaughlin moved. Cavender could see her shadow rise above his, bend, then merge into one form. There were some loud writhings, and Basil lifted his head to see what was going on. He seemed to find out and dropped it to go back to sleep. McLaughlin's gruff voice slipped out the words "Oh, my Irish girl." There were some *shshsh*'s from Rose, more twistings, and in a few minutes it was over, with some of the usual stifled sounds.

Cavender watched the whole thing. His eyes had adjusted to the darkness and a small moon had risen through the clouds. The room had a pale glow. McLaughlin rolled off Rose and faced her on his side. His back was to Cavender.

Again Cavender heard Rose call "Alec?" He did not stir. She began to talk to McLaughlin in low but clear whispers. Cavender heard it all.

"It's been a long time, hasn't it," she whispered.

"It has, my fine girl, it has. And I thank you kindly for this. It restores a man to know he hasn't forgotten how and still can. I'm grateful to you."

"Shhhh. Not so loud. He's a heavy sleeper and we can

118

talk, but no need to wake him deliberately. You'll want to do it again soon, I can tell. It's the least I can do for a man who's doing so much for the Brotherhood. We're the ones who're grateful and I'm just showing you one little piece of it." She kissed him and added, "And don't be thinking I didn't enjoy it, too. You're a man, McLaughlin. There aren't many like you, I'll tell you."

"I'll bet there ain't," the Irishman agreed.

"Do you think," she said hesitantly, "we'll at all be seeing each other when we're in Ireland? It'll please me some if we did."

"Now that's an invitation no man will spurn," he said. "There won't be many young ladies like you to be interested in an old goat like me. When I turn over to the IRB what I've got, it'll be some time you and I can have, won't we?"

"Then it is the IRB, is it? You haven't changed your mind?"

"It's the IRB, it is. And you," said McLaughlin. "Now . . ." He rose above and over her.

"Oh," Rose grunted in surprise.

Cavender did not detect much pleasure in that sound. He looked toward the ceiling this time and gave them their privacy. But he couldn't shut his ears. When they were through there were a few more whispers about how wonderful it was and how she was doing it for herself and how important their joining up like this was for the IRB.

"Ay, it is, my lovely girl."

Cavender felt like pinning an NSM on each of them for national spirit and national sacrifice. He almost thought of going to sleep. Until he heard Rose speak his name again. This time she was not calling him to see if he was awake. He came wide awake. She was saying:

"He does not trust you, Brendan, at all, and he doesn't say he trusts me. I'm afraid of him. Tonight he told me to watch you. We're taking turns. Will you look at him there sleeping, a man who works only for money. He's here now for the money. What's going on between him and that Russian I'd like to know. And the Greek. There are things going on between them."

"Ay," said McLaughlin, "he's a detective and a detective is only a businessman selling his talents and his time. What d'you expect?"

"How, for the love of God, can you trust him? If he's not for the Irish, won't he be dealing with those other two for more money? If he doesn't trust us, you see, how can we trust him? Is he really your friend?"

"An old acquaintance is more like it," replied McLaughlin, twisting his head for a short look across at Cavender. Their whispers had grown louder as though Cavender were gone. "He owes me nothing from the past. He's working for us for his fee, that's sure."

"Then listen to me, McLa—Brendan, darling. I don't know really what to call you now."

"Brendan darling is fine, my girl."

Rose sat up and leaned over McLaughlin, looking down. Cavender could see her shadow clearly outlined in the moonlight. Her heavy breast barely grazed McLaughlin's chest.

She said, "Seeing how he owes you nothing, you owe him the same. It's sure he's taking money from those men already as a bribe to get the scrolls for them one way or another. Ask him and he'd deny it."

"That doesn't mean he'll persuade me. He can try and more power to him, but my mind's fixed. They'll go to neither one of them."

"Brendan . . ." She hesitated. "Brendan, what I'm really afraid of is the man's greed. He likes money too much. I've been with him for almost a month. I think the Council's been misled to hire him. He's going to steal the scrolls from us when you dig them up. I mean deliver them to the Russian and keep everything. Just take them by force. And who knows what he could do to us. He carries two guns with him almost always. One in his waist, and one, a big one, in that leather bag he never lets go of."

McLaughlin grunted as though he were thinking that one over.

She waited a few moments. Then she said, "I'm thinking what the Council would do. What do you think the Council would do?"

"Get rid of him first, is that what you're thinking they'd do?"

"Yes," said Rose quickly, exhaling as though she had been holding her breath, "that's exactly what they'd be doing. But I didn't—I couldn't say it. But you see how right it would be to do that. He's a threat to us all and we really don't need him now, do we?"

McLaughlin moved Rose aside and sat up. Their shadows touched now along the shoulders and arms. He said, "So, the IRB has taken up killing, has it? Times have changed, I guess. And so they must."

"Yes," said Rose, "and there'll be more, I'm afraid. But I don't mean to kill him at all. I know you wouldn't want that."

"And what if I would?"

"No, I know you wouldn't. It would be a bother to you some day. Don't test me. I mean, we could just tie him up. Overpower him, right now even, he's sleeping. It wouldn't be hard, would it? Tied up, Farashah could watch him with a gun while you and I go to wherever the scrolls are. That's all there would be to it. We'd leave him here and send someone later after we've gotten out to the train. Or the people here would find him soon enough. Sure he needn't be hurt at all."

McLaughlin scratched his head with both hands. "You think he's that dangerous to my plans, do you? You've got some points. There are no obligations between us and I don't really know the man. Thought I knew him once, but sixteen years can change any man."

Rose's voice dropped lower. "You'll do it then," she whispered anxiously.

He thought about it for a while and then he said, "This kind of riding I've been doing tires a man when he ain't used to it. Thinking is jumbled. But I'll tell you, my beautiful Rose, I've got to hand it to you for what you'd do for freeing the Irish. I envy you the devotion. I'll think about it in the morning."

Rose grew quiet. Cavender could almost sense her confusion.

McLaughlin thanked her again for what he called the "fine fun."

She spoke last. "Whatever you decide, Brendan, I'll support it. But he could ruin everything. Oh, and if I were a man I would do something myself, but I haven't come that far yet."

When she left, Cavender heard McLaughlin emit one low "Huh!" and fall back onto his mat.

Cavender turned onto his side and went to sleep. He needed the rest.

25

Dawn was still minutes away when Cavender awoke feeling almost completely refreshed. He had slept less than four hours, but he was fortunate to have a body that needed little rest. If he had to, he could stay awake for seventy-two hours or more, and, with only a few ten-minute naps here and there, he could stay awake alert. He could take those naps even in the saddle, if he were traveling.

Everybody else was asleep. The bungalow was in semi-darkness. He got up, lit an oil lantern, and put on some clothes. The bull terrier stood up and shook himself awake and stretched. In the yellow light the powerful muscles in his neck and hind quarters rippled prettily under the white coat. He looked at Cavender getting dressed and wagged his tail.

Cavender let him out the front door and drew some fresh water for him at the well.

The sun was breaking visibly at the horizon and the sky reddened. The clouds were scattered thin and a cool drying breeze came in from the north. The breeze carried the smell of the ocean from beyond the low hills to the east.

Cavender checked the horses, fed and watered them. When he came back to the bungalow, McLaughlin was in the doorway studying the sky.

"It's going to be a fine one, do you think?" McLaughlin half asked.

"It looks fine. I'll pack in whatever food's left. You saddle up. The horses have been fed and watered. It doesn't make sense to wait."

Rose slept through their leaving. She had worn herself out trying to tire Cavender. Farashah was up and outside before Cavender finished packing the few things he wanted to take. She behaved badly over seeing her father go off. Cavender heard her pleading. She asked to go and argued when he refused. She wanted to know when he would be back. She asked him to promise he would not desert her. She said she was frightened.

McLaughlin folded her in his arms. "Frightened of what, my little Farashah? There's nothing to be frightened of. And how could you think I'd be leaving my own dear daughter? You're coming back to Dublin with me all the way." He pointed a thumb over his shoulder toward the sea. "This is going to be easy, my girl. Make us a fine lunch, will you. We'll be back in time to eat it."

When Cavender was alone for a few minutes he drew his big Broomhandle Mauser from his pouch and removed it from its wooden holster. The fine walnut holster was designed to be attached to the butt of the pistol, converting the weapon into a short rifle if needed. He packed the shoulder stock into the bottom of the pouch, laid a few articles of soft clothing over it, and, after checking the mechanism and cartridges of the pistol, placed the pistol on top, where it was handy. He closed the flap and drew the leather drawstring. He swung the pouch around his neck and over one shoulder. Once mounted, he shifted the bag so that it rode on the right side of his back where it would not interfere with his handling of the horse.

McLaughlin rode in the lead again. Cavender followed.

Basil roamed up and down between them, sometimes running ahead, sometimes falling to the rear.

The ride should have been easy. The weather was cool and the air grew fresher as they rode toward the shore. The trail left Puri straight east for three miles through gentle coastal hills hardly taxing the horses or McLaughlin. Cavender was the only sufferer, and he suffered only in his inside thighs.

Before they could see the ocean the trail bent northwest and drifted closer to the water, as the bus driver had described it. A half mile beyond the bend Cavender could distinctly hear the softly grating ebb and flow of the surf. As they rode farther the ground dropped now and then and the beach and ocean came into view. Finally they rode through a shallow gully toward the water.

The beach was wide and flat and hard. The tide was ebbing and the surf gently rolled a wide ribbon of pebbles up and down the shore. The empty flats stretched in both directions as far as Cavender could see. There was white sand stretching up the slope where sea grass grew in clumps sparser than those on the land side of the rise. Closer to the water line the ground was a wet-looking dark gray. It was smooth as glass.

McLaughlin suggested they stay on the beach and they walked the horses for two miles along the water. Basil was tempted to the water's edge but stayed close to McLaughlin's side. When they came to another scoop in the low ridge to their left, they returned to the horse trail.

McLaughlin asked, "Would you like to rest, lad?"

Cavender removed his Panama to let the breeze cool his head. "No," he said, "keep on. The legs are getting used to it—or they've gone numb."

They rode for another few miles, never drifting out of earshot of the surf and never seeing it again. Finally McLaughlin stopped and dismounted. He urinated in the sand, holding his horse.

Cavender slid off his horse, rubbed the inside of his thighs with his hands. While he was going he heard McLaughlin walk up to the left of his horse behind him. He listened intently and kept going. Nothing happened.

124

He finished and heard McLaughlin walk back to his own horse. He relaxed his grip on the Mauser pistol, which he had been squeezing tightly in front of him, and put it away. He swung up on his horse again, feeling relieved in more ways than the one they had stopped for. He had given McLaughlin his chance and the old Irishman had come through.

McLaughin called the bull terrier. Basil came trotting back down the trail. McLaughlin picked him up, placed him sideways across his saddle, and swung up after him.

"He's a heavy one, he is. What a chest!"

Cavender watched curiously.

Once up and secure, the Irishman maneuvered the dog so that the bull terrier was sitting comfortably up in front of him. "I don't want him too tired when we get there," he said to Cavender. "Look at him sittin' here as though he's done this a thousand times."

The dog did sit perfectly poised on the saddle, not seeming to need McLaughlin's arm to keep him there. He looked straight ahead.

Cavender began to form an idea why the bull terrier had been brought all this way to Konarak from England.

They traveled at a straight walk. The dog was good but he would have had to be acrobatic to stay aboard at a trot.

"Not much farther," said McLaughlin soon. There was a trace of excitement in his voice. "Not much farther at all. I'm beginning to remember a few things now. That stand of stump trees and those toddy palms. Only a mile or two beyond them."

Cavender was about to say something insignificant. Then he heard it. He stopped his horse and listened hard.

"There it is again. What I heard yesterday. It *is* an engine. Listen."

McLaughlin halted. "Aye, I hear it right clear now. A boat, do you suppose?"

Cavender listened and looked toward the sea. The low ridge was too steep to climb. He listened for a few more seconds.

"Not a boat, McLaughlin. That's an aeroplane."

"Holy Christ, it's not! Where?" shouted the Irishman. The bull terrier's ears perked up.

Cavender scanned the sky toward the sea.

The beating of the engine grew louder. Suddenly, it was there beyond the ridge directly opposite Cavender. It looked like a great moth. It soared, dropped, leveled off, and then disappeared out of sight.

"By Jesus Christ!" McLaughlin muttered excitedly. "I've heard about those bloody flying things, but I never thought I'd ever see one. What the hell d'ye think that bloody thing—God, there it is again!"

The machine swooped up into sight, tilted its near wing up, and slipped back out of sight. Cavender recognized the aeroplane as a Blériot, the most popular sport and military machine in Europe. Cavender had seen them win at Rheims and he had flown in one from Brussels to Paris once, on the trail of a cache of illegal diamonds.

It was a low-wing monoplane with open-framed fuselage and gracefully scalloped wings. It was usually equipped to carry only the pilot, but Cavender had gone up in a Blériot modified to carry a passenger and powered by a slightly larger Gnome engine. Hiring an aeroplane than had been an inspiration. It had put him in a place the smugglers had least expected. After that he had taken enough lessons to fly it himself, although he had never gone after his license.

Now Cavender listened to the engine's beat fade away until there was only silence. McLaughlin was already moving away along the trail. Cavender kicked his horse and cantered up close.

McLaughlin asked, "Now who in bloody hell could that be and how could he get that thing out here to India? Could he fly it that far?"

"In good weather he could," said Cavender, "if he had fuel stations set up along the way. It flies about two hundred miles on its fuel, perhaps more if he carries extra cans. But my guess is that he packed it down here in pieces. I've seen two or three men take the machine apart in two hours. It's all wood, canvas, and wire, and only the engine is heavy. Some screws, turnbuckles, a few bolts.

It doesn't take up much space. I've gone up in one like that."

"By God!" said McLaughlin, shaking his head and urging his horse into a faster walk. After a while he said, "You don't suppose that fellow has anything to do with us!"

"At your age would it surprise you?" Cavender replied.

"I don't know," McLaughlin grunted back. "You surprise me. Basil there surprised me. But I wouldn't be liking it if that flying fellow up there surprised me."

"I wouldn't let anything surprise me, if I could help it," said Cavender. He was adding up a few things. Count Borodin was an experienced pilot and very rich. He traveled with servants and what he wanted was clear and defined. If he carried a Blériot around when he went anywhere, Cavender would not be surprised. He wondered why McLaughlin didn't add up the same facts.

Before they reached the great Black Pagoda, they heard the aeroplane twice more but did not see it. Heavy low cumulus clouds had grown in the sky and the pilot was staying in them. Cavender heard the Blériot going by down the coast toward Puri and then return and pass them heading up the coast toward Konarak. The second time she passed he thought the engine's sound died faster than before, as though the pilot had cut it. He was not sure.

And he could not think long about it, either, because just then McLaughlin shouted,

"There she is, boy, there she is. Beautiful and deserted. And waiting for me."

26

It stood in the open at the end of the horse trail, blocked from the sea by the same low sand bank that followed the beach all the way from Puri. From the distance when Cavender first caught sight of it, the Pagoda looked as though it had been hewed out of great blocks of honeycombed black stone.

It was massively shaped in the form of a great chariot on huge wheels ten feet in diameter. Magnificent stone horses stood in stone traces dragging the carriage toward the sea but not getting any closer. Before the front and rear entrances, poised on guard, were heavily maned lions and gigantic elephants, unmoving and unmovable. The lions lay crouched, ready to spring. The elephants held their trunks skyward, their long dark tusks ready to strike. What they were protecting rose from the roof of the chariot—twelve identical figures of a god, forming a huge sundial. The temple belonged to the sun-god the Indians called Surya. Cavender recognized it easily.

McLaughlin had described it with remarkable accuracy sixteen years ago and the image had stuck somewhere in the back of Cavender's mind. Outside the library on Alipore Road it had risen into his consciousness, telling Cavender where McLaughlin had hidden the scrolls.

As Cavender followed the Irishman closer, he saw that the stones were not completely black but darkly streaked and stained in broad areas. The stone was really gray going black under some natural transformation.

And what looked like honeycomb perforations in the stone was really the maze of carvings McLaughlin had

128

once so vividly spent his words on, and made his listeners' tongues hang out. At first Cavender could only see that almost every square foot of stone had been carved into figures of humans and animals. He dismounted and, ignoring the ache in his legs, approached the temple slowly, leading the animal by the reins. As he got closer the figures emerged from the stone in pairs. A few more yards and he could see what poses the pairs stood in.

"What d'ye say to such fucking, lad!" said McLaughlin. "Does it take your breath and make your tongue hang, huh!"

Cavender shook his head. He had seen sexuality displayed before—in the flesh and through the arts—but none so riotously and stunningly.

The temple honored a sun-god. It was a statuary hymn to the flesh. Couples five inches tall or five feet tall grappled with each other in every posture conceivable and some, Cavender swore, inconceivable. Sex organs were rampant, male and female, in every size and mostly outrageously exaggerated. But probable or not, in every face of man and woman, the joys of sex spilled out in grins, grimaces, mouthings ecstatic, eyes closed or rolling upward. The stonecutters, and McLaughlin said there had been twelve hundred of them, had caught every figure in a moment of climax.

As Cavendar's eye roved over the sculpture he began to sense a mystical ecstasy flowing from the grotesque animalism of the forms. The carvings did not really arouse him as McLaughlin's descriptions had—there was something holy about them—but they did stir some memories around in his mind as he recalled some strange positions he had gotten into himself.

He looked over at McLaughlin. McLaughlin was running his hand over the back of a lion and contemplating the statues. In his other hand he held a small canteen. On the ground at his side was a small oil lamp. He had come to this place prepared, but he had never said anything to Cavender about needing canteens or oil lamps. He had never really expected Cavender to be standing there with him.

129

The Irishman seemed to feel Cavender's eyes on him. He turned, offered him the canteen, and said, "Well, my lad, is it enough to distract a Catholic votary, would you say? Or maybe even corrupt her?" He chuckled deeply.

Cavender drank from the canteen. He expected water but it was Irish whiskey.

McLaughlin said, "A decent hiding place, would you say? Who would ever care to set foot inside with this to look at out here?"

Cavender nodded, said "Mmmmm," and watched the bull terrier, who was beginning to act strangely. The dog had his nose on the ground and tracked around the stone lions and horses nervously. Several times he started toward one of the open portals and stopped when McLaughlin called him.

Cavender was pretty much certain about what was inside the temple, what the driver had meant when he said there was reason for not going inside, and what Basil was there to do.

McLaughlin handed Cavender the oil lamp. "You have a match?"

"Yes."

"Don't light the lamp until I need it."

He picked up the bull terrier, who grew quiet in his arms but remained tense. Cavender stayed behind them.

The main room inside was about fifty feet long and forty feet wide. The floor was stone. The air was dank in spite of the half-dozen slit windows on each side letting in air and some slivers of sun. The dampness came from the ground.

As they walked in, Cavender heard things running around on the floor. Basil began to whimper. Before they reached the center of the hall the things had stopped running and the temple grew still.

"Do you have that match, Alec?"

"Yes."

"Don't light the lamp until I need it."

Cavender fished a big match from a watch pocket and held it in the hand holding the lamp. With his right hand he drew his small Mauser pistol and kept it inconspicuously

130

at his side. He had turned his back to McLaughlin several times since last night and nothing had happened. But he had prepared himself in case something did, as he was doing now. He liked the big old Irishman but that did not mean he would act carelessly. He was never careless. It sometimes seemed to him that he was born cautious. And there was no sense in relying on McLaughlin's resistance level. Rose was a tempting piece in any man's eye.

"We're going downstairs, Alec. Over there, you can see the opening near the wall. When we start down the stairs, light the lamp. And hold it over my head."

A wide set of stairs had been built down through a hole in the floor. Beyond the first step the hole was empty blackness. Without waiting for the lantern, McLaughlin stepped down, keeping his shoulder to the wall on his right. His shoes resounded on the first two steps. Cavender followed. He touched the wall with the back of his gun hand. The wall felt slimy. Down below him to his left and to the rear there was a wild scramble of squealing and scurrying. It sounded as though a sea of living things had been stirred awake.

The dog grew wild. Cavender could see a ghostly white squirming form in McLaughlin's arms. He struck his thumbnail across the head of the match, tucking his Mauser pistol under his left armpit. The smell of sulphur struck his nostrils and faded quickly in the heavy mustiness of the staircase. As the light flared up, McLaughlin let the bull terrier down. Cavender touched the match to the oil wick and turned it up high. Weak yellow light pushed the darkness back toward the bottom of the steps. He took the Mauser in his right hand again.

The screeching and rushing grew wilder. The sounds were like hundreds of feet running over layers of finely broken thin glass. Cavender moved downwards spilling the light into the room. The floor looked as though it were heaving alive with a will of its own. It surged upwards at one point and then receded, and rose again somewhere else. Small things came rushing up the stairs, swarming over his feet and brushing his trousers. He froze. A light wave of nausea came and went in his stomach.

He heard McLaughlin chuckle aloud and slap his side with satisfaction. The great sea of rats flowing madly around them meant that no one had come prowling into this part of the Pagoda out of casual curiosity.

Cavender watched Basil. The white bull terrier had gone down the steps in a white blur. He waded into the swarming sea doing what no other animal could do so well. His jaws worked faster than the human eye could follow, his head jerking from side to side with blinding swiftness, seizing a rat by the neck to snap it, seizing another, breaking it, then another.

In less than two minutes the rats were gone, thousands of them, disappearing as if by magic through unseen exits or up the stairs. Dozens of rats lay around the floor dead, their necks broken or their heads crushed in. The bull terrier made two searches of the whole chamber, found another rat or two, killed them, and came back to McLaughlin.

There was blood on the dog's jaws and a few dark spots on his body where he had been bitten. McLaughlin took the lamp from Cavender and examined the dog carefully, murmuring words of praise over and over.

"Sure he's not hurt bad, do you like that! A few nips is all he's taken and look at those bloody bastards."

He stood up and handed the lantern back to Cavender.

"Well, Alec, let's a have a look at what we've come for . . . And you can put your gun away now. I'll need your help."

27

Cavender set the lantern on the ground near a small stone altar about four feet high, six feet long, and two feet wide.

It was a single block of stone fully carved with the sexual contortions of dozens of couples. But Cavender was no longer interested in the art. Or the act.

He watched McLaughlin lean a shoulder against the altar and heave. The stone barely moved.

"I was a bit stronger when I was down here last," said McLaughlin, out of breath.

Cavender put his Mauser away in its holster. He crouched next to McLaughlin and put a heavy shoulder against the block. At a signal he brought the power from his strong legs through his body into the shoulder. McLaughlin grunted. The stone block gave an inch, scraped harshly on the floor, and started to slip forward screeching. Cavender was carried forward by his own momentum. He almost toppled flat into the hole that appeared under the altar. He groped with the foot, found the rim of the hole, and continued heaving forward, moving his other foot out and around the opening. The stone block screeched along for another few feet when McLaughlin grunted, "Good," and relaxed.

The hole was about three feet deep and big enough to contain a large traveling case. When McLaughlin held the lamp above it, Cavender could see a crate of some kind that fit almost perfectly into the hole except for the depth. There was a good foot between the rim of the hole and the top of the crate.

"It was already there when I moved that altar sixteen years ago," said McLaughlin, wiping his face with the back of his hand. "Made to order for me, like an omen. Brought my shovel down here for nothing, except to kill some of those rats with. They nearly killed me. That's what I wanted a ratter for. And Basil here—good boy, Basil, good boy—was the best you could have gotten."

Neither man moved to reach into the hole. It seemed that the moment required a little silence, a little savoring of the touch of awe in their feelings. Basil tilted his head and looked down into the hole puzzled.

Then McLaughlin spoke. "Well, there they are, Alec, my boy. The scrolls of Homer. And the hand of Alexander himself on them."

In the glimmer of the lantern Cavender's gray eyes were bright. The muscles in his face were tight and the flesh bulged along the jawline. The dimple in his left cheek was long and deep. The weeks of wondering what the Calcutta job was really all about were over.

Not that he had lost any sleep wondering. He did not suffer from impatience. But he had been curious and he was not phlegmatic. Experience had not dulled his senses or the leading edges of his mind. He could still indulge himself in excitement when the exciting appeared. And the anticipation of rubbing what Alexander had rubbed and holding what, perhaps, Aristotle, too, had held, even if he could not read their words, stirred his blood quietly.

Cavender was a man who loved the exotic and the remote, and the scene he saw himself in at that moment was as strange and exhilarating as he could have wished. A dungeonlike chamber of an almost forgotten Indian love temple, the distant east coast of India, an old Irish ex-soldier and convict, a young English bull terrier, and Cavender himself about to reach back into history to touch two of the most famous men who ever lived.

It was the kind of bizarre moment that he had never lost a taste for.

He said, "Let's see what they are."

He crouched again with his back to McLaughlin and listened and braced himself. McLaughlin kneeled next to him, and together, gripping the crate by its corners, they worked it out of the hole.

Almost lovingly McLaughlin brushed the dirt off the crate. Then, cradling it in his arms, he started up the steps. Cavender followed with the lantern. The bull terrier was still sniffing around until McLaughlin called him up.

Outside, Cavender suggested they go down and move the altar back over the hole. McLaughlin shook his head. He placed the crate gingerly on the ground near the great stone horses.

"Will you look at it," he said softly.

The crate was made of cypress wood, tongued and grooved to form a tight, almost seamless fit, and even the fine seams were carefully caulked. There was no sign of

134

rot from dampness. The crate looked as though it had been put into the ground yesterday.

"Waterproof, Alec, and airtight. Completely, I hope. When we open her up and see the scrolls you'll know what a bloody crime it would be to ruin them in sixteen years when they stood up to time for twenty-four hundred years. I learned how to make that box in Delhi on the run. Best waterproofing there is, that cypress. There's a pride I have in that job."

Cavender said, "Let's take a look inside now. This is as good a private place as any, and we ought to know what's in there is what we expect to be in there."

McLaughlin shook his head slowly. "It's a shame to break it. But you're right. *I* know what's in there and you don't. You've been going along with me, all right, that's what you've been doing, and it's time you think you should be seeing what it's all about. Me serving sixteen years, you and that Rose girl coming ten thousand miles out here, those Sikhs hanging about making threats. Do you have a knife?"

Cavender handed him a folding knife with a handle shaped like a dolphin. It was a beautiful object. On the blade were the words, "May Allah cut with you only in kindness," engraved in Arabic.

McLaughlin tried to close the blade, couldn't find the lock release, and handed it back to Cavender opened.

"Too nice a piece to be doing gritty work like this. I've got something better in my bags."

He went over to where their horses were tied under some trees thirty yards away toward the beach and brought back an old, heavy carving knife. Using it as a chisel, first, and the palm of his hand as a hammer, he gouged out the caulking along three seams. Then, making the blade serve as a small jimmy, he pried out the end slot of wood and the two next to it.

Cavender could see the dull glint of metal inside. In a few minutes McLaughlin had torn off the top of the crate piece by piece. His hands trembled a bit when he lifted out the dull copper box inside. It was just slightly smaller than the crate.

The copper had completely gone to a dark greenish, almost black patina. Tiny hammer marks were still visible pimpling the metal. Cavender ran his eye over the box. It looked seamless. He picked it up from McLaughlin's hands. It weighed about ten pounds. He could not find a lid or a seam. He bent his head closer. Along the top of one long side he found a hairline. It ran along the full length of that side down both shorter sides.

"It's ingenious," he said. "One piece of copper folded, hammered, and no cuts. And this lid."

"That's it, lad. Sure the box is old as the scrolls. It's almost airtight as a plugged jar. Here, let me show you what the genius did who made it. I'll need that fancy blade now. This is fragile work."

With Cavender's knife held like a scalpel, McLaughlin worked the blade along the hairline, applying slightly upward pressure toward the box's center. In five minutes he pried a three-sided lid free from slits in the front and sides of the base of the box. He lifted it higher.

There were six rolls of dark gray parchment in the box, each tied in two places with thin green copper strands twisted in one place to lock them.

"Go ahead, Alec. I've handled them before. They're not that fragile."

Carefully Cavender reached in with a steady hand and lifted one scroll out. It was a little more than two feet wide and about as thick as his forearm. He laid it gently on a flat stone in the shade of a statue of a horse.

A simple twist of the copper bands freed the dark gray parchment. The parchment fell away as a separate piece. It was a blank cover for a deep brown, almost black leather scroll. Cavender touched the leather. It was soft and supple under his fingers except at the outside edges, where it had suffered some stiffening and cracking.

Cavender started to unroll it. When it had stretched to about five feet, he stopped. Only half the roll was open. He moved his hands slowly over the surface to flatten it. He could see that the scroll had been made of smaller pieces of leather several feet in length and about six inches wide, neatly and almost invisibly sewn together. Age had blurred the seams so that the scroll at first examination almost appeared to be one unbroken piece of leather.

The writing was in black ink, appearing in four columns, each on a separate strip of leather. The lettering was small enough, he judged, to get five lines to an inch. He did some quick figuring, estimating the roll to be about ten feet long. That would be six hundred lines to a column and twenty-four hundred lines to a scroll. He did not know how long the *Iliads* of Homer were but he guessed that six scrolls covered a pretty big chunk of it, if it didn't contain it all.

The Greek lettering was startling. It was almost completely decipherable on a first reading. And the passages that were obscured to his own eye would probably give very little trouble to any Greek scholar who could read and understand the good ones.

What took Cavender's mind next—he wanted to savor the thought last—was the handwriting in the margins. It was aslant, unlike the perpendicular stroke in the text, and the stylus that had been used was broader and threw more ink. Even the formation of some letters had some obvious differences. In the text the omegas were clearly open at the bottom. In the margin they were closed. The margin writer and the textual scribe were different people.

Cavender felt his temples throb a little. He touched the ink in the margin and could feel it raised above the leather surface, as though it had been put there yesterday. He had a sensation of setting his hand directly into the past.

He felt McLaughlin's hand on his shoulder, breaking the strange mood he had passed into. He nodded his head. McLaughlin said, "I can guess how you feel, lad. I felt the same when I first touched them. I knew you'd have it. In the old days I could sense it in the way you tasted old wine. There was the connoisseur in you then, too. Not every one has it. Most men would see only the gold in that piece of leather. Stathopolous, that O'Connell girl. The IRB'll look at them and see only Mauser rifles. Borodin, he may be different. He may feel something, too, but he wants them too damn badly. He goes too far."

McLaughlin did not go quite far enough in his assessment of Cavender. The English-Belgian agent did have the sensitivity he referred to. But Cavender also liked money. Rose had not been completely wrong. He seldom did a job for ideals. Now, having enjoyed the intellectual side of the scrolls, he was thinking of how much they were worth. There was no longer any doubt in his mind that they were worth a great deal. They looked ancient. Bids for their purchase could be inestimable.

But there was a problem. It was a big problem, and it wasn't his. But he thought about it anyway. What kind of bids could there be on an open market if the legal ownership of the scrolls was doubtful?

The question of ownership Cavender resolved for himself as he sat fingering the scrolls. He had been hired to bring the man McLaughlin and the scrolls back to Dublin. He had not asked anybody about legalities. Rose had played dumb. McLaughlin claimed them as his. The Russian believed they belonged to the world. Local law would give them back to the Sikhs. But conventional, local law had never blindly shaped Cavender's business codes, and he had done things that were completely outside such law.

Part of his code was simply this: If in the long run something of a high good could be gotten only by breaking local laws on the way, then the local law got broken. He had once accepted a job, for example, to get rid of an Austrian spy who was corrupting Belgian officials. The Austrian spy had shortly afterward taken a fall from a moving train and probably died. Had the spy been arrested in the usual way, a national scandal would have been harmful to many people. In another case Cavender had disposed of a man who was keeping his wife and four daughters as a virtual harem. The daughters ranged in age from ten to seventeen. The woman could not prove her charges in public without destroying her daughters, two of whom were already pregnant by their father. Cavender's solution was private and permanent.

Now he was thinking about the scrolls. Few people in Taxila knew anything about the scrolls or cared, and fewer understood what they contained. To most they were only a mystery surrounded by a few aging Sikhs. Legally, the scrolls belonged to them. But in the longer run more good could be done if the scrolls reached the outside.

Before he closed the box, Cavender fingered the other scrolls. He picked another one at random, opened and scanned it. Like the first one the handwritings in the margin and in the text were different. The scrolls looked good. He replaced the second scroll and fitted the lid carefully back into its slots.

He stood up and handed the copper box to McLaughlin. "Well, McLaughlin, they are something. I've never seen anything like them. Even the British Museum has nothing like it. They'll buy your Irish some arsenal, I'd say."

"Seein' them there again, I was thinking the same thing," McLaughlin said, looking around for the bull terrier. "Here, Basil, come here, boy." He petted the dog. "There's more than enough there to buy an Irish regiment or two what it needs of basic stuff. And still be money left over." He was rubbing the dog's neck and not looking at Cavender. "Supposin' I give them four or five of those scrolls. That would be worth the trouble they've had sending you out here—and that girl."

He looked up. Cavender stared him in the eye without saying anything.

"Oh, I'm not going to do it, mind," McLaughlin grinned. "I was just supposing. It would bring the two of us a pretty penny, if we had just one scroll to peddle on our own and split."

"Listen, Black Dog," said Cavender. "It's you that's got an agreement with someone you don't think you can fool. Not me. You can tell your God what you want to. I can tell the IRB anything and they'll have to believe me. Just say so, and we'll keep two apiece and hand over two. Or keep all six and tell them there were none. That'll put us on easy street for a while. We'll have to do something about Rose."

"No need to talk that way, Alec. I wasn't suggesting it. I was supposing." He straightened up. "They're all going to Dublin in this pretty copper box, and that's the truth of it."

He lowered the copper box into the cypress crate, fitted

the top slats on, hammering them in place with his fist, and walked toward the grove where the horses were tied.

Cavender watched his back for a while, frowning, removed his Panama and wiped his forehead. When he approached McLaughlin near the horses, the frown was gone. His face was covered by a scowl.

There in the grove, waiting for them against a tree, smoking from his black onyx holder, was Count Borodin, wearing a big white duster open over a white suit and tie. On his head was a pair of heavy goggles raised over a leather helmet.

28

"You see," said Borodin in his suave, matter-of-fact tones, "I do not give up. I have been with you since you left the train at Bhubaneswar. And I must say I was happy you quit yesterday morning. It was getting dangerous for me up there."

"So that was you, was it, in that flying thing," growled McLaughlin. The big Irishman had gotten red in the face. "You must know what I think about you. I've killed your kind before. You threatened my girl once, Borodin. I've nothing to do with you."

Basil came over to McLaughlin's side and crouched low, his ears back as though he understood McLaughlin's anger.

Borodin did not blanch. "Believe that foolishness if you wish, Major, but I have had nothing to do with your daughter." For the count that seemed to settle that. He brushed the subject away like a speck of beach sand. "The important thing is that we are here, the two, three of us,

Mr. Cavender included. And the scrolls. I presume the scrolls are in that crate. They are there, are they not?"

"If they are or if they're not won't have much to do with you," snapped McLaughlin. "Now if you don't want some bad trouble, you'll go back to that contraption and fly away somewhere else. But leave me be."

Cavender placed a hand on McLaughlin's arm. There were twenty-five hundred pounds of the count's money in his breast pocket. "Let's just hear what the count has to say, McLaughlin. He's talked about a lot of money. Maybe he's ready to show some of it."

Borodin nodded his head, acknowledging Cavender. He smiled.

"Now that is what I call being sensible, Major. Mr. Cavender is sensible. And showing you money is exactly what I do plan."

The Russian reached into a pocket somewhere under his white duster and produced a piece of paper, folded. He started to hand it to McLaughlin, thought better of it when he looked at his face, and gave it to Cavender.

It was a British India Bank cashier's check for £25,000. All it needed was Borodin's endorsement. Cavender held it up and showed it to McLaughlin.

Count Borodin threw his cigarette away and pocketed the mouthpiece. He thrust his hands into the deep pockets of his white duster. He spoke with his usual quiet confidence.

"If the scrolls contain all that I expect, in the margins and in the text, there'll be another check for you in Calcutta matching that one."

McLaughlin grunted. "Not on your life, Russkie. Money's not the whole business here. I don't like Russians."

"Aha," said Borodin in slightly tighter voice. "Dealing with this Russian, Major McLaughlin, will save everyone much trouble." He pushed his hands deeper into his pockets. "My aeroplane is right beyond that knoll. I can fly those scrolls out of India with little difficulty. Borders, British inspectors, the Sikhs—they are still after you— they will mean nothing. But if you try to get them out

141

yourself, I can assure you, the British police will give you much grief. There is a young inspector in Calcutta who wants to make a reputation. I hear."

Cavender rubbed his jaw thoughtfully, studying the Russian count, short, neat, confident, hands thrust stiffly in the duster's pockets. Cavender said, "If the scrolls were mine to sell, Count Borodin, I'd probably take your offer. But Black Dog here has more invested in them than I do, sixteen years more."

The count looked back at McLaughlin for an answer. Cavender was staring at the count's arms sticking out of the pockets of the duster. Just as he made out the faint traces of shapes in those pockets, McLaughlin suddenly tucked the crate under one arm, grabbed the bank check from his hand, tore it in two and threw the pieces at the Russian. The pieces floated slowly to the ground. Cavender's hand went inside his coat toward his small Mauser.

"Take your hand out empty, please, Mr. Cavender," said the count. He need not have said anything. His own hands were now in sight. They had appeared there without any apparent movement of his arms. In each hand was a big American revolver, nickel-plated and big-bored. They were Smith and Wesson Russians. Cavender had seen one before, once in the hands of a Russian Jew on Madagascar, who also pointed it at him, but in a more casual, less ominous way.

The hammers of both revolvers were cocked, the count's manicured thumbs resting on the spurs. Cavender brought his hand back into sight empty.

"I am going to take that crate, Major, if you will place it on the ground and back up until I tell you to stop. That check is still good. I will sign it now and leave it. A little glue will make it negotiable. I am not a thief, you see, or a kidnapper. The other twenty-five thousand pounds will be sent to you if you will give me an address."

McLaughlin's face was bright red. His cheek muscles bunched into knots as he bit down with his teeth. His fists were clenched.

"Now be reasonable," the count was saying, "and set the crate down."

142

Suddenly, McLaughlin, bending as though to obey the order, shouted, "Get him, Basil, get him."

The bull terrier leaped forward and growled deeply. But the dog was not sure exactly what he was supposed to do. He took three or four steps toward Borodin, stopped and barked, then lunged forward. Borodin's eyes were off Cavender just long enough for him to reach out and wrap a large hand around each revolver, locking the hammers back with his thumbs.

For a moment it looked like a stalemate between Cavender and Borodin. Their eyes were locked on each other's face, their hands fastened to the revolvers. If Cavender relaxed his grip for a second Borodin would drop the hammer in a part of that second and kill him. But he was stronger than the Russian. His hands held fast.

"I'll handle him, McLaughlin," Cavender said. "Stay where you are." He spoke to Borodin through tight lips. "I said that I'd try to get you two together. I didn't say that I'd let you take the scrolls this way."

With a quick movement he spread his arms wide, forcing Borodin to open his. He let go with his right hand, closed his fist, and brought it up and across, clipping Borodin's chin right on the tip of his short aristocratic beard. The .44 revolver to his left roared in a cloud of white smoke as the Russian's knees buckled. Borodin fell to his knees and lowered his arms without dropping the revolvers. His hands relaxed.

Cavender bent and took the guns away. Borodin looked at Cavender with glazed eyes. Cavender walked over to McLaughlin, who was holding his big four-barreled Lancaster pointed at Borodin. Basil was crouched beside him, growling low.

"The bloody bastard wanted to kill us," McLaughlin muttered.

"I don't think so," said Cavender quickly. "He wanted to scare us into selling him the scrolls. I don't think he would have killed anyone coldly. He could have shot us as we walked up here. He didn't. Did you see those guns come out? He's used them before. And that check was real."

143

Cavender picked up the two pieces of the check and went back to Borodin, who was getting shakily to his feet. He stuffed the check into the Russian's breast pocket.

"That's not a china jaw you've got there," he said.

Borodin was rubbing his chin carefully. "It feels broken. You did not have to do that—quite so hard. I am sorry about that shot. It was not intentional, I assure you."

"When guns are out intention is always there," said Cavender. "I think you had better get back to your aeroplane and go home. He's not interested."

Borodin brushed his clothes, composed himself, and strode over to within three feet of McLaughlin. McLaughlin kept his pistol pointed at him.

"Major, if you won't sell them to me, at the least, you could let me examine one of them right here and now. Who knows, I may never have an opportunity to be this close again. What do you say?" He hesitated, and then added "—sir."

A cloud passed before the sun and cast a shadow across McLaughlin's face. Now he looked sinister.

"You heard what Cavender said. You'd better be going now before I forget myself."

Borodin shrugged. He walked by Cavender and stopped.

"May I have my Smith and Wessons? There will be no further shooting."

"I'll keep them as mementos," said Cavender, holding the big revolvers by the barrels in one hand.

"As you wish," said Borodin. "And the money?"

Cavender shook his head. "You got what I promised."

"I see. Then *au revoir,* Mr. Cavender."

He walked on and stopped again, turned and called, "And you, Major McLaughlin. You will regret this foolishness in rejecting my offer this day. You may not again receive one so generous."

The words could be construed as the first threat the Russian had made, although the threat was more in the tone.

It did not bother Cavender. There was so much control in the Russian that Cavender could not help admiring him in spite of himself.

144

But McLaughlin cursed softly. The count was just beginning the short climb up the low hill toward the beach. McLaughlin cursed again, louder, raised his Lancaster, and took aim on Borodin's back.

Cavender jumped toward him and struck his arm aside. The heavy gun roared, throwing McLaughlin's arm upward. A small geyser of sand rose a few yards to Count Borodin's front.

The count twisted his head and looked at the two men as though he were waiting for the next shot. McLaughlin's hand holding the pistol was down at his side, pinned by Cavender's grasp.

The count raised his hand to his leather helmet. He turned away and climbed to the top of the rise and disappeared down the other side.

As Cavender and McLaughlin rode their horses back down the trail away from the knotted couples of the Black Pagoda, they heard the fluttering beat of a motor. They looked up to their left. Climbing slowly into the sky like an outsized bird was the Blériot, heading south toward Puri. Its scalloped wings glistened silvery in the early afternoon sun. Once when the plane dipped, Cavender caught sight of two small heads, one behind the other, above the open frame of the fuselage.

"I hope it's not sorry we're going to be about letting him go like that," grumbled McLaughlin. "And it'll be on your head if he gives us trouble again. You know how I feel about Russians. Kipling may have thought a Russian could be a gentleman. I don't believe it. We lost too many good men in '97, and the bloody Russians were behind that trouble."

Lighting a Suerdieck, Cavender said, "But this is 1913 and the Russian showed some pretty cold cash in a decent sum." He blew a cloud of smoke into the air. "I'd say he was rather legitimate."

That ended the conversation. McLaughlin rode in a quiet, grumpy mood, balancing the crate on the saddle in front of him. Cavender rode more easily than he had on the way down. His legs were getting used to the pounding and his mind was more relaxed. McLaughlin had not tried anything against him, and the Russian had not been too hard to handle. Cavender stayed to the rear. Basil trotted along with his head down. He moved wearily alongside McLaughlin.

Halfway to the bungalow, McLaughlin pulled up on his reins, dismounted, and handed Cavender the crate. "He'll ride with me the rest of the way."

Two hours later, with Cavender riding in the lead, they rode up to the bungalow. Everything was quiet. Cavender called out Rose's name. He expected both girls to have been outside waiting for them. They weren't. McLaughlin came up alongside and shouted Farashah's name. Basil scrambled down the side of the horse and ran ahead. He stopped outside the bungalow and sniffed at the doorway. No one appeared.

Inside in the first room where the men had slept, they found Rose semiconscious on the floor, moaning. There was a slight bruise on her forehead.

In the women's room, her legs sprawled across the doorway, was Farashah. A small dark hole showed in her temple where the hair was pulled back. A thread of blood laced along the side of her face. She was dead.

29

Twice in four days!

Cavender thought it bitterly. He pressed a wet handkerchief to Rose's forehead to bring her around. McLaughlin was groaning in the other room.

Rose opened her eyes. "The Russians. It was the Russian Borodin. They've taken his daughter again." She sat up on her side with her legs drawn up under her.

146

McLaughlin came back into the room and seized Cavender by the shoulders and shouted, "By God, man, you said he was legitimate. Legitimate. Will you look at what your legitimate does, is it? The bastard. This is on your soul, Alec. I'll not be listening to you again, d'ya hear. You can get the bloody hell out of here now. D'ya hear."

He went back to his daughter's side, picked her body up and laid it on a cot. He knelt there, holding her hand. His eyes were dry.

Cavender's face was grim and lined. He glowered. The dimple in his cheek was a raw crevice that looked like a knife wound. It gave his face a touch of brutality. He felt brutal but he was not certain toward whom. He was not accustomed to the feeling and he did not like it. By training, discipline, and instinct he was used to having his feelings under control of his mind. Anger caused mistakes and mistakes in his business were dangerous to make. He had made few, and they were too many.

He waited patiently for Rose to pull herself together enough to tell everything that happened. She remained on the floor, sitting up. He poured some whisky for her and himself. He did not try to console McLaughlin. What was there to say? That he had misjudged the Russian?

He had misjudged people before, but seldom so completely. He usually preferred to make no judgments about people at all, but to believe only what was true at the moment. At times, though, circumstances forced him to judge and rely on the judgment. McLaughlin's big pistol pointed at Borodin's back was one of those times. To have been wrong so badly shook him a bit. He sipped some whisky and waited moodily for Rose to explain.

After a while Rose, sitting on the floor, began to talk. McLaughlin came and sat down on a stool.

"Farashah?" Rose asked, looking at McLaughlin.

"She's in there, dead," answered Cavender.

Rose twisted the back of her fist in her mouth. Her eyes fluttered.

McLaughlin muttered, "Out with it."

Rose spoke in short spurts broken by what seemed

147

like painful gasps for breath. "We heard an aeroplane. I couldn't believe it. We both ran outside and saw it landing in the field out a little ways behind the house. It was Borodin and a woman he said was his wife. He told us you had the scrolls and refused to sell them. He wanted me to help. He wasn't sure who it was I am, but he guessed I had something to do with Dublin. That wasn't hard to tell from my talk."

"What did you tell him?" asked Cavender.

"Nothing," she snapped quickly. "I told him nothing. That I was with you, that I was McLaughlin's niece or something like that. I didn't know exactly what was best to tell him. He knew about the Brotherhood. I said I had no influence over what either one of you did."

She drank two fingers of whisky without making a touch of a face. She rubbed her head. Her hands were shaky. Her skin was paler than Cavender had ever seen it.

He asked, "What was the countess doing?"

"She said nothing. Now and then she spoke Russian to him. When they saw they couldn't get much through me, they started on Farashah. I told them to leave. That's when the countess took out a pistol, a small thing it was. One of us was to go with them, they said. I told them to take me. They had the poor girl once before, did they not? The woman wanted Farashah. They took hold of her. The girl struggled and I tried to help. Maybe—oh, Alec— maybe if I had done nothing they would have just taken her. But when I struck the woman, the man hit me with something hard. I heard Farashah screaming. Then I think I heard a shot. That's all I remember."

She dropped her head down and was silent.

McLaughlin got up and came over to her. He bent forward and seized her chin in his hand and lifted her face near his.

"Is that the truth, girl, is that the whole truth? It was the countess shot my daughter, is that it? Not the count?"

"I don't know, Brendan, I don't know," Rose groaned. "I thought it was Borodin hit me and a shot was fired. I was dazed. The shot might have been fired later. He hit
148

me again before he left and the next thing was Alec bending over me."

McLaughlin released her chin with a short savage jerk sideways and a deep, throaty growl. "Ahhhr, you know a lot and you know nothing. It was convenient to be out of it, wasn't it?"

Rose's dark eyes widened. "What do you mean by that?"

"Ah, nothing, girl, you mustn't mind me now."

The Irishman went outside.

Rose got to her feet. Cavender took her by the arm and led her toward the doorway to the other room. She held back. "I'd rather not, do you mind. I don't want to see her," she said.

"Squeamish? Not you, Rose," Cavender said. "I thought you'd like to pay a last respect. You had gotten friendly with her these few days, haven't you? Very quickly friendly. Loving friendly, I'd say, weren't you?"

His voice was hard.

She put a puzzled look on her face.

"You know what I mean. The smell of her was on you whenever I came near. How the hell did you manage that so fast, answer me that, Rose? You don't really like men, but you fake pretty well. That's become plain. But Farashah? She took you less than a day, I think."

The scorn on Rose's face did not hurt her beauty. Her voice was scornful. "Alec, you're a pig for this, you are. It should be none of your mind what happened between us. The girl knew what I did right away. When we met she knew because she was like that herself." A look of pain crossed her face. "Beautiful it was and could have been. Something no man could ever know, especially a . . . a . . ." She was searching for the right word.

He shook a finger at her. She visibly braced herself and walked over to the cot where the girl lay. Cavender came to her side.

She said, "It was sweet and beautiful she was. You'll never know anything like it. I'll miss her." She kept her face from Cavender and walked quickly out of the room.

Alone in the room, Cavender bent over the girl and drew her outer robe back. Her sari underneath was damp.

Cavender touched the dampness, and then, with his knife, cut a slit in the sari near the breast. He ripped the sari open wider. There, two or three inches under the girl's right breast, was another small bullet hole.

Two bullet holes. The one in the temple to be sure she was dead. Why would the Russians want her dead? It did not make much sense. It stank. He covered the girl's body carefully, turned her head so that the bullet hole in the temple was down, and left her there, looking peacefully asleep. A suitcase lay open on the floor. Quickly, Cavender went through it, found nothing.

Rose was sitting stonily outside when he came out. McLaughlin was somewhere in back of the bungalow. Cavender heard someone digging there. He went to the horses. Rose got up and came after him. The copper box was nowhere in sight. He mounted McLaughlin's horse that had been left saddled.

Rose came over and placed a hand on his knee. He sat there motionless and she took it away. "The scrolls, Alec. You did get them. Borodin said so. We're still in this together, for that anyway?"

"We've got them," Cavender said. "You'd better go round the back there and see what he's digging. Who knows? He may be putting them back into the ground."

Cavender could see a question come into her face, but she didn't ask it. He rode off toward the village.

30

The natives in the town were helpful—up to a point. Cavender spoke to a dozen people, asking the same questions. They had all heard the Blériot come down and many of them had seen it and gone over to where it landed. Some had been frightened into their bungalows.

The more curious ones said there had been a man and a woman in the machine. They had asked for the English visitors. Then the two women who had come with the Englishmen ran out into the field and the man and woman from the flying machine had greeted them. Before they all went off to the bungalow together, the man in the goggles had paid two villagers to stand near the machine and keep the others away.

Cavender asked about noises, any unusual noises. The villagers nodded their heads. They hadn't heard anything unusual. The motor's noise was strange enough. A big tall farmer started to say something, but an older man silenced him with a word and a look. They had heard nothing. The man and the woman returned to the machine many minutes later and flew away to the north.

Cavender found the two men who had guarded the aeroplane. Neither one had heard or seen anything the others hadn't. When the man and woman came back from the bungalow, they came alone. In a hurry? No, they were not in any hurry. Their faces were covered with their goggles and scarves. The men knew nothing else.

On his way back to the bungalow Cavender overtook three men walking in the same direction and carrying shotguns. One of them was the talkative driver of the bus. Cavender nodded and greeted them. The bus driver smiled back broadly. They were going pigeon-shooting, he said, explaining the muzzle-loading shotguns they carried on their shoulders.

At the bungalow McLaughlin, soaked through to the skin with sweat, met him outside. He leaned a short shovel against the house.

"I'm burying her right out there under the sky, with the sun and the stars. The hell with the laws."

"You'd better do it fast then," said Cavender. "Some people may be by here any minute."

"Who?"

"The bus driver with the patter," said Cavender. "And a

151

couple of his friends. Going pigeon-shooting in the fields up here somewhere."

"They'd better stay clear of here," said McLaughlin bitterly. "And we're not saying anything of this to the police anywhere. I'll take care of the Russians when we meet again. And we'll meet again when they come for the scrolls. He hasn't given up yet."

McLaughlin went back into the bungalow and reappeared carrying the girl's body wrapped entirely in her own saris. Her face was carefully shielded by veils tied behind her head. Cavender did not offer to help. McLaughlin stepped in front of him and said:

"You're right, man. I'll not be needing your help with this. You and I still have the business of the scrolls, I suppose, and we'll be taking them back to Dublin together, but never again had you better interfere with Brendan McLaughlin when I'm going to do something."

Cavender's eyes hardly changed. He stared back at McLaughlin, unintimidated, almost uninterested. "I'm sorry it's come to this, McLaughlin. There'll be difficulties between us. You're doing what you think you've got to do, and I'll be doing the same."

"So be it," said McLaughlin. "Now I'll thank you to leave me be alone."

"I think we've got trouble right now," said Cavender, spotting the bus driver and his two companions coming around the bungalow. "And not between us."

The three villagers approached on the run. They were pointing their shotguns at McLaughlin and Cavender.

"I was right, I was right," shouted the bus driver gleefully. His brown false tooth glinted as he grinned. "You were up to no good." He pointed his finger at the body McLaughlin was holding. "Who is that? The Indian girl? Aiieee! It is the Indian girl." He ordered one of his two men to go into the house. The man returned, pushing Rose in front of him. He reported that there was no one else there.

The driver waved his shotgun threateningly at Cavender. "You three English come here to the Pagoda with the young Indian girl, and she is dead. The shots were heard

152

by some in the village. They came to me and I knew there was trouble here. The Moslem warned me. You will not bury her in that hole, sahib."

He came up close to McLaughlin, who was still holding Farashah's body, and reached out to draw the veil from the girl's face. McLaughlin twisted away, but the driver pressed the shotgun against his face and drew back a hammer. He yanked the veil away, yelped "Yiii!" and replaced it.

"We will await the arrival of the police for this."

"Police?" said Cavender calmly. "That's exactly what we need here."

"Ah, do not fool with me," said the driver. "You think we have no police here. That makes you so brave. We have police. Every two days in Puri they come. They tour the district for bandits and pass here every two days. Today they will be here. Two Indian constables and an Englishman. They will know what to do with you."

He backed away from McLaughlin and approached Cavender, keeping the shotgun pointed at Cavender's stomach. He grinned widely. "We can let you go now, all three of you, if you give us the treasure."

"Treasure?" Cavender grinned back. Then he laughed. "Your Moslem informer was dreaming. Our dog pissed on his robe. He wants a little revenge and you're it." Cavender laughed again. "We'll wait for the police."

The bus driver thrust the muzzle of the shotgun into Cavender's stomach. The tall farmer shouted a warning. He did not like the whole business. For a moment Cavender thought McLaughlin was going to drop his daughter and go for his gun. It would have been a bad move. Very bad for Cavender. All three shotguns were pointed in his direction. He stood very little chance of not becoming a sieve. The other farmer was growing nervous.

McLaughlin did nothing.

The bus driver barked an order. "Take the dead girl inside."

McLaughlin obeyed. The villager who had looked through the bungalow before followed him. They came out.

The bus driver told his companions he was going inside to search the bungalow. They began to quarrel. They did not want to be left alone with the Englishmen. Cavender knew from the first that the two farmers were nervous about pointing their guns at Englishmen. The bus driver had given them the courage and the courage was slipping.

Where were the police, one wailed.

There was nothing inside, no money, no gold, nothing but old rubbish, the other swore.

The result was that they all stayed outside and waited.

The bus driver thought of something and said to McLaughlin, "Your gun, please."

McLaughlin looked at Cavender. Cavender handed his Mauser over without being asked for it. McLaughlin drew his big Lancaster and handed it to the bus driver.

Then the villagers drifted away and sat down but kept a watch on them. Cavender, McLaughlin, and Rose sat down and faced the three men. Occasionally they smiled across the ground at each other.

Cavender spoke softly. "Where are they?"

"In the room, under Farashah's cot," said McLaughlin.

Cavender lighted a cigar. He gave one to McLaughlin.

"If there are police coming here," he said, "and I'm beginning to think he's telling the truth, we're going to lose the scrolls. Listen carefully. Are they all as soft as the two I looked at?"

"Soft as lamb skin when I looked at them."

Cavender moved closer to Rose and spoke quietly, smiling all the while. "Listen to what I'm going to tell you and don't say a word—if you want to save the scrolls."

He put an arm around her as though to comfort her and talked gently. She smoked a cigarette and listened. Then he got up and left her and stretched out near some logs to lean against. McLaughlin was sitting on his haunches, his head between his hands. Once he got up and brought some whisky outside. A farmer followed him to the door. He offered the villagers some but they refused. They kept glancing toward the road leading down from the village.

Rose got up and went inside. Their guards shifted around a little but left her alone. Cavender stretched out on some dry grass. He began to talk idly to the bus driver about what he had seen at the Black Pagoda. Basil slept near McLaughlin.

The afternoon faded slowly. The air was damp and cool. The sky was weak blue and the sun was dull from a high overcast. The farmers grew more nervous as the time passed. One got up and started for the bungalow, but Rose came out and he went back to his friends. The bus driver had to cajole the other two to stay with him. They wanted to go home. He resorted to threats to keep them there.

At four-thirty the police arrived in a small Austin with its top down. Everybody got off the ground. The bus driver rushed over and spoke to the English officer. The Englishman dismissed the two farmers with his thanks and the thanks of the Indian government. He told them their testimony would be needed later. He spoke further to the bus driver.

When the three villagers were gone, the English officer introduced himself as Captain Forsythe of the British Police Guard Unit of Orissa. He introduced the two Indian constables with him. Cavender made the introductions for his party, lying somewhat about McLaughlin and Rose, telling most of the truth about himself. He called McLaughlin "Major" and mentioned his service in the Guides Infantry during the uprising. That got some added respect from the English officer.

Forsythe was in his mid-thirties, spoke with an Eton accent, and had been with the colonial police, Cavender judged, long enough to have learned how to mix gratitude and authority in dealing with the natives so effectively.

When Cavender told their story, he told it exactly as it happened, leaving nothing out except the part about the scrolls. One of the Indian constables named Ram Sind took notes on a small pad.

Afterwards, Forsythe offered his sympathy, waited just the right length of time for it to seem sincere, and then questioned McLaughlin.

"It all happened just as Cavender told it," said McLaughlin. "What they wanted with my daughter, damned

155

if I know. Mixed me up with someone else, they did. The bastards."

"They will be caught, Major, you can be sure of that. But right now I'm afraid I must look at your daughter." He nodded his head at one of the Indian constables. "Ram Sind, ask your man to check for the tracks of an aeroplane in the field out back. We'll authenticate that bit first." He addressed Cavender. "Your story sounds quite reasonable to me, you understand that quite. But I *am* here to train these Indians, you know. We might as well go full procedure for the official report. Shall we go in now."

"There's no reason you shouldn't," said Cavender. He went in first, hesitating at the doorway, blocking Forsythe for a moment. He viewed the room quickly and then relaxed. Rose had done the job perfectly.

Over in a corner was the long low table they had eaten on. Worn strips of leather covered the entire table and hung crudely over the edges. They blended perfectly into the bare simplicity of the rest of the room. Dishes and cups were strewn on the leather table-covering as though a meal had been recently interrupted. A half loaf of bread rested on the leather itself. Some leftover greasy food was on the plates. A water pitcher stood on a small platter. Flies were all over the dishes and above the table.

Walking by the table, Cavender saw that Rose had been careful to put the writing on the scrolls face down. In another corner standing on its side against a wall was the old copper box, looking nicely like a cheap makeshift table. Some pieces of pottery stood on it. The cypress crate was near the table upside down, resembling a crude seat.

Cavender relaxed. He sat at the table with Rose and ran his hand over the back of the leather.

Forsythe spent nearly ten minutes with his Indian constable in the room with Farashah's body. He came out alone, shaking his head grimly. Cavender offered him a small whisky. He refused, saying something about duty. Cavender smiled to himself and remembered his own ascetic code during his early years in the service. They went outside. Rose walked down to the well.

"Nasty business, that kind of killing," said Forsythe. "Deliberate and conscious. The first shot was into the body. That probably would have done it eventually, but the head shot made it quite certain. Very close up, too. Small caliber, very small. I'd say .22, maybe .25." He looked around to see where McLaughlin was. The tall Irishman was out in the fields with the second constable, searching for the aeroplane tracks.

"Good, he's out there," said Forsythe. "Ram Sind is looking for the bullet in the body. The one in the head we'll not find. I'm very sorry about this, Mr. Cavender, but we have no time to send for a doctor. Don't let the major in for a while." He started to go back inside. "We'll have to burn her, you know. This is Hindu country—Ram Sind will demand that and he's the real authority out here. Not me. I'm the advisor."

"We'll be free to go then, of course," said Cavender.

"I don't see why not," said Forsythe. "But Ram Sind will have to decide that, too. I'll do what I can with him."

The Indian officer came outside at that moment, shaking his head. His eyes were keen and intelligent.

"Good," Forsythe said to Cavender, "he's got the bullet." He held his hand out and weighed what the Indian dropped onto his palm. He showed it to Cavender, who moved it around the officer's hand with a finger.

"It's a .25, all right."

Forsythe dropped the bullet into a shirt pocket and buttoned the flap.

Rose came back up from the well carrying a bucket of water.

Ram Sind stepped over to Forsythe and put his face close to his and whispered something.

"You're right, of course," said Forsythe, following Rose with his eyes. "Ram Sind here believes we ought to ask Miss O'Connell a few questions alone since she was here when the attack occurred." He reached out to take the bucket from the woman. "Miss O'Connell, would you be good enough to talk with us privately for a moment. We do have a few questions." Rose nodded and went inside. They went in after her.

Fifteen minutes passed while they talked. Cavender spent part of that time thinking about Rose, of her opinion of him, of her request last night to McLaughlin. He thought of stories she could concoct for Forsythe that might detain Cavender and let her off with McLaughlin, or even hold them both up without implicating herself. He couldn't think of a story that would sound that convincing, but you could never tell what a policeman might believe, and especially a local one. Rose could overestimate her persuasiveness and Ram Sind might hold them all. Good-bye scrolls.

Bothered by that possibility, he spent some time devising alternatives he could use if she somehow pulled off that kind of play. There was a way with guns—there almost always was a way with guns, sometimes the only way, and when it was the only way he did not mind using it. But now he thought there was a way with words, easier and cleaner.

He was working on some modifications of both ways when Forsythe and Rose came through the doorway talking. He knew immediately he could forget his alternatives. She had repeated her story the way she had told it to Cavender and Forsythe, and Ram Sind had accepted it.

"Well, Mr. Cavender," said Forsythe happily. "Ram Sind agrees. You and Mr. McLaughlin and his niece here may leave when you wish. But we are leaving, too, and we must see to the poor girl before we do. They don't last long down here, and for the sake of health it's got to be done at once. Ram Sind is going out there to arrange it. Do you think Major McLaughlin should be around?"

"I'll ask him. I think he'll stay."

Cavender found McLaughlin and told him what was being done.

"She was my real only daughter. I'm not going to take a walk."

"I didn't think you would," replied Cavender.

The Indian police officers laid Farashah's fully wrapped body on a low mound of heavy brush and sticks they had built. The five men gathered around the pyre. Rose was watching from inside the bungalow through the same door she had watched the men washing the day before. Dark clouds had come up but the air was clean and fresh.

Ram Sind struck a match and walked around the mound touching the flame here and there to the brush. He lit another and another. Soon the brush and sticks were roaring. Flames rose around the body, obscuring it. Shortly the garments covering the body peeled away in curling flames. The smoke cleared and the girl's naked flesh could be seen clearly through the rising and falling flames. As the body began to blacken, McLaughlin caught a sob in his throat, coughed to cover it, and left the scene.

The Hindus chanted a few prayers. Captain Forsythe stood with head bowed and pith helmet in hand. Rose had moved away from the door. Cavender finally left, the sweet smell of burning flesh in his nose, assailing his stomach again as it had three days ago.

McLaughlin was finishing the last of the whisky when Cavender found him down near the well. He offered Cavender the last three fingers in the bottle. Cavender shook his head and McLaughlin emptied the bottle and dropped it.

"D'ya mean he's missed the box? We haven't lost the scrolls, too?" asked McLaughlin, slurring his speech slightly.

"Come on inside," said Cavender.

McLaughlin stopped at the doorway and stared in. "Bloody hell!" he exclaimed. "What goddam nerve you've got, Alec." Some fibre had gotten back into his voice.

Forsythe came around the corner. McLaughlin did not seem to want to face him. He went inside.

"I'm sorry for the old man," said Forsythe. "It's not quite finished, but we've got to be leaving. There's been bandit activity in the area and we've been having rotten luck running them down. Which reminds me. Here are your guns."

He handed Cavender the small Mauser pistol and the Lancaster. "Haven't seen one like that for years. Hope you don't have to use it getting out of here. Good luck."

He shook Cavender's hand and began to walk toward

the Austin. Cavender walked along with him. "Your investigation here in the village isn't complete, I suppose."

"Hardly. We'll be back to talk to some of the villagers. We have enough for a preliminary. Ram Sind has your statement and Miss O'Connell's. I haven't bothered the major. I don't think he could add much more."

Forsythe climbed into the rear of the Austin. The Indian sergeant slid behind the wheel. Ram Sind came up and sat next to the driver.

"Will you do something for me, Captain?" asked Cavender.

"Anything I can, sir."

"If anything turns up out of the ordinary would you let me know? If we're gone before you get back here, will you send word to me in Brussels? I'll give you an address there. The major and I would appreciate it."

"Be glad to do anything for the major," said Forsythe. He handed Cavender a card. "Put the address on this. I'll wire you anything I find."

Cavender scribbled his office address in Brussels on the card. He handed Forsythe the card and a five-pound note.

"Not necessary, old man," said Forsythe, passing the note back.

They shook hands again. "Even if you find nothing, I'd like to know that."

Forsythe nodded his head. The machine churned down the road in a small cloud of dust and disappeared into the heavy forest growth surrounding the village.

That night Cavender waited well into the darkness before he rolled the scrolls and packed them in the old copper box. McLaughlin was outside with a small lamp transferring the ashes from the pyre into the hole he had dug. Once Cavender peered through the doorway and saw him bending over the ground brushing something with his hand. It was an eerie sight in the moonlight.

Rose prepared some food and spoke very little. Only once did she remark about the scrolls when Cavender began to roll them gently along their original folds.

"Do you think the man had any idea about these and is waiting for us to bring them out?"

160

"No, we played our parts pretty well. But we're getting out before he gets back. We'd have a hard time explaining this box to him."

"And how will you be explaining it to that nosy bus driver who'll be taking us out?"

Cavender stopped rolling the precious leather scrolls and looked at the wall in front of him and frowned. He spoke almost to himself.

"Right now I don't know. But I won't be surprised if he asks."

31

And Cavender was not surprised.

But this time the bus driver was not nosy and did not ask. He was greedy and tried to take.

The copper box was the problem. Cavender had wanted to discard the box and pack the scrolls in their suitcases. Each suitcase could have room made for two scrolls, and they would leave Puri as inconspicuously as they had come. There was Farashah's case, also. It could have held all six. Cavender decided not to mention it.

It didn't matter. McLaughlin would not listen to him. He refused stubbornly. "We'll take our chances with the box," he said surlily. "I'll not have the scrolls separated. They're like a family, Alec, and they'll be staying together like a family. They belong in that box like a home. We'll just be taking our chances."

To Cavender it seemed more likely that McLaughlin wanted to have it his way simply for the sake of having it his way. It was a bad time to argue with him. He let him have his way and agreed to keep the box. But before they left he found a large piece of old burlap and wrapped it around the copper box. It looked like nothing they had brought in with them and there was no way to conceal it.

Cavender had to think of the keen-eyed bus driver, who had taken note of everything carried aboard his bus, and he wondered how good his memory was. It didn't take long to find out that it was good enough.

The driver and his spectral omnibus were already at the café when they arrived after leaving the horses where they belonged. Only nine other people were aboard this time, six men and three women, and all of them carried produce for the markets in Bhubaneswar. None of them seemed too happy. There was little talk and no laughter.

When the driver spotted Cavender and McLaughlin and Rose heading for his bus, he climbed out and ran to greet them with his brown-toothed smile, offering his apologies for his interference the day before, but not making any excuses for it. He was the happiest of men to see that the chief constables had let them free. He bowed several times, offered to help them with their baggage, and when they demurred, disappeared into the café-bar.

The passengers sat in the sun for a while until two men rolled out the canvas top and fixed it in place to the four corner poles. It was cool under its shade. Cavender stacked their bags in a group alongside the crates and baggage of the other passengers. The burlap bundle looked innocent and inconspicuous but he felt almost certain the driver had picked it out.

He kept his own pouch with the big Mauser on top close to his right hand. The big pistol was fully loaded, hammer back, safety on, and directly under the flap, which he had untied. His small Mauser was where he always kept it.

A tea man appeared from the café and boiled some tea beside the bus. Ten minutes later, just as Cavender was about to go into the café looking for him, the driver reappeared, grinning and greeting everyone again as though he had not seen them before. He climbed onto the back of the bus and moved among the benches, seeming to be interested in everyone but not their baggage. Cavender

162

watched him carefully. Not a package escaped his quick, subtle scrutiny. Not a crate was overlooked. His grin never left his face, his mouth never stopped moving. His hand pumped up and down. And his eyes kept shifting back to the four bags nearest Cavender. When he passed them on the way back to the steps, he neatly managed to dig a toe into the burlapped box.

Not a trace of a change showed in his face. The cheerful grin stood there as though cut of wax. Cavender repressed a sigh. This was going to be one of those times when words would not work. It was going to be guns. He would wait until later to tell McLaughlin. He felt the pulse in his thick neck begin to beat a little harder. His mind felt clear and sharp, the muscles in his body were relaxed and ready. He enjoyed the control he had over himself and over what was going to happen. It was not new and it never made him overconfident and careless. Readiness was simply his pleasure.

The bus driver drove exactly as he had two days ago. He talked incessantly over his shoulder and drove so cautiously they were making poorer time than on the trip out. But the load was much lighter and the bus took the pounding worse. The rear of the machine rocked back and forth and flew up and down and shook everybody to pieces. He seemed to be fighting every rut and hole in the dirt road.

The village women began to complain. They shouted to the driver. It had never been so bad as this, they scolded. What was he doing? The village men looked at each other and at the women and shrugged and held on.

The driver laughed. The ride was worse, he said to Cavender, because few were aboard. The bus was getting old. The springs were bad. People were getting soft. They expected too much.

"You've forgotten when you walked your bullocks and carts to the city," he shouted back at them. He grinned at Cavender and McLaughlin.

The bus rattled onward. Once it almost capsized. It struck a high spot on one side of the road, went up too far on that side, and the wheels came up off the ground. The driver gunned the engine and twisted the wheel savagely.

163

The old bus settled back onto all four wheels with a violent jolt that shook everybody off his seat. Luggage scrambled about and several crates loaded with vegetables overturned.

The women squawked and gabbled. The men began to mumble angrily and tried to collect the vegetables. The driver reassured them all was well. Just as he spoke the words he struck a boulder and the rear of the lorry rode up into the air like the tail of a longboat catching a sudden swell. Somebody slid off the bench and along the floor a few feet. The women screamed and cursed.

The whole thing smelled bad to Cavender. He managed to whisper a warning to McLaughlin. Basil was crouched under McLaughlin's bench. His ears were pinched down onto his head. He didn't like the ride any more than anybody else.

When they reached the small cluster of huts halfway to Bhubaneswar, two older men crept forward and leaned over the rail to reach the driver. They pounded him on the shoulder and shouted. He threw his hands into the air in disgust, laughed, and pulled the bus over to a halt. He climbed down from his seat and told them to get off. He shouted. It was unnecessary to say anything, for as soon as the lorry had stopped every villager began to take his goods off and left.

There was no haggling. The driver went with his passengers to the shade of some trees near a bungalow and paid them back the fare they had not used.

Cavender watched the proceedings and said to McLaughlin softly, "Something's going to happen soon. Are you ready?"

"I'm ready," growled McLaughlin. He opened his coat and showed Cavender his Lancaster lying in his fist on his lap. Cavender took the big Mauser from his leather pouch and held it under his coat in the same way.

"What's happening?" Rose asked.

"Do you keep a gun?" asked Cavender.

"Why?" she asked in return. Then, "You know I don't. Is it trouble?"

"It is," he said. "Right now sit tight and be natural and then flop down flat when it starts. Here it comes."

Four strange men were with the bus driver when he returned. Two carried old single-shot muskets that looked like the kind Cavender had seen made by Afghan tribesmen. The barrels were colorfully decorated by bright strips of leather woven around them. They were copies of an old nineteenth-century Enfield.

The other two carried outside-hammer double-barrel shotguns similar to the bus driver's. With the exception of the bus driver they all carried their guns on their shoulders or across the back of their necks, gripping them by stock and barrel. No hand was anywhere near a trigger. They looked as innocent as another party of afternoon grouse shooters. The bus driver carried nothing except his grin. Cavender thought that was something.

The bus driver said, "Always you see me with men like these. But these really are hunters. They have asked for a ride a few miles north to shoot a leopard that has been molesting the villages. They are paid well to kill such an animal."

He waved them onto the bus and, with a bigger grin than ever, climbed up to his driver's seat. The four men climbed onto the back and sat on a bench on the far side of the platform opposite Cavender and McLaughlin. Rose was sitting up from McLaughlin. The three of them were facing the four natives. The hunters placed their weapons butt down between their feet and embraced them with their knees. Three of them threw their arms out behind them to grip the rail. The fourth dropped his limply on his lap, nearer to his shotgun.

They smiled and nodded at Cavender and McLaughlin and grinned at Rose. In the grins Cavender thought he saw some lewdness they didn't show in their smiles at him. He guessed they were thinking of what they could do with her when they got rid of her two men. Rose was taking their eyes pretty well, probably thinking of the same thing. She kept her own eyes on the floor at her feet. There was an unusual tightness around her chin, but Cavender couldn't tell whether she was afraid or angry.

The bus lurched and crept away from the tiny village. The villagers who had left the bus were grouped together talking and vigorously making gestures to one another. One woman kept waving her hand in disgust at the lorry.

Miraculously, Cavender thought wryly, the road became much smoother as the bus left the village behind. The springs beneath the axles seemed to have become rejuvenated and the sickening swaying almost disappeared. The leopard-hunters had charmed the machine or the road or both, and the driver picked up speed and made four or five miles in short order. There was nothing subtle about what had happened. The driver was no professional bandit but not any less dangerous because he was obvious. He was an opportunist who thought he was fooling some watery-brained Englishmen who had walked into his trap.

A little beyond five miles from the village they entered a heavy forest that darkened the sky and held the road in a deep gloom. The driver was singing loudly to himself when he suddenly let out a cry of alarm and a few seconds later struck his brakes hard. The big machine skidded in the rear and started to drift off the road to the right. The driver accelerated hard enough to break the skid and toss the machine forward with a sharp lurch.

It was the kind of signal Cavender expected from a grinning Hindu amateur bandit who was a pretty good driver. Through half-closed eyes, as though he were trying to sleep, he watched the natives across from him. The man with his hands in his lap near the trigger and hammers of his shotgun was the most dangerous. He watched him most of all, especially his face.

Cavender was no English paladin, no knightly fighter. He would laugh at the Marquess of Queensberry when there was blood to be let, especially his own. Yet he didn't want to shoot four innocent men for nothing. He had to be absolutely certain.

He waited a fraction of a second for the man's hand to move to his gun and his thumb to reach for the hammer before he shot him. And then he shot him three times so rapidly the roar of the big Mauser blended into a single sound. He shot him without lifting the Mauser from his lap.

He shot the next two Hindus twice each from the same position before they could move their arms from the railing. The fourth Hindu was already dead, blasted half over the railing by McLaughlin's heavy pistol.

McLaughlin was leaning over the side of the railing and had his pistol pressed against the side of the bus driver's face. There was still a grin on the face but now it was a weak and sickly grin.

He ordered the bus driver to stop the bus. The man obeyed almost immediately, slowing the machine to an easy halt. He left the motor running and got out with his hands over his head.

"Wha . . . what . . . what happened?" he asked, shaking. His face was pale and twitchy. His teeth showed in a kind of snarling grin. He looked disbelievingly at the four Indians crumpled on the back of the lorry. "Aiieeee! Why did you kill these men? You are evil men, you are bad. Now you will kill me." He suddenly fell to the ground and bowed to them. "In back of the head, sahib, make it easy on this poor innocent. In back of the head."

Cavender placed a foot on the man's side and kicked hard. The man toppled over onto his side. "Get up," Cavender ordered. "Get up or you'll get one in your stomach. Those thugs were yours. Admit it or I'll give it to you right now. And stop that sniveling."

He leaned over and pointed the Mauser at the middle of the man's belly.

"No, please, sahib, do not shoot. I meant no harm. Those men would not shoot you. I wanted only that box." He got to his feet and stood in a half-bowed position. Cavender moved around him, came up close, felt through his clothes, and took away a small thin-bladed dagger. He threw the knife onto the seat in the cab of the Lorry. On the floor in front of the seat was the bus driver's shotgun.

Cavender took it out. Fresh percussion caps were under the hammers. He cocked the hammers and fired both barrels into the air and threw the shotgun into the back of the lorry.

The driver was back on his knees, mumbling and whimpering for mercy. Rose came over to stand near Cavender while McLaughlin was dumping the bodies of the four bandits. The driver crawled to her feet and pleaded with her. He lifted his head and begged her not to let him die.

Cavender hadn't decided what to do about him. He took out his small Mauser pocket pistol, pressed the safety release and handed the compact weapon to Rose.

"If he moves, just squeeze that trigger at him, release it and squeeze it again, and keep on doing that until it stops shooting. We don't want him running off into the woods. Can you do it?"

"I can do it," she said, holding the pistol out at arm's length. She leaned back against the bus and stiffened her stocky body in a pose of determination. Her face was deadly grim; to Cavender it looked somehow comical.

In Hindi, Cavender repeated the exact words he had just spoken to make the driver understand clearly what he had told the woman. Then he went up onto the lorry to help McLaughlin. The Irishman had already dropped two of the bandits onto the ground. Cavender helped him with the other two. The bodies hit the ground like sacks of potatoes.

"We'll have to get them a bit into the woods, won't we," said McLaughlin.

"Bury them, you mean. If we're going to get out of the country without talking to the police again."

McLaughlin grumbled and began to drag the bodies one at a time into the underbrush.

Cavender found a spade with a long handle tied under the carriage. He looked over at the bus driver across the lorry bed. The driver was now standing five or six feet away from Rose's outstretched arm. He had stopped whimpering. He had just finished saying something to her that Cavender did not catch.

"Don't let him get any closer to you," he said to her calmly. "Do what I said if he moves again." He raised his voice. "You, driver. You heard what I told her. Keep your mouth shut and stand there or she'll kill you."

"Aiee, sahib," said the driver, managing a weak grin. "I am not moving. I do not wish to die."

There was a touch of confidence in his voice, Cavender thought, as though he had been promised another chance. Cavender had an impulse to shoot him right now and get it over with. How else were they going to keep him quiet until they got free of the country? By sparing him and expecting gratitude? With threats? Money? How much would guarantee anything? In Cavender's mind it looked bad for this driver-bandit who liked to grin.

He thought about it during the next fifteen minutes while he and McLaughlin were burying the dead bandits and their weapons in a shallow grave. McLaughlin was for the easiest way.

"If he's a threat to our getting out of here, I'll kill him, Alec. He'd kill us, give him a chance. We'll be doing it my way."

Cavender said nothing. They covered the grave with brush and began to work their way back to the road, covering their trail as well as they could. They shook at bushes they had bent, straightened branches, and kicked around the growth on the ground. In a few days the jungle would do the rest to hide their passage from even the sharpest eyes.

They had covered twenty-five yards when the first shot sounded. There was a pause. Then came the second. Five more sharp cracks followed in rapid succession.

"Bloody hell," muttered Cavender, starting to run. "I didn't think she'd do it." He headed in a straight line for the road.

"Do what?" yelled McLaughlin, following after him at a trot.

"That was our bus-driver problem," panted Cavender. "I don't think we've got one anymore."

32

The first thing he saw when he hit the road a few yards up from the bus was Rose bending over the driver's body. She heard him coming and straightened up and stood facing him as though she were dazed. His Mauser was in her right hand at her side, its action locked open by the last shot. He made a few sounds deep in his throat, shook his head, but not in disapproval, and took the pistol away from her. Like a soldier she had followed his directions literally, unaware that he had given them for the driver's sake, not hers. They were supposed to make him behave.

"He went into the truck for his knife, Alec," Rose said, speaking defensively and trembling. "What was I to do. He didn't think it was in me to do it. But I did. I did what you told me to." She looked down at the dead, grinless face of the bus driver. Her own face showed little if any after-effects of shock. Then she turned away.

"Yes, indeed you did," said Cavender. He knelt and examined the body. "It was good shooting, too. Did you say you never shot a gun before?"

He opened the driver's shirt. The holes in his chest could be covered with one handspread.

"Sure now I didn't say that," she said, "and you never did ask it. But I never have."

"Well, I haven't counted but I think you hit him with every one of them."

He could have spared her that but he did not feel like sparing her anything. He thought she would flinch. She didn't. That bothered him. Something was developing about her that was beginning to rankle in him. It wasn't just her seduction of McLaughlin or her queerness with Farashah or even her wild proposal to get rid of him in the name of Ireland. All of that made her much less endearing, of course, but the shooting added something else. It blooded her. He wished he could send her back to Dublin and forget her for a while.

"By God!" exclaimed McLaughlin, kneeling for a close look. "Will you look at the way she's blown him open with that toy of yours. The only problem he'll give us now is to get him under the ground with his bloody friends."

A faint smile of satisfaction crossed Rose's face. "If you were going to get him out of the way yourself, Alec, why did you look at me like that?"

Cavender's voice hardened. "I didn't think you needed to shoot him seven times. We might have gotten him to tell us some things."

"About what?" she complained.

"About how to get that white beauty into Bhubaneswar without attracting too much attention, for one thing."

Rose went sullen and stared at him through her dark penetrating eyes. "And what else?"

He thought of something else but said, "That's enough, for one thing. Let's get him out of here, McLaughlin, and in there."

33

They made it to Bhubaneswar with no further trouble. Cavender drove, wearing the skullcap he had taken from the driver. He removed his coat and tie, rolled his shirt-sleeves, and passed for a native. McLaughlin and Rose sat in back with the bull terrier, who had not left the bus during the entire trip.

Once in the city, Cavender tried to remember where the train stop was, headed in that direction, and finally left the lorry on a side street when he thought he was close enough. The three of them walked around until they found the station and learned that the Calcutta train was due in four hours, at 7:00. That meant it might not arrive in the next twelve.

It arrived within eight, just before eleven. Waiting for it, they had found a decent local eating place and usable toilets. Then they took turns sleeping in the station against their bags. Cavender spent an hour in the nearby streets hunting for something better in which to conceal the copper box. In a factotum shop he found an old paperboard suitcase that would just take it without the burlap wrapping. They made the change quickly and unobserved. Cavender knew it was not exactly inconspicuous carried next to his alligator bag, but some things couldn't be helped.

The Calcutta train had its usual crowds and the first-class compartments were all occupied. But the trip was saved by a good-hearted quiet Hindu lawyer who shared his compartment with them, even allowing Basil floor space. If not for the man's offer they would have spent the ten hours in the passageway on the floor.

The lawyer was about forty. He was a merchant-caste Hindu, political but private about his person. He spoke seldom during the first hours, asked no questions, and neither shared his food nor accepted Cavender's when he offered it. Cavender and McLaughlin passed up the slices of meat they had bought for the trip, and when Rose took her piece to stuff it into a flat roll, Cavender motioned to her to put it away. She pushed it back into her bag and began to eat a piece of dried fruit.

"Thank you, my good sir," said the Hindu in perfect English. "It is not only against my faith that meat goes, it is against my body. The fruits and breads you have will be much better for you."

Throughout the night this brief exchange was all the talk. As day broke, Cavender found the Hindu sitting cross-legged on the floor, doing his morning prayers. Mc-

Laughlin and Basil were up watching him. When he finished, the Hindu addressed himself to McLaughlin.

"Your speech says you are Irish. Your Mr. Parnell was a great man."

"Aye, that he was," answered McLaughlin.

"His cause is my cause," said the Hindu. "It is a great cause, freedom for one's people. Mr. Parnell saw the way as I once did—talk and talk. Now I hear the people in your land talk of conflict, talk of arming. That is not a good way."

"It may not be a good way," said McLaughlin gruffly, "but it is as good as the only way. And it's not the talking I mean but the arming and the fighting."

The smooth, spectacled, big-nosed face of the Hindu lawyer winced.

"No, my good friend, I cannot agree. You are going to be in Calcutta these next few days. I invite you to the Maidan on the day beyond tomorrow. We are going to show the British something new. It will astound them and they will not know what to do. They will do nothing."

He spoke then to Cavender, kindly and softly. "You are English. You may think of forewarning the authorities. Do not trouble. I have told them myself. There will be no fighting, no bloodshed. We are going to walk and then we are going to sit. They will give us our country back."

McLaughlin stared steadily at the quiet, serious Hindu. His face started to break into a laugh, but then he reconsidered and the laugh faded. "Ahhrrr," he growled almost politely, "you don't think that walking and sitting will persuade the British, do you? The Americans in the old colonies should have taught you better than that."

For the next ten minutes Cavender listened to the Hindu lawyer quietly and confidently expound a view of political resistance without arms, of political pressure without force, of revolution without blood. When McLaughlin spoke of arrest and imprisonment, the Hindu smiled and replied that both were essential courses in the strategy.

"And you've been in a British prison?" asked McLaughlin.

173

"Not I personally, but my friends have. I expect to share their experience soon."

"You'll change your tune when you've been inside a while. But good luck, my friend."

Rose awoke and the conversation died as though women were not fit for it, and they all sat back and waited for Calcutta.

In the southern outlying districts of the city the train made an unexpected stop at a small-platformed freight station. Cavender, in his usual curious reaction to anything out of the ordinary, leaned out of the window in time to see two British constables and a man in mufti boarding their carriage. One of the constables boarded at the rear and the man in mufti and the second constable at the front. The other constables remained outside the carriage to guard the compartment doors.

The distance between the two constables was about thirty feet, and though they carried side arms Cavender thought he might be able to make a run for it with the scrolls. With McLaughlin's help in creating a diversion he could get by them. But before he could signal to McLaughlin, the engineer hit his whistles and the train jerked into motion and pulled away from the station. The two constables stayed on the platform and stared after it.

Cavender frowned and muttered to himself, "What the hell?" and started to get up with the cheap suitcase. Alone in the passageway, he might bluff his way by the constable who had boarded at the rear.

"It's the police," he said casually to McLaughlin, who was looking puzzled at him. The Irishman grew red and had a curse and his Lancaster half out.

"The son of—"

"Rest at ease, my friends," said the Hindu lawyer, sitting up a little straighter and holding his hand up. "It is most certainly I they have come for. Please, please, sit down. You will not be involved."

The door slid open without a knock. The man in mufti was there in a spotless tan suit, brown striped shirt, and light tie drawn tight under his collar. He wore a white-strapped pith helmet which he did not remove and the air

174

of a man on official state business of some importance. The constable paraded past him smartly and strode across the compartment to its exterior door.

The man in mufti addressed Cavender, McLaughlin, and Rose. "You will have to excuse this intrusion, gentlemen, and you, ma'am. Apologies of His Majesty's government, you understand. Unavoidable, I assure you."

The Hindu lawyer folded his hands on his lap. The man in mufti squared his shoulders to face him. His voice dropped its courtesy.

"Mr. M. K. Gandhi?"

"Yes," said the Hindu lawyer, undisturbed. "I am Mohandas Gandhi."

"Good, sir. Now that's what I call not giving us trouble. I have a warrant issued by Calcutta Government House for your arrest, Mr. Gandhi."

"And the charges, please?" asked the Hindu lawyer as calmly as before.

The man in mufti produced an official-looking piece of paper and read from it. "Illegal organization of a public meeting with the intention of disrupting civil routines."

"I see no demonstrations here," replied the Hindu. "Unless my talking with these three English citizens is to be considered one."

"That's not for me to say, Mr. Gandhi," said the man in mufti.

Cavender could detect the effort he was making to be civil himself.

"He thinks he's making me look rather bad in front of you, sir," said the English officer. "But Government House knows what it's doing. We received this warrant an hour ago. When we get to the rail center you'll know what the charge means."

Howrah Station was not quite packed to its four walls, but Cavender wouldn't bet he could find standing place for another six people. As the train coasted in, the density of the crowd shifted along the tracks like a crescent wave to keep alongside the first-class carriages. There was no way to get off. The two uniformed constables heaved to open the side doors but the crowd drew itself tightly to-

175

gether and the doors would not open more than a few inches. There was shouting and deep chanting in Hindi that sounded like "India free, India free."

A few minutes later there was a great uproar as three or four units of white-capped British sepoys burst into the station and charged into the crowd, opening up a narrow corridor from the main station entrance to the door of the Hindu lawyer's compartment.

When the corridor was passable the man in mufti said to the Hindu lawyer, "Please, Mr. Gandhi, do not give us any more trouble."

The Hindu lawyer looked at Cavender and McLaughlin. "You see, sirs, I give nobody any trouble or very much trouble." He turned back to the man in mufti. "The only trouble you will have, my good sir, is the trouble of carrying me. I will not resist you. But I will not assist you either. You will have to carry me if you want me to go to your gaol. That should cause you little trouble. I do not weigh very much."

With those words he sat back and folded his hands on his lap. He was quiet and soft and very harmless looking, Cavender thought. And very tough and almost likable. He waited to see what the man in mufti would do.

"All right, corporal, pick him up," said the man in mufti.

"Constable Williams!" said the corporal.

The two constables took the slender Hindu lawyer on either side by one arm and one leg and effortlessly propelled him upward into the air and marched with him down the carriage steps into the open corridor.

Cavender could have laughed at the absurdity of the sight. But as soon as the Hindu lawyer was brought down into the corridor, a great roar came from the crowd and savage fighting broke out near the train. Two British soldiers fell into the corridor, one bleeding from a face wound and the other from his head. Their companions retaliated by swinging the butts of their rifles into the crowd and driving back the attackers.

McLaughlin called down to the Hindu lawyer, who had been carried only a few yards away.

"No bloodshed, is that it, my boyo?"

The Hindu lawyer heard him above the row and twisted slightly and said something as calmly as though he were being carried to his wedding. To Cavender it sounded like, "They'll learn, my Irish friend. In time, they'll learn."

Then the corridor closed behind him and the mob swirled crazily and followed.

Cavender gripped the old suitcase, swung his leather pouch over his shoulder, and started to step off. Suddenly he ducked back in.

"Did you see him—BPO Bentley. He's out there with some of his men. Maybe he's here for that Gandhi fellow. Or maybe he's here for us. We'll split up. We'll never stay together in that mob anyway. Now listen, both of you. In twenty minutes we'll meet at the foot of the Howrah Bridge, left side. All right? But don't let the police tag along."

Cavender was half off the carriage when he felt a strong hand on his shoulder spinning him around. McLaughlin's face was dark red and his eyes were harder than Cavender had seen before.

"Go ahead," Cavender said angrily. "Settle who's running things right here. Go ahead, Black Dog, settle it now—and throw it all away—or start trusting somebody. And I'm the only one you've got."

"Like the devil you are," Rose protested. "I'll stick with him, Brendan." She squeezed by McLaughlin onto the steps. McLaughlin swept his hand off Cavender's shoulder and against Rose's breast, toppling her backwards onto her seat.

"Like hell you will, lass. He's going out there alone, then I'm going, then you do what you want. We'll meet where he said." He was facing Cavender all the time. "How long?"

"Twenty minutes. Don't waste your time. The alligator bag there. Take it along for me, will you?"

He jumped off, squeezed his heavy body into the mass of Hindus, and fought his way across the station to the baggage room at the far end. A British railway baggage room was the next best thing to a British bank, perhaps better, for some things. He handed the suitcase to a small, tough-looking English clerk who tied a large heavy ticket to it, tore off half for Cavender, and stored it somewhere among the crowded racks in the rear. Unless the claim ticket passed over that counter, the suitcase would stay there undisturbed for one year, the property and responsibility of the British government, protected by the weight and authority of its Commonwealth.

34

Two hours later Cavender left Rose and McLaughlin upstairs in a small hotel near Old Court House Street on his way to the docks on the Hooghly. A telephone call had informed him that a steamer was leaving for England the following day. He wanted to be on it with the scrolls. Calcutta was too crowded with people who wanted them.

As he reached the sidewalk outside his hotel he checked his inside pocket for his half of the claim ticket to the suitcase. The other half was with McLaughlin. He had offered the half before the Irishman asked anything about the suitcase. That made things comfortable between them. Rose was told nothing.

He fingered the smooth thin piece of stiffened paper and started up the street. That was as far as he got.

Up toward Strand Road a familiar figure was climbing out of a rickshaw. Scowling, Cavender dropped back into the shadow of the building and watched the man looking up and down the street. His gaze paused too long on the clean white front of Cavender's hotel. Cavender swore softly.

When the man turned to settle with his wallah Cavender went back upstairs fast.

"Prepare yourselves," he said, coming through the door of their rooms. "You're about to have a visitor."

McLaughlin got to his feet. Cavender watched Rose. She was combing her hair. She glanced at him sideways and continued to comb vigorously. Her breasts looked good stretched up. For a moment he was sorry he had given her up, and that was a strange feeling to have right now. She moved a big floppy hat she had worn off the train, and tossed it on a bed.

"Who?" she asked, combing again. "Bentley?"

McLaughlin was drawing his gun.

"Put that bloody thing away," Cavender said gruffly. "It's not the police and that wouldn't be a bright thing to do if it were. It's Stathopolous—and I'd like to know how the hell he found this place."

"What are you going to do?" McLaughlin asked. He put the Lancaster on the table and covered it with his coat.

"I'm not staying. Someone's got to get us out of this city—and soon. Get rid of him. Tell him a story. Promise him something. But keep him out of our hair until the boat sails tomorrow. And for your sake, don't use the gun. Right?"

McLaughlin looked gloomy. Rose looked anxious. Basil lay on the floor, indifferent to the change in moods. Cavender left them and went down to the floor below and stopped around a corner near the stairs and waited. The building had no lift.

Except for the street noise drifting in through an open window somewhere, the hallways were quiet. Then after a while a girl started crying downstairs, a quiet, steady sobbing. Five minutes passed slowly before he heard steps above the crying. He waited until the fat man turned toward the next flight, putting one hand on the railing and pausing for a breath. He breathed audibly.

When he took the first step up, Cavender came up quickly and quietly behind him. He placed his Mauser pistol against the back of the Greek's fat neck and pushed the muzzle deep into the flesh. With his other arm he circled the Greek's neck and drew him backwards off balance, taking his weight off his feet. He braced himself

179

hard for the vast weight. His thick shoulders and arms knotted under the strain but he held the Greek high and helpless on his tiptoes.

"Wha . . . at?" was all Stathopolous could say.

Cavender put a growl into his voice and spoke into the Greek's ear. "We're sick of you, do you hear. How did you find us this time?"

Stathopolous gurgled until Cavender relaxed his grip. "Talk," Cavender repeated, "or you'll get no further. You'll stay right here forever."

"The girl," gurgled Stathopolous. Cavender's eyes grew brighter. "It was her big hat. I spied it at the train station. I've been waiting there for you, Mr. Cavender. You have my money. You can't shoot me."

Cavender grunted in disgust. He slid his left hand from the Greek's throat over his chest, around his great belly, until he found a pistol in his right pocket. He took it away. He could find no other weapon.

"Go ahead up now," he said harshly. "That's what your five hundred is buying. A skin in one piece and another chance with McLaughlin. And feel lucky if he doesn't open you up himself. He's tired of you, too. Go ahead. Don't talk to me. I'm through with it."

Cavender pocketed the Greek's pistol, holstered his own gun, and walked away. He heard the Greek continue his laborious climb up toward the next floor.

35

The liner was a twin-stacker called the *Prince Albert*, thirty years old, medium tonnage, moderate speed, modest accommodations with the exception of two first-class suites. Cavender saw the passenger list as he was picking a cabin from a numbered diagram.

One of the first-class suites had been taken by the Countess Irene Borodin.

Cavender ran his fingers over the entire list. He did not recognize any other name.

"Everybody on this list sails tomorrow," he observed.

"If they're not on the list," said the booking agent, "they do not sail."

"I'll take these three," said Cavender. He pointed to an empty block on the port side, gave the names of the occupants, paid for the tickets, and left.

He took a taxi to the Empress-Gresham Hotel. The count and countess had checked out four days ago. He went to four other first-class hotels. Nothing. At the fifth he found that the countess had checked in two days ago and checked out that morning.

As he was about to leave he was stopped by another desk man, spotlessly dressed in an English tailored suit, which Indian managers preferred to wear. In a helpful voice the manager said, "You may know the countess's husband, the count, was keeping an air machine at the flying field in Dum Dum. I suspect they may very well be there, if your business is important."

Cavender thanked him. It was still early. He knew he ought to talk to the Russians before McLaughlin did. And if the countess boarded the *Prince Albert,* the Irishman was certainly going to talk to her. It wouldn't be easy to prevent it or stop him from wringing her neck. Once the scrolls were delivered in Dublin he would say the devil with them. Let McLaughlin do what he wanted to. But not before then.

He asked to be driven to Dum Dum. He had never been there, but he knew the name—every British soldier knew it. Dum Dum, the town made famous by its military arsenal there, which years ago had developed the expanding bullet, now known as the dumdum. When the British began to use it against their enemies there was a great fuss stirred up about it. Finally at a conference in The Hague the bullet had been internationally condemned and banned. As if it mattered whether a man died from a small hole in his body or a big one.

Cavender still used a dumdum bullet himself in his big Mauser, a copper-clad lead bullet with a small hole bored into its nose. It was more efficient when the situation needed that kind of efficiency, like the executions the day before on the bus.

That thought brought him around to thinking of the way Rose had shot the driver and the way the countess— or count—had shot the Indian girl, the way people sometimes shot other people because they had to and sometimes because they wanted to. The Hague Conference, hell, acting as if people were humane.

Suddenly Cavender stopped thinking of those things. He was looking out the rear window for the third time. He was being followed.

When he had left the Empress-Gresham he had been conscious of a taxi leaving directly after his. He had noticed it, or a machine just like it, a block away, and then had not seen it for the next several blocks. He ignored it for the next half hour and mused about bullets and killings. Now there it was again. It was the same taxi.

They were out of the heavily settled city and rolling through open countryside toward the town of Dum Dum. It was bright midafternoon. Farmers were in their fields and machines and lorries occasionally squeezed by on the narrow dirt road.

Once Cavender told the driver to pull off the road and stop. He got out, walked a few feet into a field and urinated with his back to the road. He stayed there long enough to force the trailing taxicab to pass him or to stop up the road and make itself conspicuous.

The shadow chose to pass. Cavender was already walking to the taxi. He could see a man sitting far back in the rear seat of the machine. The light was good and the angle clear. The man was bearded and turbaned and Cavender knew he was wearing a steel bracelet on his right wrist— and the other hidden accoutrements of the Sikh.

They hadn't given up. None of them. The Greek had

182

showed up with a gun in his pocket and was probably badgering McLaughlin right now. The Russian had booked his wife aboard the *Prince Albert,* gambling that it would be the boat taking the scrolls to Ireland—and he himself was probably at Dum Dum arranging to fly somewhere to beat the boat and get there to wait for it. Bentley had been at the train station and was still nosing around. And now he had the Sikh on his tail who had probably picked him at the Gresham looking for the Russian. Nothing had changed except to get a little warmer now that the scrolls were nearby.

No one had dropped out of the game. The affair had developed into a steeplechase—he didn't like the image and thought of a better one. More like a dog race—hounds coursing the field after a rabbit or fox. With a difference, he suspected. In the end the hounds tear the prize apart. Not each other.

A half mile farther the Sikh's taxi was parked at the side of the road and someone was standing in the fields behind a low tree. As Cavender's machine went past, the man was climbing back into the taxi and the order of shadow and shadowed was restored. The stratagem, Cavender mused, was not very original. But then, the Sikh was not a professional.

He lit a Suerdieck and concentrated on watching the tobacco turn into silver ash. When they reached Dum Dum his mind was at ease. He watched the aerodrome approaching. It was a small flat field covered with short cut grass resembling a Scottish putting green. At the south end of the field was a long, low building with an air sock blowing full out high above it. Two more small hangars stood at the east end.

They drove along the road behind the building and onto the grass around to the doors opening to the full length of the field. Three aircraft stood on the field, two monoplanes and a small biplane. Six men were there either working on them or lounging idly by. There was no Blériot in sight.

The men were English, easy, chatty, and open. They

183

told Cavender that the Russian count and the countess had flown the Blériot out three or four days ago, carrying several extra tanks of fuel for an extended trip.

"Four, five hundred miles," said a short grease-stained man whose accent was cockney. "Ten, twelve hours flying time taken all together, with a stop down somewhere to get the extra fuel in. The spare tanks couldn't be rigged into the main lines. He's got to syphon it on the ground."

The cockney warmed up talking about the Blériot, saying it was a beauty, modified to carry two, and could fly faster and farther than most other machines its size.

"And 'e's a top pilot if you ever needed one, that Cossack," added another mechanic. "One of the best bloomin' airmen I've ever known. And an amateur, too. No professional. Just rich."

Cavender asked a few other questions. Yes, they had returned two days after they left, returned on a Thursday almost at dark. No, none of the English mechanics had ever worked on the machine. The Cossack had his own people, two good mechanics who knew the machine backward and forward, inside and out, who could tear it apart in the dark, engine and all, and put it together and not lose a washer. One of them had seen them do it. Yesterday, as a matter of fact, the two Russians had dismantled the machine, loaded the parts into two medium lorries, and driven out of there. They didn't expect they'd ever see it again or another like it with a team like theirs. If that Cossack wanted some trophies he could get them in just about any race he chose.

The cockney mechanic walked along with Cavender back toward Cavender's taxi, all the while talking about the machines. He began to explain the difference between the Russian's Blériot and the two monoplanes on the field. Cavender listened to his words but all the while was looking around for the Sikh.

"Those monos over there," the cockney was saying, "can lug four-fifty, five hundred pounds up, but they're creepy slow with that weight. The Morane with the wires on its wings is a bit better. Now the Blériot can't lift anywhere near that weight but it'll fly circles around those."

184

The aeroplane he had named was a mid-wing monoplane with a sleek round fuselage with two open cockpits. Between them a short pole rose, from the top of which guy wires stretched to the wings to stiffen the support. The craft was painted bright blue. A mechanic had turned the engine over and climbed down to listen to it from up front and make some adjustments. Cavender could hear the soft rhythmical flutter of its engine.

"Fly circles around that bird coming in now, too," added the cockney.

They were near the taxi and the cockney was pointing to a biplane sweeping over the field. The aeroplane banked swiftly and dropped for a landing.

"You better be flyin' yourself," said the cockney. "There's a Metro bobby wi' rank in that bipe and 'e's lookin' for your Cossack, too. Thought maybe you might not want to be talkin' to 'im, would you?"

Cavender said thanks and handed the cockney a fivepounder. He called to the driver to start the engine. The man was already bent over the crank.

"Having trouble, sir," said the driver, giving the crank a vicious turn. "She's dead. I've been trying. We'll need a push."

Cavender had to make the decision fast. He did not want to talk with Bentley and it would be Bentley on that plane. He looked over toward the Sikh's taxi, which had stopped farther down the road. The Sikh was boldly walking straight toward him. He was the man who had accosted McLaughlin outside the prison and had been stabbed a little later. He walked with a noticeable stiffness in his upper body.

Off to the right the biplane had hit the ground, bounced slightly, and was taxiing toward the far hangar.

Cavender made the decision. He jogged down toward the Sikh. He met him halfway between the motorcars.

"We've seen each other before," began Cavender, speaking Punjabi, "and you have business with me. Or with McLaughlin. But if we don't get out of here now—immediately—there'll be no business between us, and your scrolls are going to fall into the hands of the police.

185

There's a Metro in that ship over there and he'll be interested in both of us. My taxi's broken. Can we use yours?"

"We have no luck, then," said the Sikh, holding himself stiffly and speaking unexcitedly. "That machine went out of petrol right over there. I was coming to share yours. Luck will have to come from this." He drew his short curved sword.

"We'll make a different kind of luck," said Cavender, a strange thrill beginning to race around his mind. At the far side of the field two men were climbing down from the biplane. One of them was in the white uniform of the Calcutta Metropolitans. From the distance it looked like Bentley.

"Come on, if you want to talk about the scrolls," said Cavender. He ran toward the monoplane whose engine was running smoothly. The mechanic was halfway up onto the wing on his way back into the first cockpit. Cavender shouted to him. He hopped down.

"How's she running?" Cavender shouted.

"Like a watch," said the mechanic.

"Fueled?" asked Cavender. He could see Bentley ambling over to his taxicab where the driver was standing forlornly by the open bonnet.

"About half full." Then with a puzzled look on his face, "What's it to you?"

Cavender shoved a crumpled ten-pounder into the startled man's fist.

"Hey, yer can't get in there," said the mechanic excitedly, grabbing Cavender's arm as he started to pull himself up the side of the fuselage.

"Sorry," said Cavender. He dropped down and threw a short right jab into the man's jaw, connecting perfectly at its tip. The mechanic's legs went rubbery and he dropped to the ground stunned.

"Get in there," yelled Cavender. He pointed to the rear cockpit. "Quickly, now. Move." His voice sounded to him vaguely familiar, like a voice from the past when he had commanded men in the field.

And the Sikh responded like a man who had been

186

trained to obey such commands. Without a word he followed Cavender up onto the wing and fairly leaped into the rear cockpit and was settled there almost before Cavender had buckled his belt.

Across the field Cavender heard a dull report above the idling motor. He glanced to see that Bentley was running toward them with his pistol drawn and pointed into the air. Another shot sounded.

Cavender removed his hat and stuffed it beside him. He found the stick between his legs, moved it forward and back and saw through a small mirror the rear stabilizer respond. With his feet he fumbled in the darkness beneath the instrument board until he struck two small pedals. He worked on them and watched the small curved rudder turn right and left.

A short lever with a knurled wooden knob on its end stuck out from the instrument board near his left hand. He eased it slowly inward, feeling the engine respond. The rhythmical flutter of the pistons deepened, the sense of a missing beat faded, transforming the flutter into a light-pitched whirr. The propeller disappeared into a silvery blur.

Cavender felt the aeroplane rock under his body. The backrest pushed lightly against his body. They began to bounce forward along the ground toward the smoother grassy field. His foot accidently jarred against a pedal and the rear of the fuselage began to slide to his right, turning his nose toward the hangar where Bentley's craft was parked. He made a quick correction with his left foot, overcorrected, the rear fuselage straightened and then skidded harshly to his left. He corrected again and straightened the craft downfield.

The air sock above the hangar stood out to show him that he was rolling downwind. He gave the Gnome engine a little more petrol and maneuvered the craft toward one corner of the field. A kick on one pedal as the craft was moving along nicely spun the tail around sharply and reversed their direction.

At the far end of the field he could see Bentley racing back toward the biplane waving his hands wildly. Cavender pushed the throttle knob completely forward. The Morane-Saulnier's propeller bit into the air and sped the light craft across the grass. The wind cut into his face, brought tears into his eyes. He crouched to keep as much below the low windscreen as possible.

Cavender had flown before under the guidance of a professional pilot but not often enough to have gotten his license. Yet he had found a natural affinity for aircraft as he had for horses and racing camels. A little practice was all he needed to master the monoplane. He had to experiment with the control stick to determine the ground speed he needed to increase the lift pressure beneath his wings. When the ground under him became a green blur, he pushed the stick forward, bringing the tail off the ground. He eased the stick back. The nose of the ship lifted, the plane rose from the ground. Suddenly it dropped back onto the grass, bounced, and picked up speed.

Across the field the biplane was beginning to roll toward him. Again he eased the stick forward and, as the tail lifted slowly, brought it back. The aeroplane shuddered, steadied, and rose easily as though being raised by an invisible hand toward the roof of the hangar. Carefully Cavender worked with the pedals and the stick to move the aeroplane away from the hanger, up over low trees into a buoyant breeze that carried them high into safety.

As the wind whipped around his head, he squinted to keep his vision clear. He brought the craft around the field again, working the controls, quickly getting the feel of the craft's response. He pushed the stick forward and brought her nose down and watched the green grass rise up to meet him. Then he pulled back and felt the craft shoot upward swiftly and gracefully. She was easy and responsive. Cavender felt exhilarated, free, almost giddy. The world below was crowded with the murky passions of the human race, greedy, cruel, petty. Up here was cleanness and the pride of the eagle. If it could last . . . but there was always the job. And Cavender had been a professional too long to succumb long to the euphoria.

He reminded himself of his passenger. The Sikh had made no complaints. Cavender twisted around and tried to tell him about his seat straps. He failed. The Sikh grinned back weakly and pointed toward the city of Calcutta not very far to the west, looking like some child's toy. Cavender nodded but pointed down.

On the ground almost directly below him the biplane was beginning its short run for a takeoff. If Bentley got into the air with a professional pilot at the controls, he would not be able to lose him.

He dropped his craft and headed straight for the biplane as it was starting its rise from the ground. He could see the pilot beneath him clearly. He was looking up and back and waving one arm furiously. Bentley drew his revolver and fired at the Morane. Cavender heard a light whack on the canvas fuselage. He kept his ship in a shallow dive and pulled off when he was thirty or forty feet away.

But he had come close enough. The pilot of the biplane reacted badly. He dropped the biplane onto the grass too hard. Something gave in the wheel carriage and the left wing of the ship tipped down and caught the ground, whipping the craft around to a stop.

Bentley jumped out quickly and fired some more at Cavender's ship and hit nothing. In front of the main hangar the five mechanics were waving their arms and hats as though they were cheering. Cavender made one more pass over the field, waving back to the mechanics, and aimed the aeroplane into the sun setting beyond the nearby city.

Fifteen minutes later he brought the Morane away from the Hooghly River he had followed, across the sprawling teeming city, and landed her softly on an empty polo field in the middle of the Maidan. He casually abandoned the aeroplane and led the Sikh, who was somewhat shaky, off the field toward a path where there were idle rickshaws waiting. The wallahs were gathered together at the edge of the field staring at the Morane, jabbering excitedly. People had begun to appear from all directions, but they were more curious about the aeroplane than about the fliers. Cavender led the Sikh through the growing crowd practically unnoticed, pried two wallahs loose from their

189

friends, and drove off in a rickshaw with the Sikh following close behind.

36

Over tea and cakes Cavender and the Sikh talked about the business of the scrolls. The unusual flight from Dum Dum was no longer of interest to either of them.

In five minutes Cavender was able to learn that the Sikhs had no idea of what was on the scrolls, not even the Nehang, the guardians knew. The copper box was revered, but no one could remember when it was last opened nor what it contained. The reverence was for the unknown.

It took Cavender fifteen minutes to tell the Sikh the story of the Alexander scrolls. He told him about Mc-Laughlin's claim to them—the rights of knowledge and possession. He told him about McLaughlin's deal with his God, about the Irish struggle against the English, about the offers already made by the Greek and the Russian. At the mention of the Greek the Sikh's face darkened in a scowl. Cavender took no notice of it and went on to say that the scrolls in the long run really belonged to the historians and to those who would read them when they were made public to the world.

In the back of his mind, however, he was feeling uneasy. He was not convinced himself. For several days now the doubts had been coming. Even as he was pushing the Sikh from the train heading to Konarak, he was thinking of the Sikh's legitimate claim to the manuscript. He was losing the comfortable belief that the interests of Irish freedom and his own bank account outweighed that claim of theirs. His feelings were now badly mixed.

The Sikh's, however, weren't. "I have made my decision, Mr. Cavender. Not an easy decision to make for me. My comrade was killed in your hotel five days ago. His killer—the fat Stathopolous—still walks free. The man who gave me this wound"—he pointed to his shoulder—"is dead. But the man who hired him—Stathopolous—still lives."

"You're quite positive it was Stathopolous, not the count?"

"We have our eyes, Mr. Cavender. Greeks cut throats. Russians do not. And we would have had our justice outside Stathopolous's hotel the night you interfered. We chose foolishly that night to use the rope instead of the sword. But I thank you for shooting so high. I know now it was a gesture of remembered comradeship that led you to do so, and I have not forgotten."

The Sikh placed his hands flat on the table before him. They were strong dark hands with silver hair along the fingers and on the backs. The steel bangle on his right wrist had a dull polished glint. The man's eyes were deep blue and cold. Cavender waited patiently for the man's decision.

The Sikh breathed slowly and fixed Cavender's gray eyes with his. It was his way to exhibit his honesty. Cavender understood that what he was about to say was not going to be easy for him. And there was a strain in his voice when he spoke.

"That gesture not to harm those who once served with you—in addition to all that you have said here—has helped me reach this point. We at first intended to take the scrolls from the major and leave him dead. Now, however, for your sake, we will pay. We will pay the major and you to deliver the copper box and its contents to us intact. We will pay you with our wealth, Mr. Cavender, and not with our swords. And, if it is money you really want, what we have to offer you will not refuse."

Cavender's gray eyes narrowed slightly and his dimple grew deeper. "The offers, my friend, have run high."

"We are not rich," said the Sikh, "but we can offer you a sum that will satisfy your Irish employers and free your

191

conscience. We have a thing of value that will please you. What would you say, Mr. Cavender, to the offer of a flawless blood ruby the size of a pullet's egg."

The Sikh formed the shape and size he had in mind with his thumb and middle finger. Cavender stared at the fingers.

The Sikh smiled faintly. "Do not answer until you see the stone. It is a bauble to us and we will part with it for the scrolls. It is here in Calcutta, and I am sure it will bring a vast sum on the market in Europe. And it will be much more negotiable than the scrolls. Could there be anything fairer than that?"

Cavender did not have to think long at all. "When can I see it?" he asked.

"Without the scrolls?" The Sikh looked doubtful.

"Without the scrolls," said Cavender. "I can't touch them without McLaughlin and he can't without me. We've both got to agree. If you show it to me right now, I can talk to him right now. But it's got to be rather appealing."

37

It was.

It was bigger than the oval formed by the Sikh's thumb and middle finger. It was deeper red than blood and to Cavender's naked eye it looked absolutely flawless.

The Sikh had taken him directly to a third-class native hotel on Mirzapur Street, a ramshackle, rundown building. Someone optimistically was attempting a repair job inside. The first three floors were empty. The hallways and stairs were covered with a mixed debris of old and new boards, half-empty paint cans, rusty tools, and a few broken ladders. The doors to all the rooms on the lower floors were open to empty dirty rooms. They had to climb with care.

On the fourth floor Cavender met another Sikh in a sparsely furnished room. He was the second man Cavender had seen in the attack on the Greek, the fourth Sikh in the affair, counting the one who had been killed and the one on the train.

The gem was produced almost immediately. They allowed Cavender to weigh it in his hand, to study it at a window. He dropped his hat onto a clean chair and rolled the stone between his thumb and forefinger. He warmed to its crimson flashes and thought about the old leather scrolls of Alexander. Those pieces of leather were worth plenty, certainly. But only to a small and select group of people. They were rare and they held scholarly importance. Their true value lay in the mind.

The ruby was different. It struck the eye and hand. It was solid, tangible, visible. It was cold and smooth and heavy. Its beauty lay as close as the nearest eye looking at it. An illiterate beggar who had never heard of Homer would marvel at it and a dowager princess would love to wear it. It looked as though it would ransom the king of a small country and it would make the beautiful more beautiful.

It was difficult not to be affected, even for Cavender who had seen gems like it around the neck of an Indian prince and had once himself carried a small satchel of more valuable diamonds around with him. The ruby brought an unaccustomed glow into his eyes.

He handed back the red stone, which had grown warm in his hand.

"It looks like it might be a fair price to pay for the scrolls," he said, "but then I'm no gem expert." He picked up his hat. "McLaughlin's got to see it, too. I think I can arrange that."

He went to the door. "I'll send someone around tonight to tell you the exact time I'll bring him over. It'll be tomorrow. Morning or afternoon I'm not sure."

The Sikh with the wound in his shoulder laid a hand on his sleeve.

"Mr. Cavender, can we have your word on this as an officer in the Punjab? We know that the *Prince Albert* is sailing tomorrow night. If we have to sail with her there will be blood on the ship. Your word that you will bring McLaughlin and the scrolls to us tomorrow—before noon."

"You have my word I'll bring McLaughlin," Cavender promised. "The scrolls are another matter. You see, Lieutenant Bentley—who tried to chase us in the other aeroplane—has got wind of this whole business and would like a bit of glory laying his hands on the manuscript. If he does, none of us will ever see it again, except maybe under glass in the British Museum."

"But you can promise that the scrolls will be in reach? Easy reach?" His dark face had begun to glower.

"Very easy reach."

"Good-bye, then," said the Sikh. "Until tomorrow morning."

Cavender adjusted his Panama hat. "I'm giving you my word that McLaughlin will come here. Do I have yours that he will be safe whether he brings the scrolls or not?"

"I am surprised, Mr. Cavender. If we had wanted to avenge Taxila, the major would have died at the gate of the prison."

"You didn't have the scrolls then and you had no idea where they were."

"You have my word, Mr. Cavender."

38

It was easier than he expected to persuade McLaughlin to take a look at the ruby before they sailed. It was not much more difficult to get him to bring the scrolls along as well. Rose had sent a wire to Dublin and had received a reply. She showed it to Cavender.

Do as you see fit, my child. Take Uncle C's advice but do what is best for you.

Mother

The message was on wireless-company paper, handwritten by the agent who took it, Rose said. She had not waited for him to typewrite it. Softened by the message, McLaughlin listened amenably to Cavender's description of the gem and his views of their situation. Cavender argued that the money was what mattered, that the stone was as valuable as the scrolls, that it could be more easily transported and converted into cash, that the wire from Dublin gave them leeway, that the Sikhs would be off their backs, and that the job, their job, would be done. Rose agreed.

McLaughlin stooped to rub the neck of Basil, who drowsed at his feet, bored with all the talk. He talked to the back of the dog's head. "All right, we'll do it—with the Sikhs. Not because it's your way, Alec, but because I think this time it's the right way."

"What about the Greek," asked Cavender. "How did you handle him?"

"He's coming back tonight thinking we'll have the scrolls here," said Rose. "He showed us a bundle of money. That's what I wired Dublin about. The money looked very good."

Cavender rubbed the back of his neck. He was beginning to feel the strain of the day. He had not stopped moving since leaving the train that morning, and the wild flight in the Morane had strained his nerves. The reaction was setting in. He squeezed the back of his neck and the muscles behind his shoulders.

"What time is he coming?"

"Ten," said McLaughlin. "Around ten." He did not seem concerned.

"All right," said Cavender. "Let him come. I'll take care of him myself."

McLaughlin said nothing. He had grown solemn again. He reached for a bottle of whisky. Cavender refused a drink. He headed for the door.

"The Sikhs have to be told we're coming. If they don't hear from me soon, they'll start on something else. I'll send someone from downstairs."

Rose asked, "Do I at least get to know where everything's happening?" There was no expectation in her voice that she was going to be answered.

Cavender did not answer. He said, "McLaughlin hasn't asked. The fewer in, the better. Trust. Trust." He grinned at her.

"Brendan gets to go along, I'll bet," she snapped back.

"You'll be going along when it's important, too," Cavender said, closing the door behind him.

Downstairs he paid one of the clerks to carry a note to the hotel on Mirzapur Street. Then he asked the desk man if there was a quiet telephone he could use.

"This way, please, sahib," said the desk man, lifting a small lid on the desk to let Cavender through. Cavender followed him into a tiny office where there were a chair and a low desk with a telephone on it. He left Cavender alone and closed the door.

Cavender asked the operator to connect him with Metropolitan Calcutta Police. When someone came on he gave his name and asked for Lieutenant Bentley. After a long wait Bentley came on.

"This is Alec Cavender, Lieutenant . . . I don't blame you. Sorry about the crash. I had no time to talk to you. . . . You're right. I did take a run down to Konarak. . . . That's right, it *is* quite an education. . . . Forget that. Just listen carefully. I'm going to give you something and I'm going to say it once. I'm in a hurry. . . . Never mind where I am. You know I don't care to see you. You're too ambitious. Just listen. If you want to put your hands onto someone who can tell you about the murder of the Sikh in the hotel off Upper Chitpur, pick up a fat Greek named Achilles Stathopolous. He probably hired someone to do it for him. And he's also connected with the attack on that other Sikh the same day. . . . I don't know. Maybe he doesn't like Sikhs. Ask him. You could probably squeeze it out of him if you squeezed hard enough. But be careful. The last time I saw him he had a pistol in his pocket. I took it away from him but he probably has more. . . . Hold on and listen. I'm not through. You might also want to talk with a Russian countess named Irene Borodin. But before you pick her up get in touch with a Captain Forsythe of British Advisory Police in Bhubaneswar . . . You have? That was fast. . . . Look harder. You might not find him but you could find her. You might even connect her to the Greek, if you're smart enough. They'll be feathers in your cap. . . . No, but it will be worth your trouble."

Cavender dropped the receiver into its cradle and broke the connection as Bentley's voice was beginning to rise into an angry shout. He smiled to himself and hoped that the lieutenant was disturbed enough to be so busy in the next twenty-four hours that he would forget McLaughlin and him for a while. And if Bentley *could* pick the Greek up he would save everybody considerable trouble. Stathopolous was too shrewd to say much. He would play dumb and try to ooze out of the whole affair.

To get Bentley to trust his tip on the Greek, Cavender had mentioned the Borodins and Forsythe, guessing that he already had that information. But he also hoped that Bentley would nab the countess.

Cavender had said nothing about her passage aboard the *Prince Albert*. He wanted Bentley out in the streets and hotels looking for her, not sitting on the gangplank tomorrow where he could pick them all up. With that thought bringing a grimace to his face, Cavender sent a message to the Sikhs that the arrangements were set, and went back upstairs to wait and see whether the Greek would make it to the hotel that night.

39

The Greek was wily enough to make it. Or lucky. Shortly after ten he knocked on the door of Cavender's room. Cavender let him in and pointed his Mauser pistol at him.

"What the devil is this, Mr. Cavender?" protested Stathopolous as Cavender went through his pockets and removed a pair of Dreyses. "These people have invited me here this evening. And now you're robbing me."

He looked in appeal to McLaughlin and Rose. The Irishman, surprised by Cavender's move, drew his own four-barreled pistol and pointed it at him. Rose averted his eyes and went to Cavender's side.

"What can I do?" she asked.

"Here," he said, and handed her the Mauser. He was about to tell her to shoot if he moved, but he remembered the bus driver in Puri and said, "If he moves shoot him in the leg. And believe me, Stathopolous, Rose does just as she's told when it comes to shooting someone. She'll probably shoot you in both legs."

Rose shot him a puzzled glance. The Greek fell silent. His lips quivered. An oily film appeared on his forehead. He followed Cavender's movements with beady, dull eyes as he deposited the two Dreyses in a drawer of a table.

When Cavender approached him with window-curtain cord he muttered, "A betrayal of trust, Mr. Cavender, the foulest of acts." He sought Rose with his eyes as though he expected her to help.

"Put your hands behind you," Cavender said unsmiling.

The Greek obeyed. Cavender tied his hands. Then he tied his ankles and strung a rope between the wrists and ankles. He placed a hand on Stathopolous's chest and with a heavy shove toppled him off his feet against the divan. He tightened the rope to bring his wrists and ankles as close together as possible. There was too much fat in between to make them touch.

Stathopolous blinked his eyes, almost losing them in the flesh of his face. "Do you expect to keep me like this for long, Mr. Cavender? It's not very comfortable."

Cavender stared at him stonily. He looked like a great stuffed trussed turkey. "You'll have to get used to it for a while. Just don't plan to go to the water closet for a while."

Something resembling a look of fear crept into the Greek's face. It was really hard to tell exactly what it was. His blue skin seemed darker, his thick lower lip quivered. The flesh on his neck pinkened. His eyes remained dark slits. He opened his mouth.

"This is wrong of you, Mr. Cavender. Untie me and take the money."

Cavender bent low and spoke bitterly into his face. He didn't like the business and didn't like the man forcing him to do it.

"Shut up, you. You were told to get out of this. Now I can't let you go running around here with guns in your pocket and what you know. Someone will find you here before you starve to death. Here, this will make you feel better. We don't want your money."

From his pants pocket he pulled a crumpled five-hundred-pound note, smoothed it on the floor, folded it, and tucked it into Stathopolous's shirt.

"That bought you just what I said it would, nothing more. And not much. But you're still in one piece. And that can't be said of everyone mixed up in this thing."

40

The next morning Cavender handed Rose one of the Greek's pistols.

"Stay away from him. If you have to use the gun, push down this lever, but for God's sake don't shoot him like the bus driver. You'll have the police all over you."

Cavender had slept well and was feeling good. The ache in his body was gone. His mind was clear and things looked good. The Greek was lying on the bed, tied to the metal headpost. He appeared to be sleeping.

Cavender dropped his voice. "Stay with him until two. Then meet us at the boat with our bags. You've got that. The *Prince Albert*. Pier 20."

Rose looked tense and paler than usual. There were lines in her face and shadows under her eyes. She had the expression of someone who had not been sleeping well or was having difficulty resolving a problem. Her hand holding the pistol shook a little too much. Cavender picked up all of the symptoms but said nothing. Rose had her uses right now. He would save his questions for later.

McLaughlin, too, was bothering him. Earlier in the morning he had seemed rested and relaxed but now, as they were about to leave, his behavior had shown an increased nervousness. He sat through breakfast hardly speaking. He smoked more frequently than he had. He kept bending to Basil, talking nonsense to the dog. He wanted Basil to come with them to the Sikhs. Cavender refused.

"There are no rats where we're going. He's better off here. Rose will take him to the boat."

Cavender finally slung his leather pouch with his special weapons in it over his shoulder and they left without good-byes. On the ride across the city, Cavender alternated between absorbing the last sensuous pressures the city made on his mind and body and reminding McLaughlin that they were making the right move. Again he sensed an increasing tension in the Irishman that might be coming from a change in mind. McLaughlin listened and agreed and stared moodily out of the window as if he, too, were saying a farewell to India.

They detoured across the Howrah Bridge to the train station and together presented the halves of the baggage ticket to the same hard-looking clerk. The man fit the halves together and disappeared into the dimness of the long room behind him. When he returned with the cheap suitcase at his side, McLaughlin brightened a little. Cavender let him carry it. McLaughlin acted calmer, holding the suitcase on his lap.

After some silent minutes recrossing the bridge Mc-Laughlin cleared his throat and said:

"You ought to know something, Alec, something I've been holding back a little. I'm letting these scrolls go for that ruby of theirs—I'm doing that when I see that stone, that is—because—well, ahhrr—you see, they've not really got anything at all to do with Alexander. That's just a pile of shit that sounded good. They're old, and they're worth something, but nothing to their worth if that writing in the sides was really Alexander's."

He held the suitcase between his legs and his big white-haired head dropped despondently like a little boy's who's been naughty. His large hand caressed the worn handle. Cavender watched the hand.

"You've known it all the time?" he asked.

"Since before I went in. When I was on the run I got to see a man at the university in Delhi. An authority he was of antiquity. I showed them to him. He said no. Just like that. No. When I got to Calcutta I heard he had died. I just kept the whole thing to myself, thinking it wouldn't hurt to have anyone interested in them going on believing they were Alexander's. Borodin wrote to me all about the

201

Alexander part. I just kept my mouth shut. If he believed it, others could, too."

Cavender controlled a frown. He said, "It won't matter to these Sikhs. They don't know what's on that leather themselves. We can keep a clear conscience when we pocket that ruby. They'll be happy about it, Alexander or no Alexander."

A while later, Cavender asked, "What was the name of the professor in Delhi?"

"I don't remember," said McLaughlin. He made a face trying to remember. "I was with him only a few hours. I think it had some O's in it. A bunch of O's is what comes through my mind."

Cavender looked up at him sharply. The dimple in his cheek was prominent. McLaughlin was back staring out of the window again. But he seemed relieved he had told it.

The hotel was deserted except for the Sikhs on the fourth floor. It was just before noon. There were clear signs of strain in their faces, in the hollows of their eyes, in the eyes themselves, and around the mouths, a strain that expressed the tension of their long wait.

Feelings in the room were heavy enough to weigh. There were no customary handshakes. Cavender kept his hands folded behind his back. McLaughlin held the suitcase across his chest in both of his. The Sikhs greeted them with arms folded across their chests, not far from the hilts of their swords but far enough not to be threatening.

"It is good that you have come, Major McLaughlin," said the Sikh who had first talked to him outside the prison. "Please remove the cloth from the plate there. We are all anxious to conclude this exchange."

On a small table near a window was a dark blue silk cloth spread out. A discernible lump rose from the middle of it. McLaughlin shifted the suitcase to one hand and lifted the blue cloth.

The ruby was as beautiful and dark and icy looking as Cavender had seen it before.

"In itself it is a treasure, McLaughlin," said the Sikh. "We offer it for the scrolls"—he paused—"along with your life."

202

"My life you are speaking of, is it?" growled McLaughlin, reddening.

Cavender could feel the muscles in his body tighten. His face remained calm and unexpressive.

The two Sikhs kept their arms folded. There was a dark grimness in their bearded faces. Their eyes were fastened on McLaughlin.

"It was promised to Cavender," said the Sikh.

The room was too small. It would not be easy to move out of the reach of their swords.

"Show them the scrolls, McLaughlin," Cavender said quietly, to head off the growing trouble. "That's what we came here for, remember?"

McLaughlin relaxed visibly. He laughed and placed the suitcase on the table near the ruby and unlatched it. He flipped the top up and stepped away.

The Sikh who had done the talking moved sideways behind the table, avoided passing between his comrade and Cavender. He leaned forward over the raised lid of the suitcase and lifted the copper box out. He produced a fine-pointed dagger and held it out to Cavender, handle forward.

"You were right, Mr. Cavender. We have never opened it, though we have found how it is done. Please."

Cavender worked the point into a seam, lifted gently, and folded the top up and back. The Sikh looked in, cautiously lowered his hand and touched the scrolls and counted them.

"They are here," he said to his comrade. He refitted the lid and replaced the box. He nodded to Cavender solemnly once.

Cavender reached for the ruby. The stone felt heavier, colder, smoother than before. His hand was moving to drop the stone into his jacket pocket.

His hand touched the flap. Suddenly there was a loud rending sound behind him. The door flew open, sending splinters of wood from the jamb onto the floor at his feet. Cavender dropped the ruby inside the flap just as Achilles Stathopolous's great form filled the room.

The two Dreyse pistols were in his hands. The door

bounced back from the wall and swung closed behind him. Without a word Stathopolous fired twice at the Sikh to Cavender's left whose sword was half out of its scabbard. The bullets puckered the man's shirt. The sword kept coming out even as the man staggered a step backward, clutching his chest. Stathopolous fired again from the same pistol in his left hand and then, extending his right arm, calmly shot the Sikh near the suitcase. The single bullet struck the Sikh somewhere in the body that made him fall back onto a chair. The first Sikh was sinking onto the floor, losing a struggle to stay on his feet. His sword had never made it completely out of its sheath.

Now both guns covered Cavender and McLaughlin. The pistol in the Greek's left hand was nearly touching Cavender's arm. The other was pointing at McLaughlin.

There was no choice for Cavender. He could smell it coming in the sweat streaming off the Greek's face. He was about to shoot both of them and was having only a slightly harder time of it than he had shooting two brown-skinned Indians. The muscles in Cavender's body tightened for the shock. He consciously fought against paralysis.

He threw his arm under the gun touching him and drove it upward, reaching for his own Mauser and charging forward against the Greek. Each movement was clear in his mind. He felt the heavy pouch slip from his shoulder to the floor. The Greek's pistol went off as the Greek danced nimbly away from Cavender. Chipped plaster from the ceiling floated down onto the three men left standing.

Out of the corner of his eye Cavender saw McLaughlin move to the side. Then the Greek, swinging his right arm in a swift tight arc, brought the other pistol across the side of Cavender's head. The barrel ripped down the side of his face as Stathopolous swung gracefully toward him. A jagged light streaked out across his brain. He grunted and staggered a step or two away from Stathopolous, but the blow was not solid and his brain remained clear. He had suspected the Greek could move like that.

McLaughlin had been unable to draw his big Lancaster from its holster before Stathopolous, whose maneuver had placed him between the two men, reached out to press a

pistol into the side of his head. It was a different Stathopolous from the man who had submitted almost timidly to
being tied up the night before.

And when he spoke his voice was several octaves higher
than his usual purr. "I will certainly put a bullet into the
major's brain, Mr. Cavender, if you do not at once produce
the ruby on the table and refrain from reaching for your
gun."

"Ruby?" asked Cavender.

"When I persuaded Rose to tell me where you went,
she told me about the ruby, too."

Cavender took out the stone.

"In the suitcase please," murmured Stathopolous in his
quieter voice. "Quickly, Mr. Cavender, quickly. You mis-
treated me badly last night and I have little patience." He
pressed the left-hand gun harder against McLaughlin's
head, forcing it to bend toward the shoulder. With the gun
in his right he flipped up the suitcase lid. He tapped the
copper box with the barrel. "I assume the scrolls are in
there. Now the stone please."

Cavender dug the stone from his pocket and carefully
tossed it a few feet into the air toward the suitcase as
though it were a bauble. The three men watched the red
twinkling arc of the gem. It was the moment for Cavender
to beat Stathopolous, but McLaughlin would take one in
the head. Cavender remembered when the situation was
reversed and McLaughlin had not moved. Cavender did
not move either.

The ruby landed on the copper box with a flat clank.

The sound signaled someone outside. There was a clatter
of footsteps in the hall rushing up toward the door. The
three men turned toward the sound in unison, Cavender,
McLaughlin, and Stathopolous between them, holding a
gun on each one.

The door, broken at its latch, swung in cautiously, and
standing there, small, stocky, wild-looking, and strangely
attractive, was Rose O'Connell, pointing a small pistol
into the room. Her eyes were wide and shifting, taking in
the scene and weighing it.

Stathopolous did not actually take a full step toward

her, but his great body seemed to move forward instinctively with a will of its own. Rose shifted slightly a few inches and fired. The first shot struck Stathopolous in the waist. Cavender could not tell exactly where. The Greek screamed words at her in Greek. He twisted sideways to bring his left hand around toward her. Cavender struck at his wrist just as Rose fired again, hitting the Greek up higher. Again came words in Greek followed by a few in English:

"You fucking bitch." The words were slow and poisonous.

Cavender shoved hard at the Greek's shoulder with his left shoulder. The Greek stumbled to his knees, losing both guns. He uttered some words including Cavender's name. Rose moved her outstretched arm and the small pistol swung toward Cavender. His eyes glared, his right arm shot out, clamped over her wrist, and forced the muzzle toward the floor. A few feet away McLaughlin was pointing his pistol at her.

"Oh, Alec," Rose burst out as Cavender took the gun away from her and put it away in his pocket, "it was awful. The bastard tricked me, almost killed me, said he had to piss or he'd go in his pants. I loosened his hands and he almost pressed me to death. It's God I'm thanking I got here in time to help. It was my fault."

Stathopolous had fallen to the floor on his left side. His right arm and leg hung awkwardly out from his great body, hardly touching the ground. He looked like a wounded clumsy animal. He was still breathing and the blood from his wounds was coming slowly. There was something unhuman about his size sprawled on the floor. He seemed unconscious.

"You're damn right it was your fault. You listen when you want to, and you didn't listen this time." He spoke angrily.

Rose saw the dead Sikh on the far side of the room. The other Sikh moved in the chair and struggled to his feet.

"Oh, my God!" Rose said. She brought the back of her hand to her mouth.

206

Cavender threw a dark, scowling look at her and went to the wounded Sikh behind the table. He motioned to McLaughlin.

"Check the hall," he ordered.

McLaughlin went into the hall and came back. He put an arm around Rose, who was beginning to tremble.

"There's no one out there, no one at all. We could have a bloody war up here and no one would bother us."

The wounded Sikh was staring morosely at his dead comrade and holding a folded cloth over a wound in his side. He waved Cavender back. Cavender checked the Greek. Stathopolous seemed to have stopped breathing. He couldn't really tell through all the flesh. Somewhere deep inside life could still be, as it had been in the elephant he had killed. The room was acrid with the smell of burnt gunpowder.

The Sikh broke the silence. "Take the ruby, Cavender, and your people, and go. Go before there is more death here. Nothing has changed."

"Yes, of course, you're right," said Cavender. "As you wish it."

He did not ask how the Sikh would manage. He did not say he was sorry because he did not feel sorry. Angry, yes, with himself, for having muffed it. Angry with Rose for—everything. And with the tiny pistol of hers in his pocket, troubled by questions he had no time to ask.

For a few seconds he stared down at the ruby lying on the copper box and then took it. He picked up his Panama hat, touched his head gingerly, and looked at his hand. There was no blood there but his head throbbed. He carefully put his Panama on and scooped up his leather pouch.

"Let's get out of here," he said flatly to McLaughlin.

The big Irishman had put away his big pistol. He stared across the room at the Sikh standing behind the table with one hand on the suitcase. He nodded at him. Before he turned away he glanced at Stathopolous's body. One of the German pistols was nearby. He stooped and pocketed it and looked for the second one. It was somewhere under the Greek. He moved the body a few inches with

207

difficulty, couldn't find it, and gave up. With his arm around Rose again, he went out.

Cavender followed without looking back. He drew the door after him gently so that it would stay closed.

41

"Basil," muttered McLaughlin suddenly as he realized the dog's absence. "Where's Basil?" he asked in a disturbed voice.

They were stalled in a taxi by heavy traffic two blocks from Mirzapur Street. A gaunt white bull was blocking their machine. Rose had been trying to explain what had happened. Her voice was mixed with bitterness and whining self-incrimination. She looked up disbelievingly at McLaughlin's interruption.

"What's the bother with a dog and things like this happening to us," she said crossly. "He's at the hotel. In the room. I left in such rush after the fat bastard broke loose, I forgot about him. Someone will find him and take him. I was just saying that he made me tell him where you were going and I had to get there to warn you."

"How did you know that?" asked Cavender.

Before she answered, McLaughlin leaned forward and struck the driver's shoulder.

"Don't be starting," he ordered the driver. "I'm leaving here. I'm going to the hotel to get him."

"Have you gone crazy?" Rose asked.

"I'm not leaving him for some Indian to spoil. He's served me—us well enough already, and I'll be thanking him for it."

Cavender had the ruby safely in his pocket. If McLaughlin wanted to risk getting picked up, it was all right with him.

"The ship sails at eight," he reminded him. He was checking his gold Dent. It's after one now."

When McLaughlin shut the door after him Cavender added, "We're sailing with or without you. Don't go getting yourself lifted by Bentley."

"Ahhrrr, Alec, my boy, you really do care about me. I'll be there all right." He charged into the crowds, avoided touching the big bull, and disappeared around a corner.

"Alec," said Rose, answering the question he had asked last, "I'm sorry about the whole thing. I went downstairs to get our bags taken to the ship and I found the man who took your message to the Sikhs. I paid him to tell me where he had gone." She touched his sleeve. "If I hadn't done that I couldn't have told Stathopolous anything and he would have bashed my head in. It was a lucky thing."

"Yeah," Cavender said sourly, "a few people killed. Bloody lucky. If Bentley gets a hold of this before we sail, your Irish Brotherhood could dissolve before we ever get to Dublin."

The sacred cow finally lumbered off into a path that opened magically through the throngs. The taxi lurched forward and moved slowly down the street.

"Alec," said Rose again. Her voice had a tremor in it he had never heard before. Again she laid a hand on his arm. "Will you see fit to do something for me now?"

"You saved me from getting shot," he said. "You got us into it, but you got us out."

"Then you owe me something. I want the scrolls back." She said that flatly as though she wanted a cigarette. "It'll be easy and we're needing them more than that Indian does."

He glared at her hard.

"We don't have to hurt him."

He continued to glare.

"If it's a conscience you're troubled by, give me my gun and take me back there. He's hurt. I'll get them myself."

"No," he said between his teeth.

"I want the scrolls," she insisted. "I'm going back there."

"Like hell you will."

She had leaned forward as though getting ready to jump from the machine. He gripped her arm and drew her back. She jerked away but couldn't break his grasp. She looked poisonously at him. He spoke angrily.

"You told me you had no gun when I asked you. What the bloody hell do you call what's in my pocket?"

"Will you listen to him who tells me everything," she flashed back.

The driver turned his head slightly.

Cavender dropped his voice. "I'd like to know what really happened down there to Farashah," he growled. "And I will find out."

Rose pushed back into the seat and stared out the window. "Just what I told you, that's what happened."

"Listen. We're going to the ship. McLaughlin told me the scrolls are fake. They were supposed to have belonged to someone important and their value depended on that. But that part of it seems to have been a lie. We're letting them go back to Taxila. That's it. The stone will have to be enough."

"I don't believe it," said Rose bitterly.

"Believe it or not, nothing is going to change."

Rose became sullen and fell silent.

When the taxicab reached the Strand Road along the river, Cavender, on impulse, told the driver to turn left in the dirction going away from the docks.

Rose looked bewildered but asked nothing.

Later when he led her into the great National Library on Alipore Road she said, "Is it an education we're going to get instead of the scrolls?" He held her by the arm on the way in.

In a few minutes he was looking at the same old newspapers he had seen before. Something then had caught his eye as he had read about McLaughlin's trial. It didn't take him long to find it again. There it was—a short article below a photograph on the same page as a story about McLaughlin. A distinguished Indian professor of Greek antiquities and history had been found dead in his university office in Delhi. Someone had broken his neck. His name was O. O. Okranah.

Cavender winced.

Saying nothing to Rose about his thoughts, he took her to the docks off North Strand Road and saw her aboard the *Prince Albert*. McLaughlin was not aboard. Cavender dropped his shoulder pouch in his cabin and searched around until he found an idle mate who accepted a fiver to see that the lady in 502 got whatever she wanted but did not leave her cabin for at least two hours or until he returned. Then he left the ship.

He headed toward the hotel on Mirzapur Street. He changed rickshaw runners twice to make good time. In half an hour he was on the street he had left a few hours ago. The street crowds this time were milling around and not flowing. There was something exciting a little way down the street that was drawing them. Cavender did not have to go far to find the cause.

He had seen the smoke from three blocks away. Flames were shooting high into the air from the roof of the Sikh's dilapidated hotel. Fire patrols were already hard at work pumping heavy streams of water into the blazing building. But nothing would be saved. The building was going to the ground. As Cavender watched thoughtfully for a while, the fire patrols changed their efforts to saving the buildings nearby.

42

On the way back to the ship Cavender stopped at the hotel they had used. No one knew whether McLaughlin had been there. Basil was not up in their room and no one had seen him either.

Cavender found them both in the ship's bar. McLaughlin was sitting high-spirited and slightly drunk at a small table with Basil at his feet. A bottle of whisky stood half empty at his elbow. He waved a glass at Cavender as he came in.

"Sure you've been saying good-bye to the city. So have I."

Cavender sat down. "Some of it's burning down right now," he said, reaching under the table to stroke Basil's head.

"What do you mean?" asked McLaughlin with a puzzled look on his face.

"Someone burned down the hotel we just left," said Cavender.

"The Sikh, do you think, getting rid of the bodies?" asked McLaughlin.

"Is that what you think?" replied Cavender.

"That's the only blessed thing to think, because it's true," said McLaughlin straightforwardly.

"If that's what you say, McLaughlin, then that's what it was," Cavender said, finishing the subject. He hoped it was that because he had liked McLaughlin from the beginning, and the idea of not liking him soured his mind. He thought about the death of the Indian professor sixteen years ago in Delhi and considered asking McLaughlin about it. But McLaughlin pushed a glass of whisky across to him and raised his own.

"Hello to Dublin," he said.

Cavender decided it would not help much knowing more right now. Rose was more of a bother to him and he was not going to probe into her on the trip back. The job came first—delivering the ruby and McLaughlin to the IRB. After that, some of the questions could be raised again.

He lifted his glass to McLaughlin's.

With the back of his hand McLaughlin wiped his lips. "She's madder than a harpy down in her cabin. The mate's given her a hard time. Locked her cabin and said he can't

212

find the key to open her door. We ought to have her up here before she raises a real storm onto somebody."

"You get her up, will you," said Cavender. He was out of his chair after a steward he saw walking by in the outside passageway. He caught him just about to descend to a lower deck.

"Has the Countess Borodin come aboard yet?"

"No, not yet, sir." As Cavender started to leave he said, "Your name, sir?"

Cavender told him.

"I have a message for you. It was just brought aboard." He gave Cavender a slip of paper.

The paper said: "It is vital for me to see you. In the Chinese tea shop at the end of the dock. I'll wait until six."

It was unsigned and the handwriting meant nothing to him. Cavender took a guess and was right.

It was the Countess Borodin.

She was standing next to a tiny booth. She held out her hand to him. It was warm, moist, and firm. They sat down. A small Chinese appeared. The countess ordered for them, and then as she took out a cigarette said,

"Ve vill have to be frank, Mr. Cavender. There is not time for equivocation. My husband is on his way to Ireland right now. He could not buy the manuscript from McLaughlin, but he will buy it from the people in Dublin. He is in Bombay by now, I am sure."

"What are you doing here, then?" Cavender asked, lighting her cigarette in its long ivory holder. He smoked a Suerdieck.

"Ve couldn't fly together. And he had to fly. It was the quickest vay and there vas too much extra fuel to carry. I am following aboard the same ship you are on. I vant to clarify our positions."

She was wearing an unadorned white dress. Her neck was long and graceful. Cavender could see the fine faint hair on its nape whenever she turned. A pleasant, definite perfume surrounded her.

"First, there is this question of the girl, Major Mc-Laughlin's daughter. Ve have heard that she is dead and ve are suspected. The suspicion is false, Mr. Cavender. Ve had nothing to do with her kidnapping and nothing to do with this. She vas alive when ve left." She talked in deep throaty tones and she pronounced his name as he had never heard it spoken before.

"That remains to be proved," he said. "And it can be proved. There was a bright, experienced British officer there and he'll find something to say about it one way or another."

"My husband and I look forvard to his findings."

The way she used the word "husband" gave Cavender second thoughts about the throaty way she said his own name. He concentrated on what she was saying and tried without success to ignore the beauty of her face.

"The scrolls, Mr. Cavender, are aboard the *Prince Albert?*" she asked.

"I've got some disappointing news for you, Countess. The scrolls are fake. At least what's supposed to be Alexander's part in their history is fake."

She blinked her almond-shaped eyes scornfully.

"Come, Mr. Cavender," she said, annoyed.

"McLaughlin admitted it to me today. He's known they were fake from the beginning. He had an authority on that kind of thing examine them."

"I don't believe it," said the countess hotly. "You are lying." Her eyes blazed darkly and her lips pressed together.

"That's what someone else just said. But you believe what you want. The scrolls are back with the Sikhs where they belong. They're probably on their way to Taxila right now. You still want them, trot up there and deal with the real owners. But I don't think you had better go on board. You may be telling the truth about McLaughlin's daughter and maybe you're not. I'm not sure. But I don't count. McLaughlin does. And he's going to stretch that beautiful white neck of yours if he finds you. So I'd clear out of it if I were you."

The countess paled. She laid a hand on Cavender's arm the way Rose liked to and looked at him with glistening black eyes touched strangely by a plea.

"I have told you the truth, Mr. Cavender. Vhy vould ve have killed his daughter?" The misplaced v's were disarming.

"I don't know. Probably you wanted to take her out of there with you—to force McLaughlin to give up the scrolls. You never proved that you hadn't tried that before. Maybe your husband was losing his control. He pulled a pistol on us at Konarak. Anything could have happened afterward."

"Ve could not have taken the girl even if ve had wanted to. The Blériot could carry the two of us. There vas not a place for a third."

Damn it, thought Cavender. He recalled the mechanic's figures about the carrying capacity of the aeroplane. New doubts upon old doubts were tumbling through his mind. Everything was pointing in the worst directions. Again he reminded himself that it was the job that counted. Turning over the murderer of a young girl would be nice but not if it meant mucking up his job. He said:

"It doesn't matter anymore. The scrolls are gone, out of your reach. At least for now. Go home and wait for your husband."

She flushed angrily.

He could almost feel her hot black eyes on his back as he walked away from her. He had nothing more to say of any use to either of them. He was angry himself because she attracted him and he could do nothing.

The ship was crowded with passengers and people seeing them off when he returned. He found Rose and McLaughlin seated several chairs apart in a dining room as dinner was being served before sailing. They ate pretending they did not know each other.

A steward approached and whispered something to Rose that put a puzzled look on her face. She followed him to a doorway. Cavender watched them. The steward handed Rose a message. She read it. She shook her head hard. Cavender could see her hair swing. She glanced across at him and said something to the steward. Then she returned to the table.

She looked at Cavender and shrugged and sat down.

Cavender repressed a snort and began to eat. The meal was solid English fare and life on the Continent had spoiled Cavender for it.

Before they finished eating, Rose excused herself to the people she had been talking to, left the table, and headed toward an area marked w.c. She went through a doorway and around a corner.

"Rather busy, isn't she?" said Cavender, looking across at McLaughlin and getting up.

"Don't be making her too unhappy, lad," said McLaughlin. He leaned over closer and spoke through a full mouth. "This is going to be a long voyage and whatever else she's up to, we've both broken her in."

Outside the dining room Cavender caught sight of her at the end of a passageway talking to the same steward. The steward handed her another piece of paper. She unfolded it, read it quickly, refolded it, and slipped it into her dress.

Cavender wondered whether the countess was trying to enlist Rose on her side. Who else did Rose know in Calcutta who could be sending her messages urgent enough to upset her?

When the steward left, Rose made her way to the open deck overlooking the dock. Cavender waited until she reached the rail and was busy searching for someone among the crowds below. The gangplank a few yards away sagged under the weight of visitors leaving. The crowds on the dock thickened.

He eased through the people along the rail until he was standing next to Rose. He circled her waist with his arm and felt her flinch. Her hand instinctively went to her bosom and stopped.

"You startled me, Alec. I thought someone was being funny."

"Can we be friends again?" he asked her, spreading his face into a smile. "It's almost all over."

"And why not," she said agreeably. "Will you look at the sight of India, will you! I'll not be seeing it again in my life."

The sun was setting over the city. The web of steel

girders in the Howrah Bridge rising high above the river glinted silver in the light. The buildings across the city were golden. The unceasing din of the million people in the streets gave the city a voice of its own. For a brief moment Cavender felt drawn to the city and the people and the romance of India herself, where so much of his own life had been drawn tight and hammered and shaped by the experience and thought in the land.

The mood was brief and almost at once he was doing his own searching among the people on the dock for that one familiar face that might answer a question rankling him about Rose. But he saw no one and he was certain she had seen no one. Together they watched the gangplank swing away from the ship and drop slowly to the dock.

The ship's great steam horns began to blow their warning and the heavy hawsers keeping her close to the dock were uncoupled from their moorings and wound onto the deck. The small tug dragging her out to a deep channel kept a steady high whistle going. Soon her own engines rumbled into life deep beneath the water line and the *Prince Albert* moved down the river toward the Indian Ocean.

43

Seven days out, the Indian Ocean behind them, the Red Sea a hundred miles ahead, Cavender asked Rose to stop by his cabin during the afternoon.

He had been having painful, yet beautiful memories of another trip he had taken aboard a sloop named *Viktor* three years ago in these same waters. There was a girl aboard then, too, and another he was searching for. The trip had been sweet. The conclusion had been tragic. He wanted the memories and he didn't want them. He thought that a woman would help him now.

He had faintly hoped to ask the Countess Borodin if she ignored his warning. But the countess had not boarded. Her luggage had been removed soon after Cavender had seen her. He asked Rose down to his cabin instead. She said no.

He had not touched her since that night in Puri she had shared herself with both men. He was not sure how she was handling McLaughlin but he gradually understood she was handling him all right.

At McLaughlin's suggestion and Rose's agreement they had decided to appear to be traveling separately. The reasons were clumsy—it was safer, they were edgy with each other—but Cavender went along and they pretended they had only met on board. The only time they deliberately spent together was with seven other passengers at the dining room table.

The talk was small but it was there that Cavender sensed the increasing closeness developing between the Irish pair. Their brogues melded across the table as her responses flowed into his talk. She laughed quickly at his stories and listened intently to his talk of himself and of India. Cavender suspected they were spending time together in her cabin but they seemed to have the freedom to meet other people as they pleased.

Before long Rose had become friendly with the ship's second officer. McLaughlin had gotten in with a group of English sportsmen and their wives. And Cavender was spending some time parrying the aimless flirtations of a mother and daughter who had discovered him. Their name was Parkington. The daughter was fine, but the arrangements that gradually emerged made the mother a prerequisite for the daughter. The combination did not appeal to him. With a charm and polish that seemed unusual for a man with his battered face and wrestler's build, he kept the ladies curious and interested, but kept them at a distance.

McLaughlin grew easy and relaxed as the days passed into each other. Cavender attributed the change partly to

Rose—lovemaking like hers, as a steady diet, could loosen a man considerably, soften him, give him a euphoric sensation. But there was something else beneath McLaughlin's quiet cheerfulness. There had to be. It was not Rose alone.

And as McLaughlin's spirits rose, Cavender's disposition fell. He felt drawn and tired inside. His sleep was not its usual refreshment. He woke restless. He spent time on the clay-pigeon deck shooting the ship's shotguns, fighting the suspicions or justifying them that he was being played for a fool. But he was a professional, thorough, self-controlled, and patient. He knew the right questions to be asked, but they would have to wait for Dublin. Now he kept quiet and watched and waited. And the more he watched them, the stronger his doubts grew.

When the three of them did meet once on the shooting deck one cool sunny morning, there was little talk about the IRB, India, or anything important. Basil was with McLaughlin. Much of the talk was about him. Then suddenly McLaughlin asked Cavender to bring out the ruby.

"For Rose here," he explained. "The lass has never had a good look at it."

They had to go to Cavender's cabin for that, although Cavender kept the stone in his pocket. Rose grew excited handling the gem. Her cheeks flushd, her eyes shone, her hand trembled. But as she passed it back uncomplainingly as Cavender held his hand out, she said it was not the same as the scrolls. They should never have been given back. The whole affair was a failure without them. McLaughlin offered some comforting words and a laughing embrace. Cavender did not answer her. She knew what his answer would have been.

It was on that day, showing the ruby to the girl in his cabin, that Cavender asked her to drop back later after middle tea was served. McLaughlin was on his way to the bar. Rose stared flatly at Cavender when he asked her.

"To get to bed with, is that it?" she said.

He made a face to say the thought had occurred to him. He would not put the question into words.

"Hard up, is it?" she mocked. "No, thank you." Her

219

voice had a hard edge to it. "That's over with us. When the scrolls were in the picture, it was different. You said we'd get them. And fake or not . . ." Then a thought changed her expression, softened her features, made her talk like a child asking for a toy. "Give me the ruby, then, to hold. Trust me that way."

"The ruby stays where it is, Rose. Unless—" He paused and stared into her face. "—you show me what you got the night we sailed. You were handed a note from someone on shore. I got a note, probably from the same person. If we compared those notes we might know something about this whole business we should know."

"Go to bloody hell, Alec."

She left him. He did not go to hell. Instead, he accepted the kinder invitations that were being subtly dropped his way by the dowager Mrs. Parkington and her Pamela, who turned out not to be her daughter at all but her traveling companion. The mother-daughter pretense was something Mrs. Parkington thought would be an added enticement to some men who liked that sort of thing. At first he spent some time alone with Mrs. Parkington, and when he found that the younger woman was not the daughter, he spent a few hours with her. Once he spent some time with them together. Neither was very pretty, but both were unorthodox and appreciative and they found him indulgent and kind. In the end it was not bad at all. They were quite good for each other, and as Rose made the journey sweet for McLaughlin, the ladies with the name of Parkington did the same for Cavender.

44

The voyage drifted into a routine. Rose spoke less and less to Cavender and more and more to McLaughlin. Her friendship with the second mate warmed discreetly. Cavender got himself up early one morning to discover the officer leaving her cabin. That added to his doubts. She was no lover of men. He was certain of that. Her body was her tool. He spent more time than he liked thinking about her.

The next fourteen days flowed into one another with a monotonous sameness that made life dull for Cavender, in spite of the Parkingtons. But dullness was restful. The quiet, almost undisturbed rhythm of sea time soothed him. And although he had no delusions that the Calcutta affair was over, he savored the lazy interlude while he could.

The complications appeared exactly as the *Prince Albert* was being maneuvered into her berth in Southampton at dusk. Cavender was strolling on the lower deck amidships watching the city come up close. He was wearing a heavy raincoat and a dark soft hat turned down around the brim. It was cold and raw and windy and people kept their hands in their pockets.

On board, people getting ready to disembark rushed around with bags and stewards. A few who were staying with the ship to Dublin lounged on deck like Cavender and stared at the great port. Suddenly Cavender heard a woman shouting angrily on a lower deck. Her voice rose above a man's voice that was trying to calm her.

He recognized Rose's Irish lilt even at the distance, and he jogged along the deck to a set of stairs down to the next deck, where Rose was stamping her feet and flailing her arms at the second mate who had become her friend. Her hair was mussed and her clothing seemed askew. A small group of people looked on, obviously embarrassed.

A string of crude oaths broke from Rose's lips that Cavender had not in a long while heard so easily used. She spared no part of the second mate's body, his family, his habits.

The mate finally seized her arms and held them stiffly at her sides to prevent her from striking him. But that did not stop her mouth.

"You filthy drop of pigshit. Your rotten mother—"

"Shut your mouth," ordered the mate, glancing around

at the growing crowd of spectators and trying to control his anger.

Cavender stepped up.

"What's happened?" he asked, speaking to the man.

"This bloody bastard tried to force me in there," screamed Rose, gesturing toward an open door. She yanked her hand away and struck the mate across the face. "He thought he should have me, seeing I was friendly to him on the trip."

"She's lying," shouted the mate. He spoke to Cavender as though he owed him the explanation. "I found her trying to get in there with that."

There was a fire ax on the floor and a broken padlock hanging on the door.

"Liar." Rose spat and seemed about to strike him again. "Fucking liar." She became aware of Cavender. "Alec, I went for that ax to fight him off. Give a man a little friendship and he thinks you're dropping to the floor when he unbuttons. You're pigs, all of you." That was intended to include Cavender.

"Here now," said the second mate, making a desperate effort to control his own temper as well as hers. "Let's calm this down. The row's not good for the ship. Let's come along to the captain's quarters and talk it over there."

Cavender thought the mate was bluffing. He wouldn't risk the accusation that he was sleeping with one of the passengers.

But Rose did not call the bluff. She said sharply, "What's there to talk about? I'll see the captain later and fill his ear. That'll cook your English goose. I'll be going to my cabin now."

She flung herself away from the mate, crashed into Cavender, and dashed for the gangway. Her heavy hips swayed vigorously as she mounted the steps, followed by the eyes of the men present.

Cavender sidled over to the mate, who was working at the padlock on the door.

"What *was* she doing?" he asked as though out of idle curiosity.

"That'll be for the captain to say, sir. Sorry."

"What's in that room anyway?" Cavender asked.

The mate kept working at the lock. It finally clicked shut.

"Storage room. Luggage not wanted on the voyage. All kinds of things people bring back home. Mailed goods, too. Christ, she had me fooled. I thought she was a lady."

45

Rose did not appear in the dining room for lunch. At their table, besides Cavender and McLaughlin only one other passenger remained, an elderly half-deaf Anglo-Irishwoman named Lady Tone, who sat next to McLaughlin. She listened but never said anything to him or anyone else, except a few necessary civilities.

Halfway through the meal Cavender said, "We can make better time to Dublin by training to Holyhead and ferrying across." The old woman leaned across the table and tapped Cavender's glass with her spoon. "No you can't, my boys. The *Prince* will get you there just as speedily and in far better comfort. I've done this before more than once, both ways. Always stick with the ship, my boys."

McLaughlin looked at her sideways in surprise and scratched his head in thought for a moment. "Thank you, mum," he said. "I agree. The time don't matter, Alec. Besides, I'm enjoying the comfort aboard, as Lady Tone says. And Basil is into a fine routine. Anyway, they'll be someone expecting us at the dock, if they got my wire from Calcutta."

Cavender did not argue.

When they finished eating he went down to Rose's cabin

and knocked. She did not answer. He tried the door and went in when it opened. He half expected what he found. The cabin was empty. The baggage was gone. Rose had flown, taking all her things. He almost felt relieved. There were too many questions he would ask her in Dublin, too many answers he was reluctant to get. Rose was up to something that smelled rotten, and he hoped he would not see her again to ask the questions. The ruby was safe in his pocket and McLaughlin was aboard. The job he had been hired to do was nearly done.

On his way up to the deck he met McLaughlin coming down.

"She's gone," he said.

"Gone?" repeated McLaughlin uncomprehendingly. "Do you mean gone—left? Oh, you do. But you've got the ruby, haven't you?"

"In my pocket," said Cavender, tapping the side of his coat.

"Then the devil with her," said McLaughlin, echoing Cavender's thoughts.

The two men walked out onto the deck despite the cold and leaned on the rail. There were a few people still scattered along the dock. One of them caught Cavender's attention immediately. It was the familiar short chunky figure of Rose heading toward the gate at the entrance.

"There she goes, Black Dog. Up there at the end of the dock." He watched her go. Her legs were pumping hard under a long coat, her hips rotating, her head held straight. The coat, fitted tight at the waist, accentuated her hips. She carried her bag in one hand.

At the end of the dock she stopped and twisted the upper half of her body round and gazed up at the ship. Cavender lifted a hand to her. She started to raise hers, changed her mind, dropped it, and disappeared around the corner. Cavender's face was deeply frowned.

"Don't despair, Alec lad," said McLaughlin, misunderstanding what was troubling him. "We haven't seen the last of that girl, I'm thinking. We'll look for her to turn up in Dublin."

"I'm not counting on it," replied Cavender, making his

response light. He was thinking of Konarak, of Mirzapur Street, of the second mate.

As they watched the dock grow deserted, a tug bull-nosed the ship out into the harbor. McLaughlin threw his arm in disgust toward the dock, repudiating Rose and all England together.

Standing a few minutes later at the ship's bar, Cavender said:

"She doesn't really work for the IRB, does she? Nothing to do with them. Right?"

McLaughlin did nothing more than raise his eyebrows and his glass. Cavender's face was serious and dark. He sipped at his drink.

"How do you come to that?" McLaughlin asked. Then, looking at Cavender, he broke into a smile and said, "You're right, Alec. I don't know how you know it, but I never believed she was them. You know the Irish, lad. If you did, you'd know they'd never send a woman like her on a job like this. Not a loose woman in Ireland's cause."

"She had me fooled a while," Cavender admitted. "I thought times could be changing. Maybe they would use a woman. She had the body for it."

"I never trusted her from the start," said McLaughlin, brushing Cavender's remark away with his hand. "Everything she did smelled bad in my nostrils. Except in bed. I was really running from her, Alec, not you, when I gave you the slip."

McLaughlin looked as though he was thinking about something for the first time. He laid a hand on Cavender's arm and tightened the grip. The thought twisted his mouth. He pushed the thought away with a visible effort. But it returned.

"Do you suppose she had something to do with Farashah?" he blurted out. "At Konarak, Alec?"

Cavender's pulse throbbed. He was hoping that wouldn't come up. And yet it could lead to a different view of everything, a view that would make him feel better about himself. But he was unsure, and so he said, "I don't know, McLaughlin. I've thought about it. We'll find out before this is over."

225

McLaughlin's face went back to normal. His grip on Cavender's arm relaxed. He emptied his glass and the bitter thought seemed to fade.

"Well, it's not the scroll we've got for them, Alec. But that ruby'll buy them a case or two of Mausers, do you think."

It was a much better subject to talk about then, for the last leg of their journey to Dublin.

46

Three IRB men were waiting for them in an old medium Standard motorcar converted from a taxi back into a private tourer. They were parked opposite Liberty Hall on the river side. Cavender saw it as he walked along the North Wall Quay, and the men sitting in it. There were few other machines on the road.

He stepped into a doorway out of a steady cold downpour that was about to turn into sleet. McLaughlin had been held up a few minutes getting Basil off the ship and by the customs people. He waited for the old Irishman, who had waited for years to meet the IRB. When he joined Cavender they hurried across the street toward the old Standard. The streets were shiny and wet.

A man climbed out of the rear of the Standard and stood poised to greet them at the door. He wore a long gray greatcoat and tweed hat. Something seemed wrong with one of his legs. He smiled handsomely and held the door for them. The two other men sat in front, one with his hands on the wheel, the other with his hands stuffed into his greatcoat pockets. They both wore soft caps.

"B. D. McLaughlin?" asked the handsome man, subtly blocking the door with part of his body.

McLaughlin nodded and growled a "Yes" nervously in his throat.

"Get in, please," said the young Irishman amicably.

They climbed in, the handsome man climbing awkwardly after them, crowding against Cavender, who sat in the middle. Basil, dripping as he was, sat on McLaughlin's lap.

As soon as the handsome man closed the door the machine sped off. The man with his hands in his greatcoat pockets twisted his body around, took one hand out and pointed a short-barreled, big-bored revolver over the seat at Cavender.

"Sure it's a bit cautious we are, you see," said the man sitting next to him. His voice had charm and warmth that hardly suited the meaning of his words. "We have to be. Until we're sure you're who you say you are. The damned RIC are becoming a pain in the arse to us. Following us around, rousting us when they feel like it. You two are dead men if you can't prove who you're supposed to be."

They drove for a block. Then he said, "Sean's my name." He nudged Cavender's arm. "You're Cavender, is that it?"

"If I can get my wallet out without your friend there shooting my hand off, I'll show you some proof."

"Go ahead," said Sean. "Be slow."

Cavender showed him a Belgian passport and his separation papers from the Punjabi regiment. Sean looked at them under the light of a small torch and handed them back.

"Not good enough," he said. "Tell me about Tommy. What does he look like? Where is he?"

"Ahhrrr, shit, lad," growled McLaughlin. "We've come to you with something rare and valuable that you need and you pointing guns at us."

"Tell me about Tommy," Sean repeated, ignoring McLaughlin. His voice had gotten chillier. "You, Cavender. You would know something."

"Tommy who?" asked Cavender, beginning to feel worried for the first time.

It was the wrong reply that pleased no one. The man in the front seat cocked his revolver slowly. Cavender watched the cylinder rotate and heard the slight, then the louder click of the mechanism, sharp and cold. In the glare of Sean's pocket torch pointing at his chest, the dimple in Cavender's cheek looked almost cavernous.

"Easy," warned Sean softly. "Give 'em the chance. Tommy Coughlin, that's who. The fellow we sent to you in Brussels. Well."

"It was no Tommy Coughlin who ever spoke to me unless he walked around in a nice dress and called himself Rose O'Connell sometimes, because a rather heavily built woman who called herself that came round to my office two months ago and hired me to go to India. She said she was McLaughlin's daughter, and when we got out there, she said she was from you. She had a letter to prove it and seemed to know whatever it was McLaughlin had written you. Even about Basil here."

Sean's handsome face expressed little belief. "We don't have a Rose O'Connell with us, now or then," he said. The warmth had slipped away from his voice. "It is strange you've got the terrier. Unless you lifted Tommy and got this all from him."

"Hey," interrupted the man driving. "Come here." Sean leaned forward. The driver tried to whisper over his shoulder but his words came into the back seat soft and clear.

"Tommy was running with a girl named Rose before he dropped out of sight. Never gave us her last name. A Dublin whore, she was, but classy, Tommy said."

Sean sat back thoughtfully.

Cavender reached for the advantage. "If you reach into my pocket, Sean," he said, beginning to feel better, "you'll find what we brought you."

Sean fished the ruby out of Cavender's side pocket wrapped in a white handkerchief. He flashed his torch on it and whistled.

Cavender put confidence into his voice. "I'm not hand-

228

ing it over to you now, you understand. It's going to your Council and only to them." He wondered how foolish that sounded with a .455 Webley pointed at his chest. He went on anyway. "McLaughlin here intends to deliver it, you see. It's cost him sixteen years to get it for you."

Just then the driver slowed almost to a stop at a busy intersection on a main street lined with shops and small hotels. Cavender sat forward and pointed toward the side window.

"Look there, see that woman getting out of the taxi. Over there. Name's Tone. Lady Tone. Who knows, maybe she's related to Wolfe Tone. She was on the boat with us all the way from Calcutta. Ask her if McLaughlin is Irish clean through and if we had a Rose at our table. Go ahead."

"Do it," ordered Sean. "I know her."

The machine slid over to the curbing and the driver jumped out into the cold rain, spoke to the old lady, who was walking under her umbrella toward a hotel. As she listened she stepped closer to him to keep the umbrella over them both. She followed him over to the Standard and peered into the back seat.

"Sure now, I told you sticking with the ship would lose you no time, Mr. Cavender. Good evening to ye, Mr. McLaughlin." She looked boldly into the faces of the two men in the front seat. "You've got some fine politic friends in the machine with you, Mr. McLaughlin. Hello, Sean McNamara. Take care of yourselves, boys."

As she started to leave Sean called out, smiling pleasantly, "Was there a Rose at your table aboard the *Prince Albert,* mum?"

"There was a Rose O'Connell. She left the ship in Southampton rather strangely, I'm afraid, in the dickens of a row."

The old woman was about to continue as though Ireland had loosened her tongue. Sean broke in so gently the old lady hardly was aware she was being interrupted. "Thanks for talkin' to us, mum. Good even to ye." The driver shot away before Lady Tone could reply and the machine turned into a busy square.

229

"Christ's glory!" said McLaughlin. "Parnell Square. It's home at last, Alec. The place's been in my mind for years and now it's in my eye." He brushed something away from his eye that Parnell Square had brought to it. That seemed to remind him of something and when he spoke he spoke harshly. "Now you can hand that ruby back to us, you Sean, you, and tell your man to put his revolver away. It's making me nervous."

Sean motioned to the man with the gun. The gunman turned back to face forward, lowered the hammer carefully, and stuffed the gun back into his pocket.

"At the next corner, drop me," said the gunman.

The driver pulled over and stopped. The gunman got out.

"Good evening, Sean."

"Good night and thanks. Beat it home and drop that thing off."

The gunman tipped his fingers to his cap and walked away rapidly.

"You find floating armaments like that safe," observed Cavender.

"Safer, at least, than having all our boys carrying guns," said Sean. "The RIC pat down anybody they suspect and them they don't suspect. Find a gun on you and it's into the slammer for a year or more—and anyone with you goes along."

Cavender was gazing out of the window.

"We've been riding around in circles now," he said, "since we left the docks. We've passed that corner over there twice before. Do you think we can get to the rest of your people to settle."

"All right, Eddie," said Sean. "Let's go to Dorset. They're the ones, I guess."

Eddie said, "Someone's following us, Sean. Picked us up on Copel Street. I made a double cut-over and they've stuck. What do you think?"

"How many?"

"I can't tell. Two in front, one or two in back. Unmarked motorcar—looks like a new Rover. Faster than us."

"Lose them, Eddie," ordered Sean. To Cavender he said, "You've got that valuable with you. If they stop us they'll lift it."

"That's not all they'll lift," said Cavender. "We're carrying guns."

Sean said: "Lose them good, Eddie. We're in for a bit of trouble. We'll have to drop them and lead that bunch away."

He looked at his wristwatch under his torch.

"It's seven. By nine get yourselves to fourteen Dorset."

Eddie took the motorcar three quarters of the way through the next major intersection and suddenly slammed the accelerator and twisted the wheel violently. The tires spun on the wet asphalt, gripped, and then whipped to the left, leaning the motorcar dangerously over onto its right wheels and spinning it into a circle. Eddie held the wheel tight until the Standard had gone through the short circle and came in behind the machine following them. Another hard twist of the wheel brought the Standard into a right turn, and then they were racing down O'Connell Street to their right, leaving the RIC's halfway through the intersection facing east.

Eddie made another right turn onto a long road, accelerated to the machine's top speed, used the brakes expertly to swing into another right, and entered a stream of traffic heading north. He stayed with it.

"Holy Mother of God!" Eddie shouted. "The sons of bitches, have they got some driver with them. The bloody bastard is still on my tail four or five machines back. It's ungodly, it is. It ain't likely I'm going to shake him this way, Sean."

"Get over to Parnell and up to Summerhill and pull down a street before they reach it. Block the road and they'll get out and we'll hold them up the road ourselves. Can you do it?"

"We'll stop the bastards," gloated Eddie. He made a sharp turn onto a side street and again began his flight across the city. The Standard was fast and Eddie was skilled, but they could not lose the RIC motorcar.

"Give us your guns," said Sean.

McLaughlin hesitated, glanced at Cavender, who gave him no signal, and then handed over his Lancaster.

"A cannon, a goddam cannon, McLaughlin," said Sean. "They'll think we've got a cannon." He held out his hand to Cavender. "Yours."

"The ruby and what you buy with it is one thing," said Cavender, shaking his head. "I can't give you my gun like this to shoot a British policeman with. That doesn't suit me."

"Have your way," muttered Sean. He bent to roll back the floor rug at his feet and removed a small metal plate under it. He probed under the floorboards with his hand and produced a small bundle wrapped in oilcloth. Inside were two break-top Webley revolvers. He handed one to Eddie over his shoulder and dropped the other one into his pocket.

"When I say go, get out the side away from the constabs and get yourself safe somewhere. Find a pub and stay there. But for God's sake hang on to that ruby and get it to Dorset Street."

Eddie drove marvelously to the near limits of the machine and gravity, just this side of catastrophe. Cavender kept his teeth clenched and his feet planted hard on the floor to keep from rolling into the men on either side of him. The rain was icy and the roads grew slicker. He wondered how Eddie and the driver somewhere to the rear could keep the machines on the streets at all. At almost every turn the wheels hit a curbing, and people on the walks jumped back startled. The weather did not keep the Irish in. Gradually, however, Eddie opened the distance between them and the Royal Irish Constabulary to a block and a half.

"Get ready," shouted Eddie above the sound of the engine. The end of the block was coming up fast where they would have to turn right or left at a T intersection. The RIC machine had not yet made the corner a block behind them.

"Here we go," said Eddie more to himself. He jammed the brakes and swung the Standard across the road to block it.

Sean jumped out and limped toward the front of the motorcar and took up a stance with McLaughlin's big pistol pointed over the bonnet. Cavender and McLaughlin were in the street as Eddie came around the other end to get behind the rear ready to shoot over the luggage lid.

"Go, man, get out of here. Good luck," shouted Sean.

Cavender was already running toward the corner. His shoulder pouch banged against his side, his alligator grip against his leg. He heard McLaughlin behind him, and Basil raced somewhere along his side. The dog barked in confusion. Before Cavender turned the corner, he yelled back. "Good luck."

Almost immediately he heard the roar of the Lancaster.

He kept running, feeling the sleet in his face, feeling his feet ready to slip from under him. The deep roar of the Lancaster came again and again, the third shot muffled by the distance growing between him and it. A few people were scattered around the walks and a motorcar or two went by. Everybody seemed deliberately not to pay attention to the two men and the dog running through the streets against a background of gunfire.

Cavender slowed into an easy jog. McLaughlin reached his side. Several more gunshots came in rapid succession. Then silence. Then a half-dozen more popping sounds sporadically spaced.

"Bloody brave lads," said McLaughlin through his wheezing breath. "I hope we see them again."

"So do I," said Cavender, meaning it. He wondered how large the IRB was and how many in it were the matches of Sean and Eddie.

They left the street at the first intersection they came to. The gunshots became fainter. Another half block and they heard nothing. A police sedan tore by them with its warning bell clanging. They found a taxi and went to a pub that McLaughlin remembered from twenty years ago. It was still there on Summerhill, a few blocks from Dorset, and still doing a lively business.

A few bottles of Guinness and forty-five minutes later, Cavender and McLaughlin left the Golden Pony, took a taxi to Dorset Street, and walked along a row of small houses.

Number 14 was like every other house on the street, small, unassuming, well-kept and innocent. Inside, four unassuming, not very well-kept and not so innocent-looking men sat casually at a table and said hello to Cavender and McLaughlin. To Cavender, as he examined their faces and felt their handshakes, they each would appear to be the match of Sean and Eddie.

47

"The scrolls that ye wrote about, then, are back in the hands of some Indians," repeated a man they called Paddy, "is that it?"

"That's right," answered Cavender, who had summarized the situation briefly.

"Now Sean said you've something else in your pocket for us."

"Sean did?" blurted McLaughlin. "We left him in a pretty tight spot an hour and a half ago."

"Oh, Sean made it, all right. Eddie, too. No one got hurt on either side, though not for want of the English bastards trying. The Standard's gone, shot up and burned. Sean telephoned half an hour ago." He removed his round steel-framed glasses and polished the glass with a large clean white handkerchief. He replaced them on his nose. "Now, Major McLaughlin—"

"Mister, will you," cut in McLaughlin. "I'm not part of that bloody force anymore. I'm here. *Brendan*'ll make me feel more at home."

"Aye, and we're glad to have you. Well, Mr. McLaughlin, Brendan, will you be showing us what we gambled on to get out of India with you."

McLaughlin laid the ruby inside Cavender's handkerchief onto the table. Dramatically he opened the handkerchief by its corners one at a time.

"Holy Mary!" someone said under his breath. "Is it real?"

"It's yours," said McLaughlin. "It's not the scrolls, but it's worth a lot more."

Paddy picked the jewel up and handed it to one of the men. "We'll see what it's worth soon enough. Patrick, will you get it over to Clark at his home. Tell him it's from me and how much we can get."

The man left immediately. Paddy turned back to Cavender and McLaughlin.

"Is that piece of glass worth more than fifty thousand pounds? That's what we hear the scrolls could get us. Isn't that right, Eamon?"

"The man was not joking, Brendan McLaughlin," said Eamon to the old Irishman. "I mean the man who told us that. I don't know how he found any of us, but he found meself and told me I'd be seeing some Homeric manuscript soon that he'd pay fifty thousand sterling for. And he showed me the whole fifty thousand. Christ, man! Do you know what fifty thousand looks like in twenty-pounders? A bloody suitcase full, it looks like. I'm telling you, if I had a pistol with me and he didn't have those servants with him, for our cause, I'd have taken away all that money from him and given him the thanks of Ireland."

"You're talking of a Russian," said Cavender, anticipating McLaughlin's question. "He's got the same story I told you. Did he tell you anything else? Like why he thought we still had them?" Cavender was asking McLaughlin although he was talking to Eamon.

"He didn't say," said Eamon. "He said only they were on the way to Dublin and us."

McLaughlin said nothing. He looked puzzled.

Cavender wondered if the countess had decided against wiring his story to her husband.

"Did he leave an address or telephone exchange?" he asked, not expecting much.

"No, I asked him and he said he would call when the *Prince Albert* was in."

Almost instinctively everybody glanced at the telephone on a table beneath a heavy lampshade. It did not ring.

For the next forty minutes, in a sort of quiet jubilation, they sat around waiting for Patrick to return. Sean came in limping. Cavender saw the limp was from an illness, not a wound. Sean handed McLaughlin his big pistol.

"It shoots like a cannon, nearly blew their engine apart."

McLaughlin removed the empties, replaced them with four fresh shells from his pockets, and holstered it. He answered questions and spoke about India. He talked about everything but he did not speak of his daughter. Cavender watched the thoughts working in his face as he passed over her when she could have been mentioned.

Sean brought Rose up but nothing was added to what had already been said.

Cavender remained the outsider. He sat and listened and smoked. The five members of the Council—Sean was the fifth—were binding a new man into the secret society of the Brotherhood. Their small talk was part of the process.

At ten o'clock Patrick came in unable to conceal his excitement. He gave the ruby back to Paddy. A small blue cloth sack had been found for it.

"Clark says it's a beauty, sure, genuine and worth a fortune—out of his class. Over forty, fifty thousand quid at least, he thinks. He knows exactly where to peddle it, for top money, quick, fair and no questions. A day or two is all."

"Well, boys," said Paddy, his round, red-cheeked face beaming, "that's settled. The gamble's paid off and we can thank her for it. That'll buy us a few Mausers, won't it, Patrick?"

"Aye it will, and the best ones, too."

"What about Tommy?" someone asked. "Do we write him off?"

236

"Rose might be able to tell us," Sean said. "If we could lay our hands on her."

Cavender offered nothing. He listened until there was a break in the talk. Then he rose. His job for them was finished. But he felt far from finished himself.

"I'll be heading back to Brussels tomorrow. You can send the rest of my fee there when you sell the stone—if you don't have it now."

"We thank you fully," said Paddy. He extended his hand. "But if you'll wait a day or two with McLaughlin we'll turn the stone into cash and pay you now. I'd prefer you to do that."

"That's fine with me," said Cavender, knowing when it was wise to be agreeable. The air had not been cleared entirely of suspicion. They had the ruby but the Russian had heightened their interest in the scrolls. And besides, his own concerns were not settled. It was just as well he stayed.

Before he left, Paddy wrote down the name of a safe place for him and McLaughlin to stay. Then he laid a hand on McLaughlin's shoulder. "At our next meeting, Brendan, you'll come in with us the way we all have. But know this, once in, never out. It's our only way."

McLaughlin shook his head in apparent agreement and went down the front steps toward a taxi Sean had brought. The air had grown colder and the sleet had let up.

Cavender stopped at the door and said, "When the Russian calls back, tell him I want to talk. Find out where he is anyway. Don't say you don't have the scrolls. If he knows what I think he does, I may find out for you what happened to Tommy Coughlin."

48

The telephone rang at ten-thirty the following morning.
Cavender was alone in a quiet room in a boardinghouse
on Marrowbone Lane. A middle-aged lady called him
down the stairs. He put the receiver to his ear.

"Eamon here. He's called just now. Wants to see you at
his hotel, Hotel Surrey on lower O'Connell."

Before Cavender left his room, he dug toward the
bottom of his leather pouch for a heavy sock. Inside the
sock was a long bulbous silencer designed to fit his small
Mauser pistol. In less than a minute he locked it to the
barrel and stuffed the now clumsy weapon inside his trouser waistband. It was awkward and uncomfortable but
the pistol would not make more noise than a cork popping
from a champagne bottle when he fired it.

He stopped at McLaughlin's door and listened to the
heavy, snoring breath of the older man inside. He heard
Basil get up and come close to sniff at the door and go
back. The dog had not asked to go out. It was snowing.

The drive to the hotel should have been fifteen minutes.
This morning's snow made it thirty. Dublin was under a
cold, damp, whitish blanket that made nothing beautiful.
The streets were a thick slushy mess. The air was heavy
and wet. It was the right weather for rotten things to happen. Cavender felt it in his bones.

But the count couldn't. Or didn't show it. Nothing
could dampen the composure of his manners. He was as
drily immaculate and unflurried as ever. He greeted Cavender graciously and thanked him for his life at Konarak.
After that he wasted some words, but not many.

"Did I tell you I do not give up when I want something?" he said as soon as Cavender sat down. "A polo victory, a woman, an art piece. It is all one, Mr. Cavender. The desire is the thing. It is the search and pursuit that exhilarates as much as the final possession. But losing that final possession—even if it is only temporary—robs the search of its thrill. I want the scrolls."

"Your wife wired you that they are probably up in the Punjab by now," Cavender explained flatly.

"In the first message, yes. The merchandise was not genuine." His tone was touched with mockery. "Trash. She had been fooled by you. Her second wire told a different story."

Borodin lit a cigarette in his holder. He blew smoke away.

"McLaughlin," he announced, training his pale blue eyes onto Cavender's deeper gray ones, "McLaughlin has the scrolls with him, right here in Dublin. Yes, your good friend."

Cavender restrained a reply. He knew it. Everything fit. Yet he fought it.

The count said, "I will not waste my own words convincing you."

From a flat wallet he drew two newspaper clippings. The paper was clean and fresh. The date on the first one he handed over was two and a half weeks old. The other was dated three days later. The dateline on both was Calcutta.

The first was a brief report of a fire that had destroyed an old, nearly deserted hotel in the center of the city. Two bodies had been found, but no identification could be made. Cavender read it blankly. It was not news.

The second news clipping was. The two bodies burned in the fire had been identified. Both were Sikhs.

That brought some furrows into Cavender's brow. He read on.

The two Sikhs were described as visitors from the North-West Frontier. Neither one had died from burns or asphyxiation. Both had been shot to death, probably—because no shots had been heard by people in the area—on

239

an upper floor. One had evidently gotten downstairs and died near the entrance. The cause for the shootings had yet to be found.

Cavender's face was dark and moody. The dimple in his left cheek was gone. In its place was a deep raw-looking crevice.

"They could have burned up in the fire," said Cavender, tracing over the events since the three of them—he, McLaughlin, and Rose—had left the hotel on Mirzapur Street. He did not like the thoughts revolving slowly in his mind—McLaughlin's lengthy disappearance to retrieve Basil, the notes Rose had received before the ship had sailed, her squabble outside the baggage room with the first mate.

As the thoughts moved around the second time, he knew the truth and hated to face it.

And so he said, "Or the Greek has them. He was up there with us."

"No, Mr. Cavender, Stathopolous did not take them, does not have them. He is here, also, in Dublin, still looking for them. I have had a man at the docks for this past week. The Greek arrived two days before you did. No, I am afraid that the good major has outfoxed us all. He has had the scrolls from the beginning and he has them now."

"You've seen the Greek yourself?"

"Yes."

Cavender calculated whether Stathopolous could have reached Dublin as fast as the count said—if his wounds had not crippled him. Train across India to Bombay, steamship to Naples, train across Europe to Calais, train ferry to Dover, train across England and train ferry to Dublin, perhaps not leaving the train from Naples once. It could be done. But why do it?

The answer was always the same. McLaughlin had gone back to the hotel as Rose had wanted to, gone back and killed the Sikh, and taken the scrolls. Then he had picked up the dog, made arrangements for the scrolls to be brought aboard, and returned to the ship. The Greek, in spite of his wounds, had sent notes to Rose. He had no choice. The scrolls had to be aboard the ship. Rose had gone after McLaughlin, failed, and had gone after the mate to get into the baggage room. She had failed at that, too. The Greek, like the Russian, had not given up.

Cavender said, "Then the scrolls are really genuine if he still has them."

"Yes," said the count. "One hundred percent genuine. There was never any doubt. Ten years ago I was on a tiger hunt in the Indian northeast when an old Sikh in the party told me about Alexander and the scrolls. He knew about the Nehang. I was curious. I hunted up the newspaper accounts of McLaughlin's trial and came across an item about the death of an Indian professor of antiquities who had been murdered coincidentally during the major's flight to Calcutta. I went to Delhi and looked up the professor's family. They were cordial enough to allow me to examine the professor's last works on Greek manuscripts. I found his notes on the Taxila scrolls he had been shown just before his death. He did not say who had brought them to him but he found there was every reason to believe they were genuine. His name was O. O. Okranah."

Borodin reached back into his wallet and drew out another folded sheet of paper. "A page from the professor's notes. I did not think the family would mind."

The handwriting was in English. The note said, "This is the most remarkable find of my life and in my memory. The Alexander *Iliad* is genuine, the handwriting is ancient, the dialect in the margins is definitely indicative of the 4th century B.C., the commentary reflects Alexander's turn of thought—marvelously, marvelously!"

There was more but Cavender handed the sheet back. He got up to leave.

"You know where McLaughlin has them," said Borodin.

"I think so. But you're not coming. He'll shoot you on sight."

"Mr. Cavender, neither my wife nor I had anything to do with the Indian girl. Are you even certain she was the major's daughter?"

Cavender looked at him blankly.

"When I spoke with Miss O'Connell in the bungalow, she and the girl had some angry words between them that made me think that they were more like partners in the affair than anything else. Were they?"

Cavender scowled. "It doesn't matter right now," he said. "Stay here. As soon as I've turned up the scrolls, I'll call."

"I mean to have them one way or another," said Borodin. "Bear that in mind, please. And the offer of money is still good."

Cavender had forgotten his words before he climbed down from a taxi in front of a British wireless office. He got off a wire to his office in Brussels. His secretary would send him what he hoped would be there.

At the boardinghouse he found McLaughlin had left some time earlier. "He's gone out, I think, to drink a little bit of Ireland back into his blood," said the landlady. "He put it that way himself."

"If he doesn't get back, will you take care of his dog?"

"Not coming back, is it? Sure, I'll be taking care of him. He's a beauty if I've ever seen one."

The local pubs were crowded with customers escaping the snow and taking cheer with that little bit of Ireland. But Cavender did not stop in. McLaughlin was not going to be among them. He found a taxi.

"The docks on North Wall Quay," he said to the driver. "As fast as you can go in this bloody weather."

49

The afternoon had grown as dark as night and the city had turned on its street lamps. The snow was falling heavier.

The *Prince Albert* was still in its slip under the glare of dock lights far down the quay. Men were loading her with light cranes and hand dollies. A few motorcars were parked along the road widely apart. The one nearest the shipping and receiving office of the P&O lines had its motor running. Its white exhaust was faint in the snowfall.

A newsboy passed hawking his papers and heading into the city. Cavender bought one and tucked it under his arm.

McLaughlin was in the shipping and receiving office. The lights were on inside and he was clearly visible through the large half-curtained windows facing the street.

Cavender turned the collar of his coat up, thrust his hands deep into his pockets for warmth, and leaned against a lamppost. The snow dashed wetly against his face. He thought back a little more than a month ago when he was waiting for McLaughlin just like this, except the weather was warm and he had leaned against a peddler's stall to escape the sun. He wished there was a sun now. He had not seen it for the last three days. His bones felt chilled from more than the weather.

There was movement inside the office. A man appeared behind a counter from the warehouse in the rear and placed a large bundle in front of McLaughlin. Cavender moved fast. He looked into the motorcar nearest him. Its engine was going but it was empty. The snow was too heavy to see into the machine up the road. He drew his Mauser pistol with the bulbous silencer attached and tucked it between the pages of the newspaper. Holding the pistol through the paper he carefully opened the door to the office, stepped in, and eased the door closed.

As the door clicked shut McLaughlin looked up from the forms he was signing. The bundle on the counter was the size of the cheap suitcase Cavender had bought in Bhubaneswar. It was now wrapped in heavy burlap and tied securely with coarse rope.

The expression on McLaughlin's face was strangely like that of a little boy whose hand was caught in the poor box.

"Ahhrrr, Alec, what did you have to go and follow me

for? You should have let things be and taken your money and gone back home."

The clerk moved tactfully to the far end of the counter and found something to keep himself busy.

Cavender opened the newspaper and let McLaughlin see the pistol pointing at his chest.

"Sorry, Black Dog, I'll do it if I have to. With immunity." He spoke softly and clearly and came close to the Irishman. "Keep your hand away from the Lancaster."

McLaughlin got the look of a hurt dog. "I'll not be shooting it out with you, Alec, my boy. And you'll not shoot me either, will you?"

"You don't really know me, Black Dog, do you," said Cavender, making his voice as cold and flat as he could. "I will shoot you if you don't do exactly as I say. And I don't worry about the police. Walk to the other side of the room."

McLaughlin looked longingly and painfully at the bundle near him and then with a conscious effort walked to the opposite wall with Cavender.

"How can you not fear trouble with the police, lad? That fellow over there looks ready to call one if you give him a reason."

"You're IRB for one thing, and you're armed, for another. They'll match that gun of yours with the damage done to their machine yesterday. And I can prove you killed that Sikh up in that hotel room, God damn you. Why the bloody hell you had to do that!"

"I didn't do that, Lad. I was on my way to do it, but the Greek had already done it. I met him downstairs in the street. The place was already burning. He was hurt and I took the suitcase away from him. It was easy in the crowds and him bleeding."

"I suppose you didn't kill Professor Okranah a long time ago. The government would send you over for that. They'll love me for what I could tell them about you."

"But you won't, lad, I know it. I'm old and foolish and you won't hand me in."

Cavender knew he wouldn't, too. But he said, "I'll shoot

you right now like a sick dog if you don't do what I tell you."

"What do you want, Alec?"

"Go over there"—he motioned to the shipping counter —"and turn that bundle around and ship it back to India. To Taxila, to the Indian governor of the district. He'll know where the scrolls should go. Write the word *Nehang* on the ticket."

McLaughlin peered down into Cavender's face to see if he was serious, stared at the bulbous silencer that looked like a long black can with a small hole at the end protruding from the edges of the newspaper, looked back into Cavender's face. He chewed on his lips for a while and then nodded.

He shuffled over to the clerk and asked for a new address tag. Cavender watched him make the ticket out, listened to his explanation, saw him pay the freight. McLaughlin surrendered the old claim ticket and took the new receipt.

"When is the *Prince Albert* sailing?" asked Cavender.

"A few days," said the clerk as he counted out some change. He picked up the suitcase in both hands and hesitated. He stared first at one man and then at the other to assure himself that he was doing what was wanted. When neither man gestured or spoke, he pivoted sharply and headed toward the open gate to the storage room.

Cavender and McLaughlin watched the scrolls disappear, McLaughlin with a mournful expression in his face, Cavender with a look of relief. Alexander's *Iliads* were on their way to where they belonged.

Outside, Cavender kept his gun on McLaughlin and asked for the receipt. He stood in a doorway a few feet away and set fire to it. He held the paper up by the corner and let it burn toward his fingers and dropped it into the snow.

Almost at once a figure emerged from the darkness of a nearby doorway and stamped the flame out. The figure stooped and picked up the charred wet piece left.

"It's for them scrolls, ain't it?" the man said to McLaughlin. He was the gunman who had pointed his pistol at Cavender in the Standard. Another man appeared in the light of the street lamp. It was Eddie, the driver.

"It's the real thing you were supposed to be bringing, right?" said the gunman. "Let's go in there and get it. This piece of paper don't look good enough anymore, but the man in there knows your face. And if he's forgotten it, we'll use this."

The heavy short revolver was in his hand.

"You're bloody crazy," McLaughlin growled, knocking the gunman's gun hand aside. "There's nothing in there we can get. You've got the stone."

Cavender was ready to fire from under the newspaper. It did not sound as though talking was going to do much good. And at such close range he would not have to kill anybody.

The gunman reached out and pushed his revolver into McLaughlin's stomach and spun the old Irishman around with his hand. Cavender fired. His pistol made a soft plopping sound. The gunman dropped his revolver and grabbed his forearm, cursing.

From up the road in the dimness a voice called out loud and clear:

"All right, you bastards, you've had your fun. Now lift those hands empty over your heads. Be quick about it."

Through the dark snowfall three shadowy figures approached. Eddie ducked behind the lamppost. The wounded gunman forgot his arm and reached down with his good hand for his revolver half-buried in snow.

Cavender shoved McLaughlin off the curbing into the street toward some shadows. Gunfire broke loose. Flames streaked out of the darkness and from behind the lamppost. The heavy snow took the hardness out of the shots.

In the first burst Eddie and the gunman went down in small dark heaps. The firing from the darkness continued. The fallen men did not fire back.

McLaughlin's Lancaster went off three times. Cavender had no choice. He fired twice—low—toward the yellow flashes up the road. He fired instinctively to protect himself, but something in him would not let him shoot at British policemen.

246

The firing from the shadowy figures stopped. There were a few moans in the darkness.

The men on the docks had disappeared. The startled face of the shipping clerk pressed against the door window. Cavender charged against the door, almost knocking the man down. The clerk fled in terror toward the rear. Cavender found a telephone and ripped the wires from it. He ran back outside toward the motorcar with the engine running. Then he came up short. McLaughlin was pointing his heavy Lancaster pistol at him. There was one .577 shell left in the gun.

Cavender said, "I suppose you *could* go back in there and take them away from that clerk."

He was close enough to see McLaughlin's grim face reflecting the mind behind it being made up. Finally the old Irishman growled in his throat:

"Ahhrrr, lad, the hell with it. Basil'll be enough for me. Let's get out of here."

50

They climbed into the motorcar, Cavender behind the wheel, and started to drive slowly into the blinding snow along the North Wall Quay. The windscreen wipers worked poorly. He kept the engine in low gear and drove without the headlamps on. The road further up the quay was empty.

Despite Cavender's careful handling, the machine skidded badly. He avoided the brake and kept his foot lightly on the accelerator. For a few yards he almost had no control. Finally the machine straightened and crawled steadily for a block.

Suddenly another motorcar turned into the quay from a side street fifty yards up to his right. It came fast fishtailing at first, then straightened and picked up speed. McLaughlin leaned through his open window to see better and guide Cavender along with directions. The windscreen on his side was completely covered with snow. The headlamps of the approaching machine caught him fully for a few seconds as Cavender lost his motorcar in a rear skid to the right.

The windscreen in front of Cavender was badly streaked with ice. He leaned forward, almost touching the glass, and peered through the snow. He drifted the machine to the left to leave plenty of room for passing.

As the two machines closed, the one approaching cut sharply toward them, bent for a head-on collision. Cavender stomped on the accelerator and felt his rear wheels spin. The rear of the machine broke away to the right. He heard McLaughlin shouting angrily at the lights boring down on them. The second machine struck them broadside, throwing them against the curbing and pinning their motorcar against a lamppost.

The impact was not great and nobody was hurt. Cavender's door was jammed, its window shattered. He was covered with splinters of glass. McLaughlin struggled for a moment with his door and then angrily hurled his body against it, throwing it open. He half fell, half stumbled out onto the walk. Cavender slid across the seat and came out after him.

It was no accident. The second machine had rammed him deliberately. He struggled to get to his Mauser, but with the bulky silencer attached he could not free it from his clothing until he stood up straight.

He was not fast enough. The silencer caught in his belt and stuck. By then, in the umbrella of light spreading around them, he recognized the huge figure of Stathopolous looming toward them in the snow. His massy shadow glided as though he were on skis. Next to him, half hidden by his bulk, was Rose.

Both of them were pointing guns, the Greek covering McLaughlin, Rose holding hers on Cavender, as though

248

they had rehearsed this scene before. Cavender swore to himself and kept both his hands outside his coat. He was facing two people he had seen kill in cold blood.

Rose's voice sounded hoarse as she spoke into the Greek's ear, "Not yet. Not yet. Watch them. I'll get the suitcase."

Without catching the eye of either man she cautiously worked her way around them and went into the front of their motorcar. She leaned into the back, searching around and cursing.

Then she came back to Cavender. Her face was filled with fury. "You fucking bloody English bastard, where are the scrolls? Where are they? If you don't give them up, you're going to die right here. In the snow. In five seconds." She extended her arm and put the gun close to him. It was not a tiny automatic now but a medium-sized, deadlier revolver.

"They're gone," said Cavender, counting the seconds. "They're on the way home. Shoot that and you'll never get them. There's no claim ticket. Your only way is to take us both back there to reclaim the bundle in person."

Rose laughed without humor. "That's it. They're in the shipping office. He had them on the ship and you're sending them back. You make me laugh, the two of you. There's no claim ticket we'll be needing. This will do well enough for that." She waved her revolver.

The snow was coming down steadily. The quay remained silent. The dock workers had not reappeared after the shooting. There were no police gongs in the air.

In the pale yellow light from above Cavender could see the pleasure Rose was having. It was in her eyes and in the twist of her mouth. The Greek's face was as inscrutable as it had always been. He was hopeless. He was ready to shoot them without another word. Cavender had to work on her.

Their positions were changed. She was enjoying herself. No longer was she following him, bowing to his wishes, listening to whatever he said and agreeing whether she liked it or not. She held the gun now, and she didn't need him. She wasn't being left behind again. She was in charge at last. He could see her savoring the reversal. The woman in her loved it as a cat loves cream. Cavender had to feed her pleasure to save himself.

"So you've been in with Stathopolous from the beginning," he said, pushing surprise into his voice. "That was pretty smart of him. How did he pick you up?"

"Tell the smug bastard, Achilles," she snapped. "Tell him who brought who in. This was mine, Alec, the whole idea was mine, me, a poor Irish lass, not fit for anything but a whore, a toy for men like you, and now finishing you off and making something of myself. Watching you dance around when I knew everything that was going on, that was bloody fun, it was. Ha! Tommy spilled it all to me and I set everything going, not Achilles, here. Right, Achilles?"

She was pleased with herself. She wanted Cavender to know she was somebody. Her face seemed flushed through the snowfall. She looked beautiful but almost crazed. She had been into everything in the affair and ahead of him all the way.

"Then you had the fat man kill him."

"No one had to do my killing. The job Tommy talked about was my chance to get out of the life. The poor slob was easy. It was almost sorry I felt about finishing him. But he was only a man."

Cavender picked up her stops without a pause. A pause might break the mood. And then good-bye. The snow was whitening their hats, their shoulders.

"Through the whole affair, then, you were in contact with Stathopolous," he said quickly. "Working together to get your hands on the scrolls, kill McLaughlin and me if you had to, and he had the contacts to sell the manuscript. Neat. That's how he kept turning up at the right places. For a woman, very neat. But I'm curious about only one thing. Why did you shoot him up in the Sikh's room?"

Her voice softened. "He knows I'm sorry for that and forgives me. He had to forgive me. We found we needed each other—and I've made it up to him, haven't I, Achilles. And let me tell you two pigs, he's more a man than the two of you together."

"You were greedy, is that it?" Cavender went on hurriedly. "Thought you could take everything yourself. When you heard the shooting you thought some of us were dead. You broke in and saw what was happening. You made up your mind fast—to get rid of him, then get rid of me. You could handle McLaughlin later in bed, right? The ruby, the scrolls would be yours. You'd get rid of him later."

"Rose," said Stathopolous, waving his gun toward Cavender. "Enough of this talk. The snow is bad. This is all bad. We're wasting time." His voice was no longer a purr in the snow. It was now womanish and a little frightened.

Ignoring him, Cavender went on, acting like a man who had a curiosity to be satisfied before he died. He put respect into his voice, even admiration for the way Rose had managed it all. It was pleasing for her to hear it.

"Everything the two of you did, every offer you made, all of the information you fed us, even Farashah's kidnapping, was just to get McLaughlin grateful enough or greedy enough to bring the scrolls into the open where you could take them away from us. But why did you kill the girl, McLaughlin's daughter? What did you do that for?"

That was the question he was leading to. Every muscle in his body was tense as he asked it. His right hand was poised to go into his coat after his gun if he had the chance. He felt McLaughlin shift restlessly next to him and heard a low growl in his throat. He was counting on the Irishman.

Rose fell for it.

"McLaughlin's daughter!" She laughed through her teeth. "That's a good one. She was a little chit Achilles picked up in that child's whorehouse to play the part, to get close to him and help us when he brought the scrolls out. Sure the little bitch turned greedy. When we were so close in Puri she got greedy when she heard the Russian's offer. Threatened to tell McLaughlin everything, she did, and after what I'd been to her, what we could be together. It was a good pair we were, the poor little fool. But she told me she wanted more, could get more from him. She laid him, you know, in Calcutta, she said, up in a room when they had given us the slip, and he let her, even thinking she was his daughter. She told me that and what he would give her. And I shot her. And now I'm going to—"

McLaughlin wasn't listening well. He exploded in a wild lunge against Rose, his hands against her throat.

She began to shoot before his fingers closed to choke her air off. She took one step backward and shot him the way she shot the bus driver. She shot him four times in the chest, and as he fell against her she squeezed her arm upward and shot him twice in the lower face. McLaughlin collapsed heavily against her, dragging her down into the snow under him. His roar had turned into a long harsh gasp that continued after he struck the ground.

Cavender had been given enough time to twist his pistol loose from inside his belt. McLaughlin had come through and was dying for it. But Cavender lived. He shot the Greek twice in the face, the hardest place to shoot a man close up. He had no other way. Rose had already shown that the Greek could absorb shots in the body like that old bull elephant. Stathopolous hardly moved. His pistol dropped and disappeared into the snow at his feet. His head tilted up toward the dark sky. Snow stuck against his eyelids and melted in the blood. The face wounds did not change the flatness of his look. His hat floated off his head and dropped into the snow where he sat on it when his legs buckled. He sat there held in position by his own spreading weight like a wax Buddha. Slowly the weight shifted and he fell to the side, face downward.

McLaughlin lay stretched out in the snow, face down also, with one arm across Rose's body. The snow around him was spattered with blood. His gasping had stopped. He lay motionless.

Taking the scene in fully now, Cavender stifled a groan. With a cold emptiness in his chest he knelt and searched hopelessly for a pulse. A tiny lump rose into his throat. He tried to swallow and couldn't. His mind was dizzy, his body fatigued and chilled. He gripped McLaughlin's shoulder with a strong cold hand and squeezed once as if to reach down through death to say one more word to him.

It was a rotten way to say good-bye to a man he had grown to love, but both men knew that in lives like theirs there was often no time for good-byes better than that.

He felt Rose struggling to free herself from McLaughlin's body. Cavender lifted the old Irishman and then let him down into the snow again. To die in an Irish snow was a lot better than to take it in the heavy dust of India. For an Irishman.

A string of cursing brought his attention to Rose. She was getting up swearing. She cursed everyone and everything, using the same old familiar phrases he had heard from her before. Then she sobered and came under control and said:

"For the love of God why did he do that, Alec? I wasn't going to shoot him or anyone. You knew that, didn't you? And she wasn't his daughter at all, someone Achilles found to help us. All we wanted was the manuscript, nothing else."

"He didn't hear you," said Cavender bitterly. He took her pistol from her and threw it under the motorcar near him. Then he turned and slapped her hard with the back of his hand, even knowing he had forced the shooting himself. She gasped, choked back a cry, and stumbled a few feet away. A trickle of blood showed at the corner of her mouth.

"You rotten bastard. He deserved what I gave him using her the way he did, thinking she was his own and not letting that stop him. I believed her." She rubbed her cheek and brushed some snow from her coat. "You didn't have to do that. But now that you did, got your system cleaned out, go up there with me, Alec, and get the scrolls. We'll neither of us work again for a long time. I'm not asking you to be with me. That's over. I've finished with men. We'll be going our own ways but let's go with some lining to our coats."

"No," said Cavender, letting the flint into his voice. "You're going to talk with some people of your own with names like Paddy and Eamon and Sean. No lawyers, no jails, no courtroom, just a little Irish fixing from your own. That's the only place you're going."

"You rotten pig," she spat at him. Then another short string of unimaginative curses. Finally she screamed, "I'll get them myself. I'll do it alone. Fuck all you men."

She tramped around in the snow near the Greek's body looking for his gun. But the snow had already obliterated its outline. She gave up. Another thought struck her. She hurled herself to her knees near the motorcar against the lamppost and crawled half beneath it. She swept her arm back and forth through the snow, her breath harsh and nearing hysteria.

Unfeelingly, Cavender watched her. His face was drawn and brutal. The snow was sticking to his skin and eyelashes. The dimple in his left cheek was a cicatrice. She was an animal hunting for something that would sharpen her claws. He waited for her to finish.

She searched frantically for a few minutes. There were ugly noises coming from her throat. The noises stopped and she wriggled out. Her clothing was soggy and she had lost her hat underneath. Her hair was wet and limp. In her right hand she held her revolver. Her face was lighted in triumph. She spoke while still on her knees.

"I've got it, you see, you know I can use it." She got to her feet.

Cavender said, "Let's go, Rose." He headed for the motorcars. "Your machine may still be running. It'll be better than walking."

She told him what he could do. She pointed her revolver at him and squeezed the trigger.

Click.

Click.

"Goddam your bloody soul and your mother's, you filth," she screamed. "I'll get the suitcase myself with an empty gun. I'll get it. I'll get it."

She spun around and started to slog through the snow. Cavender watched her heading across the circle of light, her step short and shaky, her long dress clinging to her legs, showing the full outline of each plump calf in turn as the other leg lifted and reached out.

He watched her struggle closer to the darkness of the road beyond the circle of light. He thought of how it had

254

been with her, of her body, her beauty, her early inno-
cence. He thought of a foolish young Irishman named
Tommy Coughlin and of an older one named Black Dog
and of an Indian girl.

Just before Rose left the glow of the lamppost Cavender
raised his pistol and pressed the safety release button. He
heard the tiny click. He could feel the snowflakes on his
hand. He hand shook slightly from the cold. Or from his
nerves. He wasn't sure.

The Mauser's report sounded like a small bulb explod-
ing. Rose pirouetted and said, "Oh, shit!" and sat down in
the snow.

She offered no struggle when Cavender picked her up
and carried her to the motorcar she had come in. The
fenders and bonnet were crumpled but the starting crank
was undamaged and accessible and the engine fired on the
second turn. Before he drove away he tied a handkerchief
around her wound. He had hit her as he hoped to do, in
the right calf. She did not complain. Whatever little she
had bled had drained her of fight. He drove her carefully
to the house on Dorset Street.

An hour later he left that house alone and drove across
Dublin to the neighborhood of his room. He deserted the
motorcar four blocks away and with his hands in his
pockets, his collar up and hat pulled down, he trudged
easily through the empty white streets toward his bed for
the night. The only trouble he now had to face was how to
console Basil.

51

Morning came with a leaden empty sky. It also brought
Cavender two messages. One was a wire from his office in

Brussels. The other was an envelope marked only with his name brought by a private messenger.

The wire was from his secretary. It was a copy of a message from Forsythe in Bhubaneswar. It confirmed Rose's guilt as the murderer of Farashah. Witnesses in the village had heard the shots after Borodin's aeroplane had left the gound. To the Irish council she had confessed to everything else including the deaths of Tommy and McLaughlin. To Cavender she had explained why she had killed the bus driver. He knew the shots killing Farashah had been fired after the aeroplane had gone. He had threatened her, too.

Rose was not on Cavender's conscience. She was probably already in a bog outside the city where no one would ever find her.

The second envelope tied the last loose end. Count Borodin, whom he had called last night as he had promised, was leaving Dublin that morning. The message was written in his own hand, clear, immaculate, confident. He and the countess would go back to India, to the North-West Frontier city of Taxila. Speaking for the countess, he was sending their warmest regards. He was enclosing, also, something harder and colder.

It was the silver Alexander tetradrachm wrapped neatly in a flannel slip.

Cavender turned the coin round and round in his fingers, tracing with his thumb the handsome curly-headed profile of the great soldier who had loved Homer so dearly. Finally he flicked his thumb and the coin spun up into the air above his head. He held out his hand. The coin landed in his palm just as it should—the head of Alexander facing upward.

He pushed the tetradrachm into a watch pocket, shouldered his leather pouch, and went out into Dublin, first to collect the rest of his fee from the faithful Irishmen and then to help them bury one of their lost.

And Basil. The last he saw of Basil was as the dog stood in the hall, next to the kindly landlady who had been happy to take him. She was bending to stroke his big white head. And his tail had just begun to move a little bit.